SHERLOCK HOLMES: FAMILIAR CRIMES

ALSO BY LYN McCONCHIE

SHERLOCK HOLMES: FAMILIAR CRIMES

*More New Stories
of the Great Detective*

LYN McCONCHIE

WILDSIDE PRESS

To my friend Cheryl Hunter,
who reads almost as many books as I do.

Published by Wildside Press LLC.
www.wildsidepress.com

TOO MANY ACCIDENTS

1

The echoes of our last case were still fresh in our minds when Holmes and I returned from a final meeting with the unfortunate family with which we had been dealing. Once out of the gloomy house, however, I cheered up. Holmes remained his usual saturnine self, of course, but I did think his step to be a trifle lighter. When we were back in our rooms, I poured us a drink each, slumped into my chair by the fire, and addressed him.

"So the elder Arthur Riggston is dead."

"A glimpse of the obvious, Watson. We can only hope so, since they buried the man."

I gave a small snort of amusement. "Yes. But do we know if his death was natural or not? That's the question."

"I am inclined to think that it was. That is, I can see no way in which it was unnatural, and therefore believe it to be the normal death of an elderly man of sedentary habits, who ate and drank too much. You know all that I do, Watson. As a doctor, did you note anything to the contrary?"

I had to admit that I had not. Our dinner arrived and we set to, but after we'd eaten I brought up the subject again.

"So why does his nephew believe otherwise?"

Holmes lit his pipe and once that was going well he spoke slowly, considering his words. "I can sum up the nephew's suspicions in three words: too many accidents. Five years ago he sat down to write a family history. He says that once he was well into that, it occurred to him that it was strange so many of the recent family had died quite young, and always by some sort of misadventure. There were also the deaths of old family friends and the firm's lawyer. He came to the conclusion that there were too many deaths over the same generations in his family and amongst those of the family's immediate friends. He came to me saying that while he could point to no definite evidence, he was of the opinion that something suspicious was occurring and he wished me to look into the matter. He was anxious since Arthur Riggston, his uncle, was also a good friend, Arthur having been much the younger of the two brothers and our Arthur's godfather."

"Did you come to any conclusion?"

"I agreed to consider any information Riggston had, and to give my opinion."

I waited.

"I could only tell him what I believed, that the elder Arthur had died naturally. Of that I was sure. However, of all the other deaths he listed I, too, found it unusual that they had either died from clear misadventure, suicide, or that those deaths listed as natural could have had other explanations. The main point, as I emphasized, is that the deaths he suspects may not have been accidental occurred over a spread of more than thirty years."

I stared. "What? He thinks that someone with a grudge against his family has been quietly murdering them for three decades? Holmes, it is inconceivable."

"Not inconceivable, Watson, but unlikely." He leaned forward, his gray eyes catching and holding my own gaze. "I believe it possible, however, and in two cases I think murder likely."

I reached to stir the fire, adding more fuel—the evening was chilly—before sitting back. "Tell me," I said simply.

Holmes began on the otherwise mundane history of the Riggston family, well-to-do people, now of the middle class, who had contributed nothing noteworthy to history, and who had lived in obscurity through their generations.

"The first James Riggston," Holmes said, "was born in a village outside London. James joined his father's coal business at sixteen, having had some education, and on the death of his father, rose to own the business, which he expanded into London." He looked at me. "Unfortunately, like a number of rising families, they think it proper to emulate the nobility and name boys of the next generation after those men of the previous one. It causes confusion not only to their acquaintances, but also to hard-working detectives. To simplify, those of the Riggston family who yet live are the fourth James, who married Mary; Jane, his younger sister who wed Scott Riggston, a cousin; Josephine, the next sister, who wed Victor Percy; and Arthur, who never married. The third James Riggston had remained content to own the business without further expansion."

His lips pursed. "From what I have been told, this lack of ambition may be attributed to drink, and while he died quite young, there is no obvious suspicion attached to that. He passed away after a bout of drinking during which he developed a fever and hallucinations and, leaving the house, dived into the river saying that he must be cooler at any cost." His voice became edged. "He could not swim and shortly thereafter he was cooler than he anticipated."

I gave a shout of laughter and Holmes eyed me blandly. He does like his occasional joke to be appreciated.

"James Riggston the fourth inherited the business. He seems to have been a tight-fisted and unpleasant man, distrusted by his workers, and while an apparent pillar of his church, as was his wife, I heard stories that suggested he was not as upright as he appeared.

"A difference of twenty years separated him and his younger brother, Arthur. They had nothing in common and little to do with each other. Their sister Jane married a cousin and remained Jane Riggston; her son is our Arthur Riggston, whose godfather was the Arthur of the previous generation. The other sister, Josephine, married late, a man named Victor Percy who owned a prosperous shop and had been married once before. From that first union there was a small daughter named May, who was somewhat younger than the fourth James's sons."

He relit his pipe, which had gone out, puffed it to life, and regarded me. I was utterly lost in this wilderness of names, so that he reached for a pen and paper, sketched quickly, blotted the lines and thrust that forward. I studied the genealogy and, with that before me, I could now see how Arthur Riggston was connected to those others.

RIGGSTON FAMILY GENEALOGY

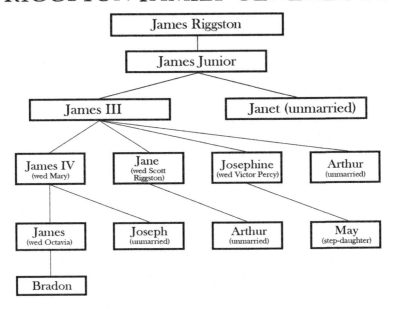

I nodded my thanks and Holmes continued.

"James the third married a woman some five years older than he, an only child who would come into the family business—which she did. The family was thus quite prosperous. You understand, Watson, I am not talking of great wealth. They had the money to live comfortably in a pleasant house in grounds of its own, and to have a maid and a gardener, while the sons went to a public school, howbeit a minor one. But neither servant lived in."

I nodded. That did indeed illustrate the families' newfound wealth. Only those not yet accustomed to being comfortably off would expect such privacy.

"Now." Holmes pointed to the genealogy. "I am told that the elder Arthur was deeply happy to have a namesake; how pleased you may understand when I tell you that upon his death everything he possessed was left to Arthur Riggston the younger. That Arthur has said that he is prepared to spend every penny of his inheritance to be certain that his uncle died a natural death, and that those other deaths also are shown to be natural."

"And those are?"

"Patience, Watson, and all shall be revealed. To sum up, of that fifth generation there were three sons and a stepdaughter. When May Percy was five, her father died. Her mother was in some difficulty as Victor Percy had left his estate to May, but it was insufficient to keep the two of them since it is in a trust and May receives only the interest. Josephine's brother James refused them assistance and she therefore married an older man named Stephens. He had two married adult children and five small grandchildren living in Cornwall, and it is most probable that his main reason for the marriage was to obtain a cheap housekeeper. Josephine Percy lived another six years but then died, and as May's stepfather did not wish her to remain with him, James Riggston reluctantly agreed that the child should live with his family. I think it unlikely that she was happy, and when she was fifteen she ran away. From that day to this no one has heard from her."

"Poor child," I said warmly.

"Yes. Passing over the next twenty years, James the fourth's sons took over the business on his death, with James as the owner and Joseph as manager."

"What of their mother?" I asked. "Did she receive nothing of the business?"

Holmes surveyed me with approval. "No, for she and her husband died together. She would otherwise have had a lifetime interest in all business and property. There is no doubt that her death was convenient for her sons."

"Then you think it may be one of them …?"

"I do not. You will understand why shortly. Next to die were an old family friend and her son. Florence Pelly had been at school with Josephine and the family had kept up the connection, not least in my opinion, because Josephine's husband was in a good way of business and now and again was of financial use to them—as they were to him. The verdict on both her death and that of her son were that the deaths were accidental."

I raised an eyebrow.

"Exactly so. Next to die after a gap of almost ten years were Joseph Riggston and the family lawyer. Both deaths were described as accidental, and no inquiries were made. Five years later, James Riggston the fifth also died accidentally."

I was counting. "James the fourth and his wife, their lawyer, two family friends, James the fifth and his younger brother. Who else?"

"Mr. David Pelly, husband of Florence, died four years after his wife and son. An elderly minister of the church that the Riggstons attended died, and Mr. Arthur has included him in the list. Mr. Arthur Riggston, uncle of my client, died last of all. I am satisfied that the last named died of natural causes, but having considered the other names, in some cases at least the possibility of murder exists. And if that is so, then while the elder Arthur may have died of natural causes, other deaths may yet be murders."

"But Homes, you are postulating a monster. Even should Arthur Riggston have died naturally, you are suggesting that someone has murdered nine people thus far."

He regarded me thoughtfully. "That is so, if all of the nine were murdered. I am suspicious of only eight of the deaths."

"Eight," I said, a tinge of sarcasm creeping into my tones. "I suppose that makes it a little better."

"By a death, Watson. I plan to begin investigations now that my last case has been concluded. Have you the time to assist me?"

"Of course. Where do we begin?"

"With the deaths of the Pelly family. They left only a cousin and his family who had little to do with them but who inherited. I have already written to them and they have no objection to our visit." His mouth turned up in a faint smile. "In fact, I suspect they hope for a murder, as they would dine out on that for years."

"Unless one of them is the murderer."

"I have no reason to think so, although I will consider them in any case. However, they believe that I do not suspect them, and are eager to cooperate."

"And we begin …?"

"Immediately after breakfast, Watson."

I went to my bed that night thinking of all those deaths, almost incredulous as to the likelihood of such slaughter, and wondering what useful information the morrow would bring.

* * * *

What the morrow brought—after we had eaten and donned scarves, gloves and overcoats—was a long cab ride. It was a pleasant if still somewhat chilly day and I asked no questions, content to follow where my friend led. He gave an address to the cabbie and we arrived at a good-sized house.

I studied it and realized that additions had been built on, perhaps when the Pelly cousins had inherited. Holmes knocked and we were greeted by a maid. We were ushered into the drawing room, and it appeared as if the entire Pelly family had gathered to meet us. I studied them with some difficulty as the room was gloomy, dark, and furnished in oak and velvet. The curtains were drawn still and the plush cushions smelled of dust.

Mr. Allan Pelly was short, rotund, and placid of face, but I noticed that his eyes were keen. His wife Bertha also appeared quiet, but she had a sensible air and I thought that she, too, missed little. The son, Charles, looked to be in his early twenties, and the daughter, Gwen, perhaps a year older. I saw both intelligence and open interest in their faces. We sat and the family frankly stared at us until Holmes spoke.

"Upon receiving your inheritance you enlarged the house. You also sent your son to university and your daughter attended a ladies' seminary to improve her chances at a favorable marriage."

I wondered where he obtained that information—despite knowing his methods—as did the family, whose mouths opened in astonishment.

Mr. Pelly gaped. "How?"

"It is of no matter."

"It is of every matter," the man said angrily. "Have the neighbors been talking about us?"

"No, sir. I merely observed that portions of your house are newer than others. They would, I believe, have been added soon after the death of your cousin. As for your children," he continued, pointing to where a photo stood on the mantelpiece, "your son stands before Oxford. Then, too, there is the yearbook I observed on a shelf when I sat down. It bears the name of a ladies' seminary on the outer cover along with a year, and is perhaps a relic of that time."

Mr. Pelly relaxed. "I see. Well then, sir, ask your questions. You think my cousin was murdered. Why and by whom?"

"I am as yet uncertain if a murder occurred. However, your cousin's wife and son died before him, with the verdict of accidental death. Good friends of theirs also had an unusual number of accidental deaths in their family, and it has been suggested that some of these deaths may not have been as accidental as they first appeared. You esteemed your cousin, I am certain. If there was murder, you would not wish it to go unpunished."

Mr. Pelly sat silent for a few minutes, and then he spoke. "I would not. However, to be frank, sir, I did not greatly esteem my cousin. He was a man who put himself first, as did his wife. After that—or in the wife's case, before her life perhaps—came their son, whom they idolized. I was told that the boy, Jonathon, went boating and fell into a pond, and Florence, although she could not swim, tried to save him and drowned also. I found that likely and enquired no further. My cousin David was well-to-do, but there was little charity in him. I think it likely he left all to me for no more reason than he had no one else to inherit and he wished the Government to have no more than it must."

He looked at his wife, who responded. "Still, we would not wish that a killer should escape justice if our cousin or any of his family had been murdered. Is that what you wish to hear?"

It was, and thereafter Holmes questioned them vigorously. Unhappily, there was little they could tell him. The son could only comment that on the handful of occasions when the families had met, his cousin Jonathon had been an unpleasant sort: patronizing, arrogant, older than Master Charles, and fancying himself to be up to any game in town.

"I didn't like him and that's the truth. But I can tell you one thing: he thought himself able to do anything he wished. No," he said as he saw the question coming. "Not only as if he could get away with things, but also as if he thought himself to be supremely competent in any physical activity. He bragged of his riding, his playing of the games at his school, and his shooting. D'you see?"

We did.

The daughter chimed in. "I didn't like him, either."

There was an undercurrent in her voice and her mother looked at her sharply. "Out with it, girl. Did he say or do something?"

She reddened, but her mother would have the truth and it came out little by little. Distressed and frightened at the time, she remembered it clearly. The year before he died, Jonathon had called at the house unexpectedly. She and her brother were alone, and Charles was engaged in the back yard building a new rabbit hutch. Only Gwen was in the house to receive her cousin. She'd made tea, brought in cake, and when he rose to go she was relieved.

"Until I was bidding him goodbye, and he snatched me against him, saying that cousins should be warmer towards each other. He kissed me. It was horrible! His mouth was all wet and he stuck ..." She broke off.

Her father made a sound best described as a snarl.

"It's all right, Papa. I bit him and he pushed me away. He said I'd be sorry for that and was reaching for me again when Charles came back into the house. He had a hammer in one hand, and I think it gave Cousin Jonathon pause."

"If I'd known, I've have hammered *him* all right," her brother growled. He looked at his sister with affection. "Why didn't you say something?"

"It would have caused trouble, Charlie. You know you'd have hit him, and his father would have made a fuss. He didn't hurt me so I said nothing. We only saw him once after that, and when he was dead it didn't matter."

I calculated. She would have been twelve or at the most just thirteen, and her brother a year younger. Jonathon would have been sixteen or so. It was perhaps fortunate for this child and for other girls that he had drowned when he did. A boy that age already willing to press unwanted attentions on a child, and moreover one related to him, is a boy showing signs of becoming a dangerous man.

Holmes asked a few more questions and we left. Once out of the house I repeated my thoughts to my friend, and he agreed.

"We have both seen what comes of that sort," he said quietly. "Pampered by his mother, spoiled by his father, believing himself all-important, and knowing they will protect him against any accusation. The girl was lucky her brother appeared when he did, but that episode tells me much, and gives rise to certain suggestions as to how he could have died. I have the direction of their graves; let us go there next."

A short time thereafter I stared down at the graves of the three Pellys. How had they really died? Had it been murder or accidents, as claimed? A step sounded behind me and I spun around. Holmes loomed, his eyes piercing, his powerful body leaning ominously towards the graves. An aura of violence pervaded the graveyard, and I faltered.

"You really think you know how they died?"

"The mother and son? Yes. And if it was murder in those cases the same motive may have held for the father. I must dig more deeply into that, but ..."

"But how *could* the mother and son have been murdered?"

"Consider this, Watson. We are told that the boy believes himself supreme in any sport. We hear that he boasts of his riding, his school sports, and his shooting. Nowhere do we hear that he swims or rows well. He is on holiday with his mother, and the greatest sport locally is rowing on a lake. Nearby is a smaller lake, the one in which he died. This small lake is full of weeds in certain parts and extremely dangerous. How if he meets someone who sneers at him and dares him to take out a boat in that part of the water? And what if the boat had been carefully damaged beforehand?"

"I see." I frowned. "But while I might expect him to drown, do I expect his mother to drown trying to save him?"

"That's the beauty of it, Watson. It doesn't matter if she doesn't die. After all, a devoted mother who watches her son perish before her eyes …. What is more likely than her suicide shortly thereafter?"

My breath caught. Yes, it was a wicked plot, but it rang true. It was possible.

"How can we prove it?"

"I think it unlikely we can," Holmes said frankly. "But if I find sufficient indications that the deaths were not accidental, I may be able to persuade the police to reopen the cases. In the morning we shall look into the death of Mr. David Pelly. His death is more recent and we may unearth clearer indications."

And with that he turned for home, I following at his heels, content to wait for further enlightenment.

2

My mood changed abruptly as a question struck me. I turned to my companion.

"Holmes," I asked. "How *did* David Pelly die?"

My friend regarded me with sardonic amusement. "I wondered when that would occur to you. Yes, that too is another death whose cause may have been misunderstood. He is said to have died by misadventure. My own belief is that the coroner declared that to avoid distressing the family."

"What family?" I asked, momentarily distracted.

"The charming people we just left in Laburnum Avenue. The four of them attended the inquest."

He waited for my comprehension and I nodded. The coroner would have seen a grieving family. He may have asked himself what would be the harm in softening his verdict to misadventure? That, I thought, depended on the actual cause of death, and I asked again.

"He drank poison," Holmes informed me.

"What? But how did they declare that misadventure?"

He laid it out for me. David Pelly had become morose and reclusive since the deaths of his wife and only child. His business was busy and he worked long hours. Four years later, he was found the morning after the sad anniversary seated at his desk, an empty glass and a small, empty, expensive bottle of cherry brandy before him. The bottle was that of a notorious brand that contains cyanide and which must be shaken before a glass is poured. When this is not done, the final glass containing all the poison that had precipitated to the bottom, kills the drinker.

I could see the conundrum. Evidence from those about him suggested that David Pelly might have taken the drink deliberately. However that was not proof, and misadventure was the kinder verdict for those left behind. Again a question struck me.

"Did he leave a letter? Had he said anything to anyone that suggested he planned to take his own life?"

"No," Holmes said concisely.

That explained the verdict. Yet how did a killer persuade or force a man to drink the final glass of so notorious a drink? I asked that, and added, "Having forced him, if that was how it was done, why were there no signs of a struggle? It would take two or three men to hold another down and force him to drink something he must have known would cause his death. Unless he drank it willingly." I warmed to that theme. "Bereft of wife and beloved son, with nothing but a sterile business to give purpose to his life, he was depressed and spent long hours at his desk. Perhaps when his enemy offered him a drink, he accepted it as an end to his barren life."

Holmes hailed a cab and we entered. He gave directions to Baker Street.

"No, Watson," he continued once we were on the move. "I suspect rather that Pelly believed he was celebrating a coup in business."

"From a lethal bottle?" I observed.

"No, say rather from a full bottle, one from which drinks were poured out before him. If he did know of that drink's reputation he would have seen a safe, new bottle, and his companion drinking with him."

In a flash I understood. "But his glass was doctored. The fatal dose was not poured into it, it was dropped in or already in the glass."

"So I think. Well done, Watson. And how cunning his enemy! A man known to be glum and depressed, who has nothing left in his life but his work, is found by his desk, the means of suicide laid out neatly. There is no note, but to whom would he write such a missive? His heirs were little-known kin; would he pour out his heart to them? No. He drank, and what then but a scurry of activity. The murderer poured away the remainder of the bottle, added sufficient cyanide to the dregs to make Pelly's death seem reasonable. He then removed the second glass and departed, leaving behind a man who had, to all appearances, decided to end his life. Nor was that ever questioned. It was accepted as suicide, and the verdict as a kindly one."

I considered that in silence as we arrived at our address and departed the cab, entering 221 and climbing the stairs. I was still thinking when I made up the fire and reclaimed my comfortable armchair. At last I spoke.

"But the doctor who examined Pelly? Should he not have questioned how a man who died from cyanide was still sitting at his desk? He would be lying on the floor, as cyanide causes convulsions. Besides, death occurs in minutes, but the man might still have time to seek aid. When he began to be ill, why did he remain in the room?"

"That," Holmes said, "is why we shall go to his place of business in the morning."

* * * *

We rose early, breakfasted well and set out for the factory that produced the sacks that held coal for the Riggston deliveries. It was within a wall of around eight feet high—presumably to prevent theft—topped by broken glass set into the concrete. There were two gates: one a double entrance that was large enough to admit any vehicle; and the other smaller, for the use of staff or visitors.

Mr. Allan Pelly was quite happy for us to examine the room in which Mr. David Pelly had died, and for us to question staff who had been employed at the time of his death. We went first to the room that had been the owner's office. It was situated on the top floor of three and was spacious, with figured curtains, oak paneling and two doors. One door led directly to the passage, and the other led to two other, much smaller rooms. I supposed them to have been rooms used by clerks.

I opened the second door and discovered an intermediate room that apparently functioned as a waiting room. A niche contained the supplies and equipment for making tea—a small urn for hot water, and various crockery—and a sink for washing, along with a shelf holding a number of biscuit tins and tea caddies. The small room beyond, however, did hold a desk and a stern-faced young woman, typing industriously. I nodded to her and closed the doors again, retreating to rejoin Holmes.

I found my friend standing, looking out of the large window that showed the busy yard below. Abruptly he strode to one side of the room and fell flat on the carpet. He lay there for several minutes, turning his head as if sighting along some invisible line, before springing to his feet again. He looked up.

"Watson, if you will? Return to that waiting room and look through all the cupboards. I want to know if there is a hand-brush there, of the kind that might be used to sweep up crumbs, or the sort of brush that may be used if ashes are spilled."

I knew the sort to which he referred and uncovered such an item in a long cupboard that also held a broom, dustpan, and minor cleaning supplies. Trays stood in a fancy rack in another cupboard. Those, I noticed with amusement, were of a graduation in importance. One tray was of prettily painted tin, the next of pewter, another of the same metal but more elaborately decorated, and two silver trays, the last a really fine affair indeed, and fit to serve a duchess. I returned and offered the brush, remarking as I did so on the trays.

Holmes turned to me. "Yes, I think he was the sort of man with a great sense of his own place in society, and determined that others should know theirs." He glanced at the brush and nodded. "Thank you, you may return that. I merely wished to know of its existence."

I replaced the brush and came back, seating myself at the desk, watching my friend as he ran sensitive fingers over the door to the passage. He examined the second door in the same manner as the first, before considering the desk.

"They've moved that from the original position."

He pointed, and I observed faint indentations in the carpet that showed he was right. I nodded and smiled. "And the chair is new."

Holmes eyed me. "Is it? And how do you know?"

Delighted to show off my own observations, I explained. "Such a desk is usually sold to the customer with a matching chair. Not only made from the same wood, but with matching detail. See here: the desk drawers have small polished wooden knobs in a contrasting wood. The chair would have the same wood in a pattern inset at the end of the arms. The desk feet are carved and the chair would have had feet carved the same way."

"Bravo, Watson. How do you know this?"

"I have seen such desks and chairs before. A specialist colleague had a similar combination. I remarked it and when, some weeks later we had been to a professional dinner and walked seeking a cab together, we passed by the very shop where he had purchased them. He paused to point out others of that type and tell me of the usual way of matching such things."

"That is excellent. You remembered pertinent information, related it to the case, and can confirm it from your own observation."

I felt a great sense of satisfaction at his words. I had contributed something new, and his praise was genuine.

"I am not surprised that they have a different chair," Holmes said thoughtfully. "The old one would probably have been stained. Besides, no man wishes to sit in the seat of his dead predecessor quite so literally. It is likely for that reason they also moved the desk. From the marks, it previously stood before the window." He moved to that position. "Yes, Mr. David Pelly would sit here, the desk at a slight angle, his back to the window. That allowed sunlight to fall on his work, and anyone that he interviewed would have that same sunlight in their eyes. And he had only to turn his head a little and he could see everything below."

I walked to join him and exclaimed. "Why, so you can. I see Mr. Allan Pelly talking to someone; there is a lady with a dog passing by on the street beyond the wall. Look, Holmes, here comes Miss Gwen Pelly. She must be about to visit her father."

"Yes, you can indeed see a lot from this aerie," was all my friend said. He opened the door into the passage, gestured that I should follow, and headed for the stairs. I hurried after him, and once I caught up we headed for another set of offices in a building by the main factory. We wound through warehouses and another group of offices, until we reached a shed that had an office at the back, with samples of sacks in a heap at the front. There we found an elderly man, upright of figure, lined of face, and with an air of some authority. Holmes approached him.

"Mr. Jacob Hearn, the yard foreman?"

He regarded us with faded blue eyes. "Are you the gentlemen Mr. Allan wishes me to talk to? He said you had questions and that I should answer them honestly, and that no anger should fall upon me if I did so."

"We are the men," Holmes said. "And he has said no more than the truth. There will be no trouble even if what you say might not be to someone's liking. Will you answer truthfully?" He received a nod and began at once. "Tell me of Mr. David Pelly. Was he a good employer; was he a fair man or not? How well did he know this business, and did he pay it the attention it required? What of those he disliked: did you know anyone he distrusted, or who disliked him?"

He paused and Jacob Hearn smiled suddenly. "A fair lot of questions, an' I'll do my best," he told us. "Yes, Mr. David knew the business, brought up to it, he was. Knew each nook and cranny here, an' every trick that could be played." He held up a hand when Holmes started to speak.

"All in good time, sir. Truth you asked for and truth I'll tell. No, he wasn't a good employer, nor was he a good man in my opinion. He liked money, and the only thing he liked more were that fancy son of his, or doing someone out of their rights. I don't know any as he really disliked. He felt himself above such a thing, but I could give you a long line of the names of those that distrusted him, whom he'd cheated, and there were even some that hated him. He was a nasty piece of work, and that's a fact. I worked here all my life and his father wasn't so bad, but Mr. David, any enemies he had he gained them honestly."

That, I thought, was truth-telling with a vengeance.

"Every trick that could be played?" Holmes asked.

"Aye. One trick is to send out a big load of sacks close to end of day. They'll be unloaded in poor light with the workers keen to finish and get home. Sacks may not be counted, and if some aren't decent quality, that'll likely be missed. If the one that bought them don't notice it for a while before he complained, Mr. David shrugged and said how could they say it was his fault? Sacks can be stolen by any worker any time, and what was to say that the damage was caused in our yard when they'd been on the buyer's place for days or weeks?"

He chuckled. "Caught cold at that, though. He sold a mighty number of them to a business right before he died, and saw to it that they went there on dusk. Someone came with a note next morning. Mr. David left it on his desk and one of our clerks read it. Said the owner had checked the sacks as they arrived and about five percent were missing, and another ten percent of worthless quality. They'd be calling on him expecting re-payment for those, and they had the exact numbers required, witnesses, and the law on their side. He'd pay or provide good items to make up for those not received or valueless, or he could explain himself in court."

"And did he meet this person?"

"I don't know, sir. I would have stayed that night to see who came but he ordered us all to go home and stood by to see we left. Once we'd gone I saw him lock the main gates and I waited until I saw the light go on in his office and there he was, looking out of his window. So I went home, walking hard by the wall where you can't be overlooked."

"Did you think that the person coming to see him could have some-thing to do with Mr. David's death?"

Jacob Hearn frowned, a crease in his forehead. "Why would I think that? Mr. David killed himself, all know about it. Likely some piece of dishonesty had caught up with him and he was afraid of the law. Coroner brought it in as an accident but we all knows that was to spare Mr. Allan and his family. Nice people they are too, and good employers," he added. "How Mr. David came to have good un's like them as kin is beyond us."

Holmes regarded him. "Was there anything in the letter that said when this person would see Mr. David?"

"No, but we all supposed it would be that night, else why was he sending us home when there was a good hour of daylight yet, when we could have been working?"

"You were last out. How dark was it then?"

"Dark enough. You could see people, but not make out their faces ...." He paused.

"You've remembered someone you saw!" Holmes stated.

"Yes, sirs. I was walking away, close under the wall. A lad passed me going the other way, just as I went around the corner. It was a cold night; he had a hat pulled down over his brow, and a scarf wrapped around his neck. There's no street lamp on that corner. All I saw was a face that showed pale under what little moonlight there was, and his clothing was dark, although of what actual color I am unable to say, it could have been any darker shade."

"Then you saw more than many would have seen or remembered. You saw no more of his face?"

"No, sirs, just a white shape. From his silhouette he weren't a big lad, slender, and maybe about five and a half feet in height. I thought him to be no more than fifteen. What would a lad like that have to do with Mr. David? No, I went on home and I daresay he did as well."

"Thank you, Mr. Hearn. Rest assured that we shall not repeat anything you have told us. Now, if you will show us the quickest way out we'll be gone."

Jacob led us between buildings and we were soon back at the main gates. Mr. Allan stood there with Miss Gwen, and he hailed us jovially. "Get everything you wanted, Doctor, Mr. Holmes?"

"Thank you, we did."

"And your opinion of my cousin's death? Do you believe he was murdered?"

Holmes glanced at the young woman. Her father, seeing the direction of his gaze, turned to her.

"Would you go to my office, Gwennie, and find that letter I spoke of? Mr. Holmes may wish to see it."

She gave us a look that said she knew she was being sent away, but departed obediently on her errand

"I think it more likely now that I have seen his office," Holmes said. "Your foreman's interesting discourse on his employer leads me to agree that the man would have had a number of enemies."

Mr. Allan flushed. "I fear that is right. David was a sharp businessman and sometimes that spilled over—well—into fraud. Since I inherited I have found four or five occasions where I have reimbursed those who had been ill done by. Florence could be more generous at times, and I know David chided her for it."

"In what way was she so?"

Miss Gwen came up just then and handed my friend a letter.

"That's the only incident I haven't been able to trace," Mr. David told us. "Maybe my cousin already repaid what was owed."

I read over Holmes's shoulder: it was the letter Jacob Hearns had mentioned. Holmes folded it and placed it in his pocket.

"It may yield useful information yet," he said. "Now, in what way was Florence more generous? Can you give an example?"

"I can give a number. She gave money to her church, at Christmas she went to help at a mission that feeds the poor, and then there was May. Josephine Percy was Florence's best friend when they were at school together. Florence was bullied and Josie stopped that. Josie helped with her studies, and was always patient with Florence. When Josephine became ill she asked Florence to take May, saying that she distrusted her brothers. Florence swore on the Bible that she would and Josie died content, but after Josephine died David refused to have the child. He said her income would not sufficiently recompense them. Florence, as ever, bowed to his wishes and the child went to James Riggston."

"From which unhappy situation she ran away as soon as she was old enough," Holmes told him quietly.

"I'm sorry to hear it. James was a cold, penny-pinching brute, as was his wife, and I never liked his sons the few times that I met them. One was a complainer, the other jovial on the surface but thoroughly selfish, and nothing mattered to him but what made his life more comfortable."

After a few more words we left and the gate shut behind us with a solid clank of iron. I turned at once to my friend.

"So you think Mr. David Pelly was murdered. I saw nothing to tell me so. What did I miss?" I asked ruefully as we walked away.

3

Holmes eyed me kindly. "You weren't looking where I was," he said, keeping his voice down as we walked along the street. "When I lay on David Pelly's office carpet, I could see slight drag marks. They had been brushed out, so they only showed if one was observing them at the correct angle. The door too showed possible clues: the handle is slightly bent, as if someone had pulled down on it strongly while falling."

I felt a chill at his words. "You think David Pelly had company when he died, don't you?"

"I am sure of it, and not such company as a man would wish. I believe that his visitor poisoned David Pelly. He then watched as Pelly staggered to the door—which had been locked. Pelly tried desperately to open the door and failed. He may have begged for help—or mercy—but he found neither and died there on the carpet. Whereupon Pelly was dragged to the desk and sat in the chair, the door unlocked, and the visitor departed."

I could see the scene as he told it; the frantic man, in agony from the ingested cyanide, already starting the convulsions that would kill him, reeling to the implacable figure to entreat help. I saw the slow shake of a head, the victim falling, writhing, gasping and uttering hoarse cries until those faded. He shivered and died. The killer did what was necessary and coolly left. A heart of stone, and …

"Holmes?" I asked. "What *could* David Pelly have done that warranted such vengeance?"

He said nothing for some moments, then—"Let the punishment fit the crime."

I stared. "What?"

"Nothing, Watson. Let us talk to Mrs. Helston."

"Who's Mrs. Helston?"

"The lady who was first on the scene when Florence and Jonathon Pelly drowned."

* * * *

I found the lady of good value. She was elderly, but sharp-eyed and sharp witted. She described the scene clearly, adding her own commentary, and we listened attentively.

"I had gone to the lakes for a holiday. I was newly a widow and the funeral and settling my husband's estate had been fatiguing. I took a month's lease on a small house near the lake. I had my maid with me, obtained the services of a local woman as housekeeper, and made the acquaintance of others staying in that area."

It had been a mostly convivial group, she said. Although she had not particularly liked the Pellys, mother and son. The mother tended to give in to the son's demands and he was "a nasty, spoiled brat, the kind who thinks the world owes him, not just a living, but anything he wants as well." She laughed. "Had his comeuppance, although," her face sobered, "a pity his mother died, too."

It had been a pleasant day, she told us, until the mist came down. Jonathon Pelly had nevertheless insisted that he was going boating. He intended to row from one side of the lake to the other and the mild objections from his mother—he said she knew nothing about it—and the more knowledgeable ones from a servant who said that the lake could be treacherous, and there was weed at the edge where he planned to finish—were ignored and finally laughed off. He went out, and after some time Florence became nervous and followed, just to be sure that all was well.

"It wasn't well," Mrs. Helston told us. "I went with her, as it was a pleasant day for a walk and I did not suppose anything to be really wrong. We rounded the edge of the lake towards the place he should come ashore. Mrs. Pelly was walking fast and was at that time a few steps ahead of me. She screamed unexpectedly and dashed forward. You must understand, the fog was still heavy and I lost sight of her at once. I heard what I thought was splashing, but I could see nothing and I could not tell from which direction it came."

"No," Holmes informed her. "Fog distorts not only sounds but the direction from which they emanate."

"I walked forward, watching the ground since I did not wish to fall into the lake. There was a minute when the fog cleared and I saw a boat floating in a broad band of reeds by the lake's edge. Mrs. Pelly was in the water, flailing about, shouting her son's name and grabbing at the reeds. Something like a log rolled in the water and then it was gone, and she was dragged under. Then the fog closed in again and I could not even see the ground under my feet. I stood still shouting for help, but it was not until some hours later that the fog finally lifted and they could retrieve the bodies."

She sat back, lost in the memories. "They said that when they found her, her hands were still gripping her son's clothing. They could not loose her grasp and the two had to be dragged into the boat together. I remained for the inquest, where the coroner spoke disapprovingly about Jonathon Pelly. He said that it was well known that that lake was extremely dangerous because of the shallow depth and the reed beds. A number of those incautious enough to swim there had been drowned, and several people had said this to Master Pelly and advised the young man against his venture. He could not imagine what had possessed the deceased to take such a foolish risk."

"He did not see it as a risk," Holmes told her. "Young men often take things literally. He was not intending to swim. He would be in a boat and thus assumed himself to be quite safe."

"Well, he wasn't, was he!" the lady snapped.

"No, he wasn't."

I saw evidence upon Holmes's countenance that some aspect of this tale had given him to think. He said all that was polite but swept me out of the house at some speed and was hailing a cab as soon as we set foot in the street.

"Where are we going now?" I asked in mild surprise. "It's late in the afternoon, and by the time we get anywhere our host is likely to be considering his dinner."

"We'll be there shortly, and I advised him that we would be calling this afternoon," was all I was told. We pulled up some twenty minutes later outside a small, pleasant block of apartments and were welcomed in by a man of late middle age. He had a quiet, unassuming look, but I noticed that, like Mrs. Helston, his eyes were remarkably keen, and from the lines on his face I thought him prone to a sense of humor.

Holmes shook his hand and introduced me. "Watson, this is Cecil Grosett. He is the Riggston family lawyer and took over from his predecessor when he died. It is of his predecessor we are inquiring. Mr. Grosett, this is my colleague, Dr. John Watson."

We were invited to sit in the drawing room, and neither man wasted any time. Mr. Grosett assumed a listening position and Holmes began.

"Mr. Arthur Riggston is interested in the death of your senior partner," he began.

"Mr. Arthur Riggston has a bee in his bonnet," our host retorted. "Yes, yes, I know his theories. He has done me the honor to share them. It is possible, just barely possible, that some could have died by design. But my senior partner was most certainly not one of them." He turned to me. "You are a doctor; bear me out in this, sir. Eli Gettes had a weak heart for much of his life. He had two minor heart attacks in the three years before he died, and his doctor told him that it was but a matter of time. Eli suffered a third and fatal heart attack over twenty years ago, soon after our client, Mr. Joseph Riggston, passed away." He shook his head at me. "Tell your friend that Eli's death was to be expected."

I nodded, and asked a number of subsidiary questions before looking at my friend. "It's as Mr. Grosett says. His partner's death could be expected at any time."

"Arthur Riggston thought it possible a heart attack could have been induced."

"With a man in that condition it is possible but …"

"It is impossible," Grosett cut in angrily. "Unless you are accusing his housekeeper or me of being responsible. She was in the house at the time and saw and heard no other person save myself, whom she had shown out only moments before. She was still at the door when she heard him gasp and fall. She screamed, ran to him, and I was back beside her almost as she reached his body. His breath failed even as I knelt beside him, and he was gone. I tell you that there was no one else around. He died in his study. The windows were latched shut, the back door was bolted, and certainly no one could have exited the door without being seen by me or his housekeeper."

"More than twenty years ago?" Holmes said thoughtfully. "Have you wound up all his affairs, discovered all his papers, and been able to reconcile all accounts?"

"Yes, I have! What are you suggesting?"

Holmes's tones were soothing. "I merely desire to satisfy Arthur Riggston that all is well. I have a report to make, you understand."

The lawyer relaxed back in his chair. "Of course. Well then, yes, I have dealt with all matters that were in Eli's hands at the time of his death and I do assure you that nothing was amiss, that all accounts were reconciled, and that there was nothing left outstanding."

"You say that Mr. Joseph Riggston died shortly before your partner? How did that come about?"

"It was all quite tragic. He was something of a social gambler, a *bon vivant*. He was yet unmarried and his own man, with all his time free beyond the business. He was no more than thirty-five, and he always said that he had time yet before he willingly donned shackles. He would come and go from his club late at night, and one evening he had won a good sum of money. He walked from the club bidding the doorman goodnight, and was later found in the Thames. He had received a blow to the head and drowned."

Holmes's eyes narrowed. "So he drowned. He still had his winnings?"

"Oh, yes. It was believed that he had stumbled, struck his head, and fallen in somewhere along his route. It could not have been a robbery gone wrong since his winnings, his pocket watch, and gentleman's jewelry were all still on him."

I caught Holmes's look and said nothing. I had assisted my friend long enough to know that the presence of these items proved nothing more than that the murderer had wanted Joseph's life, not his valuables.

"Distressing. He and his brother were only young men when their parents died?"

"Ah yes, yes indeed. I did not know them myself, you understand. But I heard all about it often from Mr. Gettes. Poor James and Mary, he used to say. James was only twenty-six and his brother twenty-five when their parents passed away. A carriage accident. The elder James Riggston was a little old-fashioned and, well, perhaps a touch close-fisted also. He had a habit of driving himself and his wife to events, relying upon his host's groom to do all that was needful for the horses once they arrived. His father had left several carriages of excellent quality and condition and he always said there was no need to replace that method of transport until they were no longer of use."

"An accident?" Holmes asked, his tone neutral.

"Yes. The horses suffered some fright and bolted and an axle broke, flinging both James and his wife onto the road. Her neck snapped in the fall, and he struck his head upon a stone. It was quite broken—his head, that is—but it was, as I believe, a mercy. Neither would have liked to linger in such a condition as they would have been had they survived their injuries."

"No, indeed," I confirmed.

Holmes opened his mouth to ask another question and was fore-stalled when Mr. Grosett stood.

"I think that is all, sir. You came to ask of my partner and I have answered. I'll see you out."

He did so firmly and closed the door behind us the second I cleared the doorway.

Holmes glanced at me in amusement. "One would think Mr. Grosett had suspicions of his own."

"Whatever do you mean?"

His amusement deepened. "It is not some anonymous killer he has in mind. In the case of James and Mary Riggston, it is their elder son he suspects."

"What? Why?"

"Think about it, Watson. Both lads had just attained their majority. Some families are old-fashioned, and I expect the father's will stipulated that they did not fully inherit until the age of twenty-five. That barely occurred when both parents die. I gained the impression that the mother would not have given her sons free rein with the business. Rather, she would have mirrored her husband's position and run it as he did."

"But the sons wanted to modernize," I said slowly. "They wanted to improve, upgrade, and not only the business but their own homes, where they wanted luxury. Their father did not waste money. He would, I imagine, pay them fairly well, but not as much as they wanted."

"And as I have heard, there has been some suggestion of arguments, then suddenly the parents are dead and the sons are in charge. They can spend as they wish. What if there was further argument? What if Joseph protested that he was not receiving his share of the spoils? It is likely, if such difficulties occurred, that Mr. Grosett would have been told of them by his partner—and then Joseph dies and James is in sole possession."

My breath caught. "James! You think he murdered his parents and then his brother? But why would he murder the Pellys? What motive could he have?"

"I could think of a number, but Watson, I did not say I suspected James. I said that I believed the lawyer to do so."

I was bewildered. "Then you think James to have done nothing?"

Holmes's lips tightened. "I think he did much, he and his brother and his father, as well as the Pellys. But I believe none were murderers. However, it may be that they led to such, and it is for that I am inquiring. Never mind, Watson," he said as he saw that my confusion had only deepened. "Let us go home, eat our dinner, and retire. I am sure you are in need of some sustenance."

And he was right as always. With all our running about, I had had little to eat all day save tea and biscuits, and I was happy to fall upon an excellent dinner once we reached our home, where a fine steak and kidney pie awaited us, courtesy of Mrs. Hudson.

* * * *

The next morning I set out alone. Holmes sought more information on the carriage accident, and I was tasked with finding someone who remembered the old minister from the elder Riggston's church. I found instead a middle-aged minister—a Jarod Wilson—who still recalled the old man and could tell me somewhat of him.

"A gentle man and a gentleman. His only fault was that he was, shall I say, a trifle too believing. If a man swore he was innocent of wrongdoing, he would believe, for the old man never accepting that a gentleman would lie to him. He was rather unworldly man. I know of a case where one of his parishioners was discovered in a brothel and convinced the minister that he'd merely called in to help someone who'd asked for his aid in unblocking a pipe."

I chuckled involuntarily.

"Yes," he told me. "It is amusing. However, another case I did not find nearly so droll. He willfully overlooked child neglect and then passed it off as due to the mother's unfortunate circumstances. 'The woman is poor,' he said. 'She only left the child to find work.'"

His eyes flashed. "She spent her money on a pretty dress and went with a man to Brighton. It was in my first year of ministering here. I found the boy, a lad of barely six, blue with cold—there was no fuel for the fire—and he was starved and barely conscious. I spoke sternly to Katy Stowe on her return and she ran to my superior saying that she should not be blamed, that her gentleman friend kept her longer than expected before she got her money and could return, and that until she was paid she could not purchase food or fuel for her son."

"That is possible," I said doubtfully.

"Possible, but untrue. I found the man and talked to him. She had been paid after two days and could have departed any time thereafter. But Reverend Mathews did not wish to hear about that." He looked at me. "He was not a bad man, but he was always unwilling to hear or accept any unpleasantness. He would pass the event off as a misunderstanding, or even a minor sin on the part of the person asking his help or support. He said to me that William should have gone in search of food or firewood, and had he done so the neighbors would have aided him. Or he could have approached one of us. Since Reverend Mathews died I have tried not to fall into that trap."

I took my leave of him thinking of all he had said and of the character of the Reverend Mathews. I could see nothing which might give rise to murder. A saintly old man who heard no evil, saw no evil, and wished to know nothing of evil. A thought struck me and I paused at the church's cemetery. There I found the graves of the elder Riggstons, their sons Joseph and James, and that of the minister. The inscription on Mr. Mathews's headstone stated that he had died in his sixty-ninth year of a stroke, and God had known His own.

I walked a while longer amidst the tombstones, but I could find nothing more than seemed relevant. By now I was hungry and becoming tired, so I hailed a cab. My mind, as I travelled, turned over the information I had received. The Riggston family was hardly extinct. Arthur the younger's mother, Mrs. Jane Riggston, might yet live—at least he had said nothing to the contrary—and what about the next generation? Joseph, we had been told, had died a bachelor, but what of James's children? Hadn't the genealogy Holmes showed me some time ago listed two sons?

I departed the cab at the door of 221, paid the driver, and hastened up the stairs to our rooms. From the savory smell that greeted me, our belated lunch was already on the table, which meant that my friend must be returned. I went hurriedly to wash up and we met at the table where I was firstly occupied in making a good meal. But once that was done I leaned back, poured myself a drink, and regarded my companion.

"I found a minister who had known his predecessor well. He told me all he could, but I fear it sheds little light on the man or why he might be murdered." I commenced my tale as Holmes listened.

Once I was done he regarded me. "You saw no reason why some person might wish to punish the man?" I shook my head. "Some do not deal well with the sins of their own class," Holmes commented. "This minister appears to have been a man who did not wish to believe in evil, but in doing so he may have encouraged it to flourish. That woman who left her son hungry in a freezing room—by his acceptance of her false excuses he absolved her of any need for improvement."

"What has that to do with murder?" I asked.

"Why, in his later years, the son might not think it so equitable."

"Ah, that might have been so, but the lad is dead. I walked for some time in the church graveyard and found his grave. He was in his twenty-ninth year, and despite all that was said of her, his mother must not have been so bad if she found the money for his monument. It was only a small stone cross, but it had his name and the dates of his birth and death, and it must have cost considerable money for a woman in her circumstances."

"If she paid for it," Holmes said cynically.

I would have responded, but for the memory of the cross. The carving was of excellent quality, the ends of the arms scrolled and bifurcated, so perhaps some other wealthier and compassionate person had provided it. I changed the subject and asked of Holmes's own discoveries. He sat back with an air that told me of revelations to come.

4

Holmes had found a newspaper report of the Riggston accident, and another of their funeral. Two of those mentioned added their long-ago recollections upon being interviewed by my friend. It was sufficient to build an interesting portrait. Neither had said outright that the Riggstons hadn't been much liked, but Holmes reads well between the lines. Once again it was clear that James Riggston the elder was miserly, his wife as mean as he was, and that James was known to be a businessman who was up to every crooked trick in town.

"'Sharp enough to cut himself,' was how one described it," Holmes said. "Another said that if you dealt with him, it was like dealing with the devil—you'd better have a long spoon." He went on to summarize the accident while I listened closely.

The Riggstons attended a party given by friends who lived only two miles from the couple's country house. James had brought out one of the old carriages and had that polished, and a pair of horses, rented for twenty-four hours, put to. James had taken the open carriage's reins and driven off. They had remained at the party until midnight, when the weather turned. If it rained and they stayed overnight, they would have to pay an extra day's hire for the horses. James wasn't risking that. He ordered his friend's groom to harness the horses again and he and his wife departed.

"I spoke to the groom," Holmes related. "He said that James was, in his words 'well to pass, sir, very well indeed.'"

"He was drunk?"

Holmes considered that. "I would say so, yes. I gained the impression of a man who, while not unsteady on his feet and slurring his words, was only refraining by an exercise of will. The groom says the horses were sidling and sidestepping as they went down the drive, and James was having trouble controlling them."

I understood. "Horses like a firm, gentle hand on the reins. They could sense his condition and felt his indecision, and it would upset them."

James had turned the carriage along the main road and only a half-mile farther something alarmed the animals and they bolted. It was pitch-dark, with solid cloud cover. It had been imprudent in the extreme to set out on a return journey in those conditions and I said so. Holmes nodded.

"They had good carriage lamps and appear to have believed them sufficient."

They had not been. The bolting horses had dragged the carriage through a fence, overturning it forcefully—from Holmes's description of the wreckage it sounded as if the vehicle had almost cartwheeled. James Riggston and his wife had been catapulted violently from the vehicle: she breaking her neck on landing, and he to strike his head against a stone so hard that the skull was smashed, the scalp torn open and the very brain exposed. It had come on to rain shortly thereafter, and when the morning light disclosed the scene all blood had been washed away, leaving only two dull-eyed corpses, a ruined carriage, and the grazing horses.

Holmes scowled. "So far as I can ascertain there was no inquiry at all. Since nothing was missing from the bodies, theft or attack was ruled out. Riggston's friends claimed that he was a businessman with no grudge against him, and that he and his wife were the most harmless of people. The Riggstons were buried in a funeral that—courtesy of their sons—was a mix of foolish pomp and cheese-paring."

I raised my eyebrows in query.

"Oh, they used one of the couple's own carriages as the hearse," Holmes said. "A pair of placid black horses was hired for a half-day from the same place as that other pair, and I was told in confidence that the headstone was the result of a bad debt. It had been cut to request but not yet inscribed, and the buyer defaulted. The sons obtained it cheaply and had the inscription added."

"And the pomp?" I asked in amusement.

"The sons borrowed horses, or used some of their own—which were not always suitable—and made a great procession with all of their father's carriage collection—some dozen, with servants and workers from their business aboard. Other locals added their own conveyances, so that in all over thirty carriages took part. The minister was arrayed like Alice in the field, or so one poetic lady informed me. (I believe her to have been referring to the Biblical verse that speaks of the lilies of the field.)"

I chuckled at this malapropism.

Holmes continued. "This seemed odd to me since ministers of the Baptist church do not normally wear elaborate vestments. I found the man and he was much amused. He told me that the sons had brought clothing and offered a sizeable donation to his church if he would wear the items 'to do their parents honor.' As there are many poor in the parish, he felt bowing to their wish would do no harm and much good. He said that he had no idea where they had obtained the garments, which were white and gold, and of fine quality."

He described them further and when he spoke of the braid-edged, open-fronted over-vest I gave a crack of laughter. As a doctor I go many places and I'd seen such clothing, Holmes gave an excellent description and I could see the garments in my mind's eye.

"Holmes, those were the vestments of a judge."

"Nonsense, Watson. No judge I know wears such a robe."

"Not a real judge, Holmes. They come from the play 'Damascus.' The sons took off the long scarlet silk scarf that is draped around the neck and a long, gold-tasseled belt, as well as a chain and medallion. But otherwise the robe and over-vest are the same."

"How is it that you recall them so well?"

I smiled. "Only a month ago I was called to Lord Temberton's London house to aid one of his guests who had slipped on the stairs. They had just finished enacting that play, and he was still dressed as the judge. I had a close view of his clothing for almost an hour, and he told me something of the play. It seems probable they were borrowed from a costumer. They must have made a fine sight, billowing and fluttering about when he stood at the graveside."

Holmes's smile was wintry. "A fine sight indeed. I wonder who loaned them, and if they knew the use to which they were put."

We sobered.

"No," I said quietly. "I doubt they did. Yet it seems to have done no harm, and at this distance what does it matter, save it shows the character of the sons. They wanted an extravagant show for their parents' funeral, and did not care if it was false."

"It shows us something else, too, Watson. One of the sons had a friend who was of a higher social strata, and also that the neither the friend nor his family were expected to attend the funeral."

I could see that. "Odd. In all that we have heard so far, there has been no mention of any noble involved."

"No," my friend said slowly. "But the sons were in their mid-twenties at the time. The father was moving his family up in society, and his sons attended a minor public school. The sons of impoverished noblemen go to such places as well."

"If they were impoverished, they would not have owned such clothing merely for a play," I said sensibly.

"The young can be irreligious, and their relations may not have been so poor," was his rejoinder. I grasped his line of thought. He believed that one of the sons had prevailed on an old school friend to borrow the garments from a wealthier relative. The young men would find the idea amusing and a good joke on the stuffy, middle-classes who would not know what they saw.

"I can see two young men doing that," I agreed. "Yet if I lost parents I loved I would not do such a thing. It makes a mockery of their deaths, and if discovered, it would do them no good in society's eyes. They are reckless at the least, and I cannot approve."

"No. Yet it throws a useful light on their characters, Watson. I see them as reckless, uncaring young men, believing themselves too clever to be found out, and believing that if what they did *should* become known, that they could talk their way out of any consequences. In short, the character of Joseph Riggston, who insisted on walking home alone in the dead of night along the river because he was convinced no harm could come to him. I must discover how the elder brother died. I think it likely we shall find his behavior was all of a piece."

I offered a suggestion on another topic. "James the elder seems to have been a blackguard in his business dealings. Is it possible that someone he cheated could have spooked the horses on purpose?"

"It is. Yet since their deaths are now thirty-three years gone, it is likely that the murderer is dead. And if Arthur Riggston's suspicions are true, then his suspect is yet alive—or was until nine years ago."

"Then you think that the elder Riggstons' deaths were an accident?"

"I did not say so. Listen. Suppose that I have a grudge against the pair. I know they will be at the party and that they will not stay the night since that would mean unnecessary expense. I wait in the darkness, and when the horses approach I panic them and run after the carriage. In such a wreck it is likely that both occupants will be injured or unconscious. I can kill them at my leisure, in such a way that my deeds are not obvious. In the event the murderer was fortunate. He found the woman dead already. The man he moved, raised his head and brought it down with all his strength on a protruding stone. Then he left the scene. It rained the remainder of the night, washing away not only blood, but also any footprints or other indications to show another person was present."

"Then he was fortunate. He took a chance."

"Not if he knew the area and the weather. He may also have muffled his footwear in cloths, so any marks would have been blurred. No one was looking for a murderer's tracks, and, since nothing was missing from the scene, the authorities did not expect or look for such indications."

It was unpleasantly convincing and I said so. "What about the lawyer? I know you to still believe his death to be suspicious. His state of health means that most likely his death was natural."

Holmes gave a small chuckle. "On the contrary, his delicate state of health makes murder easier. Suppose I approach his window, waiting until he is standing right before it, with his back to me. I scratch at the glass gently until he hears it and turns. I wear a horrific mask, perhaps the image of something he fears. I step forward so that the creature seems to leap at him, and his heart gives a great spasm of fear—then stops. He falls, dying, to the carpet in his room with its latched windows and guarded door. I hide the mask under my coat and stroll from the garden by the back of the property. I have committed murder—unseen and unsuspected."

"Holmes," I said, with great conviction, "it is well you have never taken to murder!"

His gray eyes regarded me with a glimmer of enjoyment. "Quite so, Watson. But you'll admit it is possible." And I could not dissent.

"Changing the subject," I said. "It is late afternoon and I presume we are done for the day. What is my task for the morrow?"

"If you would, Watson, I would like you to inquire on the disposition of the estate of Joseph Riggston. Then discover the heirs to James Riggston, the brother of Joseph. How the money went may have some bearing on the matter."

* * * *

After breakfast the next morning, I went to the Pelly's business. They still dealt with the Riggstons and would know who inherited. With that information I moved on to the records office to read the contents of Joseph Riggston's will. It bore nothing at all surprising, for he had left "all of which he died possessed to his beloved brother, James Riggston." I returned the copy of the will and was leaving the building when I became conscious of a presence at my shoulder. I stepped outside and a hand seized me by the arm, while a man demanded to know why I had been nosing into Riggston business.

I was shaken savagely, while the man raised his voice.

"I will have an answer! Who are you? Why were you reading that will? By what right do you come here? By God, you're the murderer!

Help! This man's a killer!" I tried to pull away, for his grip on my arm was painful, and his fingers tightened. "Oh, yes, trying to escape are you? I'll stop that."

A blow to my temple half-stunned me. I turned to see a young face distorted with fear and anger, and a second blow dropped me to the pavement. Another young man, fair-haired and snub-nosed, attempted to pull my assailant away and I dimly heard an authoritative voice asking what was going on before I slid into unconsciousness.

I came to, still on the pavement. Upon opening my eyes I saw a crowd of people standing about me, with a familiar form keeping them from moving too close.

"Harrison?" I asked weakly, venturing to sit up as my head cleared. The detective nodded.

"Doctor. Have you any idea what's going on?"

I blinked doubtfully. "I thought you would know?"

"Someone shouted for help, crying that he had a murderer in his grip and when I got to the spot you were lying there. I exclaimed …"

"What did you say, exactly?" I demanded.

"Why, that you were no murderer, but a doctor and an honest man well known to me. How had you come to be lying there? There was some pushing and shoving amid the crowd, and I could discover no one who admitted to calling for help."

"Ah," I said, thinking rapidly. I could guess who had leapt to conclusions and struck me down, however, I would rather confront him personally. "I was accosted from behind by a man who shouted I was a murderer, and before I could turn to see him clearly he knocked me down. I can only think it was mistaken identity."

Harrison eyed me skeptically. "As you say, Dr. Watson. Obviously someone who did not know you and thought you another. Here, let me help you." He aided me to rise and brushed me down. "Do you need medical assistance?"

My head hurt, but not so badly that I could not walk. I shook my head—and immediately wished I hadn't. "No, I shall be well enough if I am careful. I'll take a cab home and all will be well. Thank you, Harrison."

"Glad to be of help, Doctor." And to the goggling crowd: "You lot can move on, there's nothing more to see here."

I hailed transport and was driven home. Walking up the stairs was tiring; my head was swimming as I entered our rooms and I all but fell into my usual armchair. I closed my eyes, and when I opened them, Holmes's concerned face peered at me.

"Watson, your face is bruised and I could not rouse you for some minutes. Have you been attacked?"

"Yes," I said baldly.

"Where?"

"At the records office, where I went to see Joseph's will," I mumbled.

"Cup of tea?"

"What? Oh, yes, of course." He shouted down the stairs and I held my aching head. His shout had gone right through it. Holmes turned to see my anguish.

"My dear fellow, how thoughtless of me."

"My medical bag?" He fetched it and I dosed myself before lying back in the chair. The tincture and the tea would deal with the headache. The tea was hot and strong, and once both items had taken hold I felt better, sitting straighter in my chair and giving a clear account to my friend.

"This fellow who struck you, you think him a Riggston? I believe you are right. Only a Riggston, or perhaps a Pelly, knows of Arthur Riggston's suspicions concerning murderous attacks on their family. His own suspicions were aroused when he saw you reading Joseph Riggston's will—although why he should suppose a murderer would go to that trouble I do not know. Doubtless he has his reasons. Describe the man to me."

I managed a pained smile. "There is no need."

"He must be brought to book," Holmes said sternly. "I care not what suspicions he harbors, he cannot go about the streets attacking innocent people because he finds them reading something concerning his family. Describe him, Watson!"

"I may do better than that," I said, drinking the last of my second cup of tea and feeling almost fully revived. "I spoke to Mr. Allan Pelly. He was able to tell me who inherited the Riggston business; it was James's son Bradon, who is now in his early thirties. A man whom, I was told, looks much like his uncle Arthur."

"I see. And it was such a man who attacked you. You are certain?"

"I can only say that the man I saw closely resembled Arthur, and is Bradon Riggston's age."

Holmes hesitated. I saw that he wished to leave, to find Bradon Riggston and berate him for his actions. But I was in no condition to accompany him, and as I was the person assaulted it would be only sensible for me to be with him when the accusation was made. He realized this and sank again into his seat.

"The morning will be sufficient. Tell me what happened after you were felled?"

I described the situation as I understood it: a gathering crowd, Detective Harrison coming at the cry of murder, and identifying me as a doctor well known to him. Then the pushing and shoving, and my attacker nowhere to be found.

"Of course not. Once he heard he had the wrong man he fled. Although…" He paused. "It could be that he has since reflected and will come to ask questions. I think you should have an early night, rise only when you wake, eat well, and then," his expression hardened, "we will take a cab to his place of business and it shall be *he* who explains his actions."

* * * *

I followed his prescription, thinking that it was a good one. With the aid of tincture of laudanum I slept well, and when I rose it was most happily without that confounded headache. I made an excellent breakfast with Holmes, as we discussed his latest monograph on various soils found in the London boroughs, before we departed in a cab. It took no more than a half hour to reach Riggston Coal Merchants, and Holmes was first to alight. He paid, and the cab rattled away while I stood looking at the impressive façade of the building where they had their offices.

"The grandfather wished them to rise in society, and they look to have done so," I said.

"That," Holmes replied austerely, "does not give the current owner the right to attack those he suspects of inquiring into the family's past."

I repressed a smile. In the course of our adventures it had been no uncommon thing for Holmes to be attacked. He accepted that as the risk inherent in his investigations. On my behalf, however, he always resented such an assault. Realizing he was in motion, I followed as he mounted the front steps, rang the bell, and demanded to speak with the business's owner.

"Mr. Bradon Riggston is busy. You must make an appointment," was the doorman's response.

"Tell Mr. Bradon Riggston that he will see me, or he will be given in charge for a violent attack on an innocent man yesterday afternoon," Holmes said evenly.

The doorman looked startled and disappeared up the stairs. He returned in a more accommodating mood.

"Mr. Bradon will be pleased to see you. He asks if you will wait in a private room briefly, however, as he is with an important client. He will be with you as quickly as he can. I can offer refreshments."

I asked for tea and biscuits. The tea arrived in a silver teapot and the biscuits were of the most expensive sort, all on a silver tray. It seemed that Mr. Bradon was pleased to placate us. We drank tea, ate chocolate biscuits, and waited.

5

I kept an eye on my watch; Bradon Riggston was a man of his word. In barely twenty minutes the door opened and the man who had struck me down walked into the room, a sheepish look on his face. He approached me, his hand outstretched. Holmes and I stood.

"My dear Dr. Watson, I am most terribly sorry for my actions yesterday." His face expressed genuine contrition and I accepted his hand. He gripped it gently. "I was in the wrong. My uncle has only recently explained his suspicions and fears to me and I thought, incorrectly as I now know, that I had by chance come upon the person of whom he spoke. We were both fortunate that my assistant, Marsden, pulled me away else I fear I may have been still more contumacious."

"When precisely did you know of your mistake?" Holmes asked, a hint of acid in his voice.

"When that detective spoke the Doctor's name. My uncle told me that he had hired you, and mentioned your colleague as well. I understood at once that I had made a frightful mistake and I …"

"Left your victim unconscious upon the pavement while you scurried to safety," Holmes finished.

Bradon Riggston flushed, made to protest, and then looked my friend directly in the eye. "Yes. That detective knew him, and he was there to see that no further ill befell your friend. I planned to meet my obligations here this morning and afterwards drive to your address and throw myself upon your mercy." His gaze fell and a flush spread over his face. "I panicked, I admit it. Arthur seems certain that this person, whoever he may be, has killed several members of my family as well as family friends. He suggested that I, too, may be in danger. In the heat of the moment I leapt to conclusions and struck out, believing I was defending myself. I am most deeply sorry for what I did and will make any reasonable reparation you demand."

I waved him to his seat—noticing with amusement the careful qualification. "I understand how it came about." I looked at my friend. "Holmes?"

He nodded. "Let us sit and discuss this. You may be able to give us useful information, and we can share with you our discoveries to date."

We sat down. Riggston rang a bell and a servant brought a fresh pot and another teacup and saucer, along with a yet wider selection of biscuits. Holmes, accepting a cup, drank a mouthful, set the cup back on the tray, and began.

"We have investigated several of the deaths in some detail, Mr. Riggston. Whoever is responsible for them has been careful, and since most of the dead succumbed some considerable time ago there is no way we could convince the police that the deaths are the result of other than the original verdicts."

Bradon Riggston understood the point being made. "But you do believe some of them were murder?"

"I do." Holmes ticked off the comments against his fingers. "I am satisfied that the carriage accident suffered by your grandparents, James and Mary, was deliberately brought about. The deaths of your Uncle Joseph and of your family lawyer, who died a bare six months after your Uncle Joseph, were both contrived, and not accidental or natural. I believe that the deaths of all three of the Pellys were murders."

Bradon Riggston's mouth opened as a look of horror spread across his features. This was obviously worse than his imaginings, and he could scarcely take it all in. However, Holmes was not done.

"Your uncle also suspected that a minister of your family's church might have been murdered. As yet I have been unable to verify that, for the man died from a stroke. He was elderly, and such a death is not unlikely. It may therefore have been natural. I am certain that the death of Mr. Arthur Riggston senior, your uncle's uncle, was entirely natural. I would like your permission to fully investigate the death of your father, however."

Bradon Riggston replied in little more than a whisper. "Then you think it possible he, too, was murdered?"

"Most things are possible. The question is not were they possible, but did they occur," Holmes stated. "It is the answer to that question I seek."

"Then seek it where, how, and as you will, Mr. Holmes. I give you leave. I will write a letter right now, saying that you have my permission to inquire into all or any of the circumstances concerning any death in my family."

He went to a small desk at the back of the room and sat down there and then, dashing off a half page that said precisely that. This he blotted before handing it to Holmes, who read it and nodded.

"That will do well. Now." He eyed our host. "Please be seated and in a moment, tell us every detail you recall of the death of your father. But before you begin I must ask, would your mother speak to us on this subject?"

"I fear not, Mr. Holmes. Her marriage was not at all a happy one. Once the funeral was over, the will read, and disposition made of the bequests and my father's possessions she has never made another reference to him. Indeed, she has discouraged others from doing so in her presence."

"A pity," Holmes said. "She may know details we shall not hear from others." He shrugged and fixed his attention upon Bradon Riggston. "Tell us how your father died."

Bradon hesitated. "It is a brief but distasteful tale. My father drank. In his cups he could be—unpleasant. I never thought him to drink to great excess, yet once or twice a week he would return home slightly the worse for alcohol. At such times his voice would be raised, he would find fault with others, and my mother, on seeing him in that condition, would retire to her room and lock the door. He was never unkind to me," he said earnestly. "You should believe that. But at such times he was loud and boisterous, as was not usual for him, and he would shout comments to my mother that put her to the blush."

"Did he strike her?" Holmes asked flatly.

"I never saw him do so," was the evasive reply.

"I see, but you are aware that he may have done so?"

Riggston nodded reluctantly.

Holmes continued. "And he may, at such times—before she began the custom of locking herself into her room when he returned in such a condition—have perhaps forced himself on her?"

A deep flush spread over the man's face, and again he nodded.

Holmes frowned. "Yes, once she was locked in she was safe. He wished to stand well in his son's esteem. What is done in privacy remains unknown. But to break down a door and assault his wife when his young son may come running to her cries, is less discreet."

"I don't know if that ever occurred. My mother has great dignity," Riggston protested, in an apparent non-sequitur.

"So much so that she would not even hint at such an event to you," I said. "But the fact that she took care not to be in his presence when he had been drinking, even to locking a door, indicates she had something to fear."

"Perhaps so," our host agreed unhappily. "If that's the case, and I swear it never occurred to me until you spoke of it, I suppose it is understandable that with his death she put him out of her mind."

"It is," Holmes intervened. "But we still have not heard how your father died, Mr. Riggston."

"Of drink," Riggston said, before elaborating. "He came home drunker than I or anyone has ever seen him. He reeked of alcohol. He staggered, shouting, flailing at what he swore were bees that buzzed about him continually. He struck at me when I tried to calm him. He screamed, cursed my mother vilely, and it was with great difficulty that his man and I got him to bed. He would not remain quiet and I finally called the doctor who gave him laudanum, and at last he slept. We were worn out and retired to our beds once he was sleeping. In the morning I went early to see how he did and found him dead. His doctor, called at once, gave a certificate saying that my father died of apoplexy—although he told me it was his private opinion that the true cause was alcohol poisoning."

He rotated his shoulders, trying to relax. "The doctor was kind. Had that been recorded as the official cause of death, it would have been embarrassing for the family."

At this I could contribute pertinent information, and I spoke gravely. "Had the doctor put that on the certificate, he would have told no more than the truth. I think your father had been administered methyl or ethyl alcohol, the former being most likely. It takes only three and a half to eight ounces to cause death. In severe poisoning, death comes from respiratory failure, which in this case would have been exacerbated by the laudanum. Hallucinations are not uncommon, and it is not unusual for a doctor to confuse it with an over-ingestion of ordinary drink, such as whiskey."

I reflected. "I have seen such things amongst the poorest of my patients, where using methyl alcohol to strengthen their drinks is not uncommon. A doctor who generally treats the middle classes might be excused this error. However, if we are seeking a murder method, I think that the most probable."

Riggston stared at me, his eyes wide in horror and distress. He turned to Holmes.

"Could that be true?"

"I agree with my colleague. It is possible, and if your father's death was murder, that method is probable. But as we have said, so far we have no proof, only suspicions."

Riggston straightened in his chair. "Then do all you can! Go where you must and ask any question, and you may read any papers that we have in our possession. I want the truth. He may not always have been a good man, but he was my father. I'll not sit by if he was murdered." He stood. "Where would you like to begin?"

"Let us talk to your mother. Ask her if she will receive us. After that, I ask you leave us alone with her."

Within minutes we were swept into the Riggston automobile, driven to their London home, and his mother joined us in the sunny parlor. As we stood for her, I observed a woman in her fifties, dressed in a pale purple dress of good style and cut but few furbelows. She was a small woman, no more than an inch or two over five feet, and her hair was light brown, now shading into mostly silver, while her eyes were of a clear hazel that was almost yellow.

"Mother, this is Mr. Sherlock Holmes, the consulting detective, and his colleague Dr. Watson. Gentlemen, my mother, Octavia Riggston. Mr. Holmes and Dr. Watson tell me Uncle Arthur's suspicions that father was murdered are probably true, and they would like to talk to you about that possibility. Unless you particularly wish me to stay, I will leave you to talk privately with them."

Her head inclined graciously. "Do so, Bradon."

He waited for Holmes's nod before he left the parlor. We heard the outer door shut, and then the sound of an automobile driving away.

Mrs. Riggston waved towards two chairs. "Please, be seated. I shall call for tea and we can be comfortable. I have no idea what you may wish to ask, for I know little, but I am prepared to answer a few questions." She laid delicate emphasis on the last three words, giving us to understand that excessive or intrusive questions would likely go unanswered.

Holmes waited until a servant had brought the heavy tray, and each of us held a filled teacup on one hand, a plate containing cake and biscuits between us on a small stand. I approved his delay since it is harder to be rude to guests who are partaking of your largesse.

Holmes spoke quietly once we were served. "I am here to ask questions, Mrs. Riggston, yes. But more to warn you that your son may stand in grave danger." She flinched. "We have little proof, but it is my opinion that Mr. Arthur Riggston is both right and wrong. After careful examination of the facts, I do not believe that his godfather was murdered, rather that he died under natural circumstances. However, I also believe that a considerable number of your family members and several family friends and associates have been murdered. Since the deaths have been, in most cases, far apart or under apparently understandable circumstances, they have been considered accidents."

"Too many accidents," Octavia Riggston murmured.

"Precisely. It was that which drew Mr. Arthur's attention. He asked us to investigate the deaths, and it is our opinion that most, if not all, have been murder."

"And my husband? I should tell you that he drank; it was common for him to return home every few days much the worse for alcohol."

"At which time you shut yourself away to prevent his abuse," Holmes stated. "Did you never fear for your son at his hands?"

Octavia regarded us calmly. We could see her considering what reply to make and after a minute she stood, walked to the window, and turned her back to us. "My husband was not interested in boys," she said, and the desolate tone of her voice was painful to me. "He preferred young women, the younger the better, but since I had made certain there were none in this house any longer, he could either seek out one elsewhere or have recourse to his wife. When he was sufficiently drunk he was prepared to lower himself to that, should I be available."

"So you took care that you were not," Holmes stated.

"I did. I could do nothing about those he might abuse outside my home, but I did not intend to permit it under my own roof. He and his brother were of a kind. His father also, and perhaps his grandfather, if the stories were true. I did not know any of it when I married. I was eighteen, sheltered, and James was good-looking. He courted me and my parents approved of him. I told my mother once I knew the truth. She simply sighed and said that a woman must endure, that I should have children to comfort me, and once my husband had his fill of me I would be mostly left alone."

She turned to stare at us and her eyes burned with rage. "I had Bradon, and after that my husband lost interest, unless he was drunk and I was foolish enough to remain in reach. I hid his behavior from my son, but I tell you this here and now." Her voice had an intensity that I would never have thought her able to attain. "I hated James, and had I not considered the consequences I would have killed him myself. I will be grateful all my days to whoever did so, if someone did. I lived for fifteen years in a hell of James's making, and my release was—paradise."

Holmes's voice was neutral. "Your husband's will? How did he leave his estate?"

"I had a portion. It is invested and I have the interest. I have this house for my lifetime, our country home for my lifetime also, and should I wish to leave these properties, the estate would pay a set sum annually for rent. I retained all jewelry and other such gifts he had given me, all of my other personal possessions, and certain items that had been left exclusively to me by my parents upon their own deaths. His will ratified that." Her lip curled in contempt. "He knew I would fight any attempt to dispossess me, and that Bradon would not allow me to be beggared. Otherwise he might have attempted to leave me as penniless as he could. Nor did he expect to die so young. He was barely forty-one, you know."

"I know. You think he disliked you as much as you disliked him? Why then did he marry you?"

"His father's will said that he must be married at the time of his father's death or within the year in order to inherit. Otherwise the business went to his father's brothers as directors, until such time as they agreed that my husband was fit to take over." Her smile was malicious. "Neither man liked their nephew. He knew that once they were in the door, they would not easily relinquish the business, and being a director would pay them a large sum each year. He would need, too, to show that I was a true wife. I bore Bradon ten months after our wedding and he was able to dismiss any suggestion they might make that he was not doing his marital duty."

"Why was his father so set on your husband's marriage?" I queried her.

She smiled bitterly. "Because he knew his son; they had much in common. I suspect he wanted James safely wed and with an heir, in case he brought public opprobrium down upon himself. After that he would find it difficult to convince a decent family to ally themselves with our name."

I asked nothing further, recalling her comments about both father and sons' liking for young women. If they obtained those by means other than payment I did not wish to put her to the blush by demanding particulars.

"And you never had any suspicion that James might have died other than by alcohol?" Holmes asked.

"None." The word was flat and unequivocal, and we believed her. "Now, if you have no more to ask, I wish to be alone."

We made our farewells and departed the house. Once outside I turned to Holmes. "You could have asked other questions."

"To which we would have received no answers. You heard her, Watson. It never occurred to her that her husband was killed, and she was happy to be free of him. She will not aid us to find his killer."

"In my opinion, she would go further. If we discover a suspect and she gets wind of that, she is likely to warn them," I said seriously.

"I agree." His eyes twinkled. "So we must be careful not to allow her son to guess or to tell him once we know, because in all likelihood he answers all of *her* questions."

I believed that probably true and nodded. I stared about the street. "There's a cab coming, Holmes. Where do you have it in mind to go now?"

"Home, for a somewhat belated lunch, my dear fellow. After that I wish to visit the Riggston's church and ask questions of that amiable fellow who is minister there now."

That we did. Lunch was excellent, and any information gained from Jarod Wilson two hours later was much less so. Holmes questioned him, but all the man could say was that Reverend Mathews had died from a stroke. So the doctor had said, and he had no reason to doubt it. He could furnish us with the direction of the old man's physician if we wished. We did, and thither we repaired, to receive no sort of a welcome as soon as he understood what we asked.

He eyed us irascibly, thick white eyebrows lowering in annoyance. "My dear sirs, the minister died of a stroke, and I will have no one making some scandal from that. Now be off with you."

I appealed to him as a brother doctor—to be told I should think shame to admit it.

Holmes tried reason and was repelled.

"Go away, sir. Leave my property before I call the police."

Any further appeal was in vain and we left, the doctor's door slamming behind us as a period to our investigations.

Once on the pavement I looked at Holmes. "I suspect he does know something. Well, nothing solid, but I think at the time he may have wondered. Not that you'd ever get him to admit it, and I know that sort. The more you press him, the more determined he'll be to contradict you."

Holmes looked back at the door. "No, I too know that type, and you are right. Well, we have time yet; let us go to the minister's former home."

We set off in a cab, and once within Holmes pursed his lips in thought. We were almost at our destination when he spoke quietly. "Watson, if you wished to give an elderly man a stroke, how would you go about it?"

On the last words we halted at the previous home of Reverend Mathews and alighted. I continued to think as the driver was paid and drove away. Holmes stood by the gate, waiting.

"I cannot be certain, Holmes. There are a number of possibilities. I need my medical books to check some information, but there are a large number of herbs and plants that could effect such an outcome. They would be available in gardens, and as you know, some city doctors are not always familiar with the symptoms of the more common poisons, let alone those of plant poisonings."

"No," Holmes agreed sardonically. "They assume them to be dyspepsia or some such, until the patient expires, that is. Then they seize on the first mention of some poison and convince themselves it must have been that. I wouldn't mind so much if it were not that they convince others, and it is all I can do to save the person maligned."

I knew the case that came to his mind; had Holmes not become involved a young woman would have gone to the gallows, innocent as she was, because a doctor listened to a man with no knowledge and the appearance of authority. Holmes's expression softened as he regarded my rueful look.

"I wasn't talking of you, my dear chap. You do know that?" I did. "Well then, let us see what the housekeeper may say. You know my thoughts on this. See if you can persuade her to discuss her master—we need to know anything out of the ordinary that he may have eaten or drunk." And with that he reached for the knocker.

I seized his arm, preventing him from doing so. "Holmes," I hissed "Look!"

He turned and stared across the neat garden to where I pointed. "What is it, Watson?"

"*Zygadenus venenosus.*" I said. "Commonly known as death camas, in the neighbor's garden. I'm not suggesting that the people here are responsible, but ..." I cudgeled my memory, and while not an exact quote, I conveyed the essence of what I had read. "As little as 15 grains of the fresh plant can kill." I paused and spoke in measured tones. "In a far higher dosage it produces strongly elevated blood pressure by direct action upon the brain."

Holmes understood at once. "Which, in an elderly man who already has high blood pressure, could cause an apparent stroke."

I corrected him. "Not an apparent stroke, Holmes. It *would* be one, merely one produced by an outside causative agent. There would normally be other symptoms, but if it acted swiftly, there might not be time for the other symptoms to show." I frowned. "It is surprising to find that plant here. It is American and cannot be common in England."

Holmes trod resolutely to the neighbor's house. "Then we shall ask."

The lady of the house was pleased to be informative. Reverend Mathews had received a visit from an American cousin some years earlier, a pleasant woman who had brought the plant as a gift. The minister, not being a gardener, had offered it to her once his cousin was gone, and she had accepted enthusiastically.

"It grows well, don't you think?"

We agreed, and I asked her if it had been divided and shared.

"Oh, yes, I gave portions of it to several friends. And it isn't as uncommon as you might think. I've seen it several times in other gardens."

We thanked her and walked back to the pavement, where we stood, considering.

6

At last Holmes spoke. "So that plant is readily available. Still, it is not commonly found in England, and that points either to a gardener or to someone who reads widely."

"That is to say, almost any one," I sighed, and Holmes glanced at me.

"No," he said softly. "Look at what we know thus far. James and his wife were killed in an accident arranged by someone who was hardy—they waited along the road for some hours in the rain—quick of mind and body, and familiar with horses. Joseph's death was again an apparent accident, caused by someone who risked being seen, gambled that it would not happen, and that Joseph would not react in time to save himself. When the time came the killer was swift and ruthless."

I began to see his point. "Direct actions, Holmes. But the minister and lawyer were not so direct, nor was the younger James."

"Precisely. To kill that generation's James as he did, he must have appeared to be of a similar class. James drank with him, and he was able to add the toxic ingredient to his glass as they drank together, using a similar method for David Pelly. The boy, Jonathon, was manipulated, the victim of his own pride, while Florence Pelly was a fortunate circumstance."

I had been thinking. "So, we have someone whose methods are two-fold. He takes direct physical action, or he stands back and acts in such a way he can observe the outcome while appearing uninvolved. Isn't that unusual, Holmes? I have heard you say that most criminals choose the method that suits them best and use that from then on."

"Yes," my friend agreed. "Yet now and again you find a criminal with his own agenda. His intention is to complete some cycle of crimes and that is what is important. Under his great desire to succeed, he will use any technique that achieves his goal. Such a system is usually that of an amateur, not a professional criminal. There is another point of interest. The crimes fall into two distinct phases, but you have not observed the meaning of that."

I looked my question.

He continued. "The more direct crimes were all committed within the first decade. The deaths of James, his wife, and his brother Joseph all occurred in that space of time. The other crimes were of the less direct type, often a poisoning that involved no great physical exertion."

I sighed. "What does that mean?"

"That our killer is growing older," Holmes said thoughtfully. "Look at the evidence. If we are right and James and his wife were the first murders, those were committed thirty-three years ago. The last death that may be murder took place twenty-four years later. That is a long time to hold a grudge. At what age, Watson, would you prowl the streets of London, follow a man, watch and wait until he is walking along the bank of a river, run forward and strike him on the head hard enough to fall into the river to drown?"

I frowned. "Why do you mention the blow to his head?"

"Because I have seen the records. Bradon Riggston's father had all the inquest notes. According to those, there was evidence of a minor blow to the head, but the doctor said drowning was the cause of death. The injury could have been caused by Joseph striking his head on something as he fell. Accidental drowning was the verdict for another reason—the body was recovered only hours after his death. Once out of the water, Joseph was easily identified …"

"Yes," I said. "He had all of his belongings still. They knew it was not robbery, for what thief strikes so gently."

Holmes's face was grave. "I fear that was the killer's whole intent, Watson. He gambled that the verdict would be thus, and he won. You realize there is no way I could convince the authorities to reopen such a case, nor that of the others. The murderer has been clever. Unless we can uncover him and force a confession, I can do nothing."

I knew him too well to think that was an abdication. "So where do we go from here, Holmes? You will not give up, nor shall I."

"Let us go to the home of the dead lawyer, Watson. I have questions I would like to put to his housekeeper and to the neighbors." He checked his pocket watch and turned away from the house. "However, it grows too late. Let us leave that for the morning. Dinner and a good night's sleep will refresh us for a new day's work."

* * * *

By nine the following morning we were at the door of Eli Gettes's home. The death of the old lawyer had occurred twenty-two years ago and I was surprised that Holmes expected to find the lady still in residence. My friend explained that the housekeeper, a distant relative whose family had come down in the world, received both house and an annuity upon Eli Gettes's death.

She answered the door, appeared pleased to have the opportunity to talk of her benefactor, and invited us in. Once we were comfortable she looked at us with a bright-eyed attentiveness. Her conversation could initially be summed up as a paean of praise to her kin. He was kind, generous, thoughtful, and tidy. I was amused at the last attribute, but the lady elaborated.

"He was always a considerate man. He never walked across a clean floor in muddy boots, never left coats or jackets lying about. He hung things up, put things away, and his shoes or boots were always placed out for cleaning. I suppose it was a result of his father's missionary service."

My companion leaned forward and began discussing the trials and tribulations of a missionary. "And the natives can be resistant to the Word."

"Oh, indeed they can. My dear cousin suffered severely as a child."

Even my own ears pricked up at this—metaphorically speaking, of course. Holmes's voice was mellow and encouraging.

"Oh? There was an uprising perhaps?"

"Terrible, it was. He was taken prisoner along with his parents and an Indian trader and his wife. My cousin saw the trader and his wife die—burned to death, they were—all from a dispute over land. He was only nine and it affected him deeply."

"But a convert freed them and they came home?" Holmes asked gently, who appeared to know the story.

"Yes, Eli was in a terrible state. During the trip he contracted a fever. When at last he arrived in England he was extremely ill, and remained so for months. Afterwards his heart was affected and it was decided that Eli would do well as a lawyer. He stayed with us while he went to school here in London. Once he was recovered from his illness he went to a boarding school and did well in his studies, eventually joining the practice of his father's friend."

"But his heart was always weak?" I asked.

"It was. He had two small attacks shortly before his death, and the doctor said he was to be careful always. He said Eli must not become over-tired or agitated. Indeed, I blame the death of Mr. Joseph Riggston for his death. He left so much to be done on his estate, and Eli was so conscientious. He worked all hours to wind up the estate, and yet Mr. Joseph's brother was always complaining to Eli that things were not done as quickly as they might be."

"So," Holmes confirmed. "Mr. Gettes was tired and overworked. Was he perhaps worried about something he found in the estate papers?"

Our hostess looked up sharply. "Now how do you know that? But yes, it was so. I came in to mend the fire the day he died and he was talking to himself. I heard him say, 'I do not know what to do. They must have known, and they allowed it to continue.' And when he realized I was there he asked me if I ever thought that sometimes an earthly duty must give way to one higher. If a moral duty was more important than one of law."

"How did you answer?"

"I said that I did not know, and that it must depend on the circumstances. But yes, sometimes a moral duty was more important than a law."

"Brava," Holmes approved. "You say it was that day he passed away. How, precisely, did he die?"

In return, we heard the same description Gettes's junior partner had given. The gasp, the sound of a fall, the hasty return of Mr. Grosett when he heard the housekeeper's scream. And that effectively the man had died in a locked room. No one could have caused his death and he was living on borrowed time.

I caught Holmes's look and assured the lady that she could not be blamed in any way.

Holmes added, "You looked after him devotedly, but only God can prolong a life. His heart was weak; rheumatic fever, I would think, from his time in Africa." His voice was quiet, sliding into her thoughts. "And of course, poor Mr. Gettes experienced trauma still from the awful events of his childhood. Not exactly mental difficulties but ..."

He allowed his voice to trail off invitingly, and our hostess stared down at the carpet.

"Yes, he saw those poor people die. Their captors told his parents that they would kill them the same way if they didn't cooperate. They only needed his father, you see. They would burn Eli, then his mother if his father didn't convince the authorities that the land was theirs. He used to wake up screaming, and to the day he died if a black man came upon him unexpectedly, he would turn pale and shy away. That was why he lived here and seldom went far out of the area. There are no black men much hereabouts, and none come to the church."

Holmes sat back with a small smile. So he was seeking Eli Gettes's greatest fear. But how could that have killed him? And then I understood. A mask. They were sold in the shops around Guy Fawkes. I had seen them myself, black grimacing faces, with large white teeth bared in a terrible smile. If our killer donned it and thrust their face against the window so that when Gettes turned at some small sound, he would see the ogre from his childhood.

I took charge, said everything that was polite to our kind hostess, assured her that she could have done no more for her cousin, and swept my friend out of the house, down the path and out of the gate, and along the pavement for some distance. There I halted and began my exposition. I explained my sudden insight and my thoughts as my friend nodded at each point.

"I believe you are right, my dear chap," he agreed once I was done. "I must confess I had not thought specifically of a mask, but now you mention it I do recall having seen such a one last November. That theory may go far to explain Gettes's death. My other question is, what was he so distressed over that last day? Of what was he speaking when he asked his cousin about a moral duty?"

I had no answer.

Holmes looked about us. "Ah! I would like, if you do not mind, Watson, to make my way to the Riggston business and search their old records. Eli Gettes may have been speaking of one of the family. James the elder is my guess."

He glanced at me and I signified my assent, only suggesting that we should eat before we appeared on the Riggston doorstep. To that proposition he agreed, and we had a pleasant lunch at a small hotel around the corner from Riggston Coal. Bread, cheese, ale, and a portion of apple pie with cream satisfied the inner man, and I was quite resigned to searching through a veritable ocean of musty papers when at last we made our way up the well-worn steps and were admitted.

On production of Bradon Riggston's letter we were led to a commodious but poorly lit cellar and left to our own devices. Holmes divided our areas of labor, and with the aid of two lamps, provided upon our request by the doorman, we began.

I decided to be as methodical as my friend and, beginning at the bottom far corner of my section I began taking down each file in turn and reading it. I discovered no file of use—although quite a number of interest—and we ceased at five p.m.

This activity continued all week until my eyes ached from reading, my back from sitting, and my brain from trying to understand yet another business deal together with all its legal demands and circumlocutions. After four days I had almost lost hope that we would discover anything that might refer to Eli Gettes's perturbation, when Holmes exclaimed softly.

I looked up. "Holmes? Have you found something?"

"I have found—something. Whether it is the papers that upset Gettes I cannot say. But it shows me a possible trail. Come now, we need to see Grosett before he leaves for home." And with that he headed briskly towards the steps while I followed in his wake.

We were fortunate to find Grosett still in his office since it was nearly nine p.m. Holmes wasted no time, showing him the letter we had obtained giving us leave to see all papers and asking if there might be anything remaining in his files that could shed light on the matter.

Grosett looked grave. "I do recall some related correspondence. It will be in the cellar and could take considerable time to uncover."

I groaned and Holmes's eyes twinkled.

"We have spent much of the week searching in such a place, and I fear my good colleague tires of files and cellars."

Grosett, who had been thinking hard if his scowl was anything to go by, then smiled. "I sympathize. I feel the same each time I must hunt out some long-buried and obscure item. However, I know the approximate date, and if I am right, then it should not take above half an hour to find." He gave my friend clear directions and Holmes turned to me.

"I will return as soon as possible. Stay here, and perhaps a cup of tea and a comfortable chair will be of benefit."

The lawyer professed himself only too happy to have my company and Holmes clattered off down the iron stairs. He returned in the time promised and bore in one dusty hand a slim and even dustier file. Holding that, he addressed Grosett.

"Allowing us access to this file could be considered a breach of confidence. However, I will remind you of this." Here he displayed Bradon Riggston's letter. "I ask that you permit me to take this file. It will be guarded most carefully, and no one save myself shall read it, but I need to verify certain events against those detailed here."

The lawyer eyed him apprehensively. "You believe that the information in the file may explain the actions against the Riggstons and certain of their circle?"

"I do. Moreover, if this matter can be resolved, those actions may end. I do not wish to alarm you, but there has been one instance of a decade between deaths."

He may not have wished to alarm Mr. Grosett, but I could see that he had. The man capitulated on the spot.

"My dear sir, you have Mr. Riggston's written authority. I daresay that to allow you to remove such a file may be stretching a point, but better that than another murder." He shivered suddenly. "I ask that you both swear not to let the file out of your possession, nor to allow any other access to it." Holmes promised, secured the file in a stout brown envelope, and we departed. He reached the street first, hailed a passing cab and, to my relief, gave our address. I could only be grateful for this. I have known him to work the clock around when his interest is fully engaged in a case, and after the long day we had worked, I was hungry, weary, and grimy. I wanted a hot bath, a good dinner, and my own bed, in that order—and got them.

7

Holmes read the file next morning over breakfast, and once we were done and the table cleared he laid it aside and glanced at me.

"You would like me to do something for you?" I asked.

"If you would be so kind, Watson." I assented and he continued. "I would like you to trace Miss May Percy, if you can."

I hastily recalled all I had heard of the girl. She was the daughter of the widower—Victor Percy—who married Josephine Riggston. She was only two when the marriage took place and three years later her father died. Josephine, who loved May, kept her and married an elderly man who, when May's step-mother died six years later, did not want her. He applied to Josephine's brother James, and he and his wife Mary had taken the child in with considerable reluctance.

She remained with them until she was almost sixteen, but one night she vanished, never to be seen or heard from again. That had been over forty years ago. How was I to find anything from such a cold trail?

"Have you any suggestions where to start, Holmes? Had the girl any money when she fled?"

"I suggest you begin by talking to a Mrs. Lizzie Davis. She was a maid at the Riggston house at the time that the child was resident. She married a footman, John Davis, whose father died and left him a small business. The Davis's have run it since. I am told that Lizzie liked the girl, and there is some suggestion she was her confidant."

After donning an overcoat—the day bid fair to be chilly—I headed for the address given me and there found the Davis's, now a couple in their sixties. They owned a good-sized emporium selling many small items for prices that—as I was told by one passerby when I inquired from him the exact site of the business—were fair, and the owners honest. I found the Davis's prepared to talk to me.

"I never felt right about May, it weren't decent," Mrs. Davis explained. "They cheated her and John and I knew it, and so did she. And that isn't even to say how she was treated."

Before I could ask for clarification I was ushered into their parlor, seated, offered something to eat and drink and even as I raised a cup to my lips she continued in a torrent of complaint and explanation.

"The Riggstons took me on because my mother was the housekeeper, and she'd given me a good grounding in how to be a proper maid. I was seventeen when May was taken into the house and I was sorry for her, poor little lass. Not quite eleven she was, used to being loved, and there was no one in that whole house that cared about her. Took her in they did, for the money, and that was all. She had the worst of everything. Her clothes would have shamed a pauper, she got food as was more scraps than anything, and the boys took advantage of her. Time and time again they did things and blamed her and she was beaten."

Her earlier words had caught my attention. "You said they took her in for the money. What money? There was none; that was why her step-mother remarried."

Lizzie Davis was off again. "Oh, yes there was. Surely Mrs. Josephine didn't have any money, but her husband, May's father, left what he had to May. It wasn't enough to keep them both, just interest on sale of his shop and some investments. But it came to May, and it was for that Mr. James took her. Should have been enough to feed and clothe her decently, even give her a good education, but he never mentioned any of that at his church, oh no!" Her eyes blazed indignantly.

"Gave out there that he'd taken her in out of the goodness of his heart, and some of the church folk gave her clothes their own daughters had outgrown. Shabby, mended, ill-fitting, poor material anyhow and years out of fashion. And the food! Oh, yes, she ate at the table with them, they made sure all of their friends heard so, but she had scraps for all that, served last she was. Got the scrapings from the bottom of pots, the heel of the loaf, the burnt meat from the outside of a roast, even the leavings from the boy's plates, and not all that much of any of it. I mind the time Cook made a mess of some fancy dish. They fed it to May and she was sick all night. Mustn't waste good food, they said, as they made her sit there until she'd eaten it to the last bite, and her choking it down. Poor little lass."

"The money?" I said, bringing her back to my question.

"Oh, yes. It was left to her, the main amount that was, she could have it when she was twenty-five. Until then the interest was hers, and by my reckoning it was a goodish sum. More than they needed to feed and clothe her, and with what little she got from them in that way I'd reckon that pretty much every penny went into their pockets."

"She disappeared?"

"That's right. She would have been about three months short of sixteen. One night she went up to bed, next morning she was nowhere to be found. Riggstons didn't make too much noise about it. It's my opinion they didn't want her found, and anyhow, a girl that age, they gave it out at church that she was always difficult and they reckoned she'd gone off with some boy."

"Was there a boy?"

"Not that I ever saw. Look, Doctor, she worked for that family. Not that they let on, but she was always at her step-aunt's beck and call, running all over the house doing whatever they told her. When could she meet a boy when she was never free, and daren't set foot outside? She went to church and that was about it. Maybe now and again to the shops on some errand—and be back when she was expected or it was a beating." Lizzie Davis looked at me, her mouth set hard. "She was always bruised. No sooner was one lot healed than they were at her again."

"She had no money herself?" I made that as a half-statement and waited.

Lizzie Davis snorted. "Ho, didn't she? She did, then. Two days afore she left I crept up to her room to give her something I snitched from cook, since the poor little lass hadn't had any dinner. They were punishing her for something the boys had done, as always, and when they did that she sat down to bread and water. I didn't want any of the family to see or hear me so I was playing least-in-sight. I opened her door real quietly, and she was counting out money on the bed."

From her description May could have had as much as twenty pounds, all in coins, a good-sized heap of them: copper, silver, and here and there a half-sovereign.

"She scrabbled it under the bedspread, looking at me like I was the Devil hisself. I swore to her, I got my Bible and swore I wouldn't tell anyone, and particularly not the family."

"Did she say where she got it?"

"No, how-some-ever I could make a guess." She smiled. "Mr. James senior and the missus, they used to go to parties in the season. Not the society ones, but aping that sort. They'd come back as late as three or four and he'd be—her, too, like as not—real merry. Times like that they'd sleep 'til after midday as if they were dead and wake sore-headed. May slept in the attics. There was a small servants' staircase that went right by a little door to his dressing room. Behind his dressing table it was, so you couldn't even see it, and—well—out of sight out of mind I'd say. It's my guess he forgot it was there. It opened into the staircase landing," she added meaningfully.

"So she could open it without making any sound or having to move anything." I understood that. "And you think that she crept into their bedrooms on such occasions and helped herself to a coin or two?"

"I do. You look at it this way, Doctor. They went to maybe as many as thirty parties in any season. She was with them for five years."

I calculated. "Let us say she began to steal from them a year after her arrival and she could go safely only two out of three times. That would mean that she averaged four or five shillings a time. That is a fair sum. Would its loss not have been noticed?"

She sneered. "Not likely. You don't understand that lot, sir. 'Deed you don't. They're not quality, but they're not short of money. Maybe it was them knowing that the quality would never take to them that made them show off. But when they went out to such parties they tipped heavy. A sovereign for the butler, like as not, and she'd spend time in the ladies' card room playing whist, putting down her cash as if it wasn't important, and coming back with coins and notes all jumbled. Once they woke next day and got their breakfast—in bed usually—they'd likely count what they had. But until then? Why, Doctor, I'd say you could safely take as much as ten shillings so long as it was coins, and they'd never find out."

I was surprised. "But if she was taking money from her step-aunt, surely the woman would have realized. I've seen women playing whist, and most keep records."

Lizzie chuckled. "Not madam. She thought it common to do such before others. And it would suggest she had to count pennies. No, she went with a wad of cash in her bag, notes and coins both. She laid her money down and never checked until the day after."

I understood the life May led, and her opportunities if she accepted the risk. "So May had twenty pounds. That would not keep her forever."

Lizzie's rich chuckle came again. "Bless me, Doctor, I don't suppose the lot she was counting was all of it."

I sat up in surprise. "You think she had more?"

"I do."

"Why?"

The rest of the story came out, then. May and Lizzie had become friends of a sort in the last two years the child had lived with her Riggston relations. She confided in her friend that night that she'd been "saving, as she called it, and I didn't argue the word. She had more than forty pounds," she told me, "and she was leaving. She was going away where she could have a decent life and make something of herself. She'd come back when she was twenty-five and claim her rights. Then she'd buy a business and get a good husband like her father. She promised to stay in touch, but I mustn't try to find her in case the family watched me, and I let her go."

I asked the question that sprang to mind. "She did stay in touch?"

"That she did. I got a Christmas card from her each year, until she was twenty-five. Then she sent a lawyer to the Riggstons, to Mr. James junior it was by then, the elder Mr. James and his wife being dead. She asked for her money. The lawyer said it was hers, and since they hadn't had the keeping of her for ten years and the interest should have acc … acc …"

"Accumulated," I offered.

"Yes, that was it. The interest would have accumulated, so the sum should be much more by now and he'd thank the master for all that was owing, every penny. He said it had been calculated." Her smile was wicked. "I was still working for them while my John looked after the business. We only needed one man before we expanded, and I saw the lawyer, guessed who he was from when I heard him announced. I listened at the door. Master Joseph said there was no money." Her smile widened. "Lawyer wasn't taking that. He said that the law would be interested to hear it. I know he got some of what was owed, for I heard Mr. James cursing about it day or two later, but he and Master James were laughing, too. Joseph said they'd tricked that fool, that he didn't know the half of it. Some investments paid higher than could be guessed.

Said their lawyer was smarter than that bitch's, no matter how clever she thought herself."

There was something in that account. Her gaze met mine and there was triumph in her eyes. I spoke without thinking.

"You told her what he said."

Her gaze fell away. "What if I did? Yes. We'd met a few times that last year. Mr. James senior and that cow of a wife were dead. Young Mr. James and his brother were too lazy to bother following me or setting someone to do that, if they even thought of it, so we met now and again. She never said where she was living, or what she was doing, but she looked well, and I'd say she was happy whatever she was doing."

I questioned her on their meetings, and she was open enough.

"I used to leave a note saying when I could meet her on a letters board at a boarding house round the corner from the Riggston's. Dunno how she got it; she wasn't living there, it was just for men, though maybe she did have a boyfriend by then, but she'd meet me where I'd said, and we'd have a nice meal and talk. I told her what young Mr. James said and she didn't seem surprised."

I was pleased. I could return to Holmes with the elusive May's address, something I'd not anticipated. "So you stayed in touch with her all those years. Where is she living now? Will you give me her direction?"

Lizzie Davis stared at me open-mouthed. "You don't think I'd have talked so free about May if I could?" she demanded incredulously. "She's dead! May's been dead since that last time I saw her, more'n twenty-five years now. She told me then where she was staying, and I knew who it was when I heard about it. I went to the police, said she'd been an old friend, and they let me look at her body. They told me her name, and I said that was her. It wasn't her name, but it was May all right. Lying there stone dead in the same clothes she'd worn to see me."

I was so taken aback that I was all but speechless, then I rallied. "Did they tell you the cause of death?"

"They said she died of a weak heart, and the only reason they advertised for relatives was that she hadn't any money. She owed for rent, and they wanted someone to pay for burying her."

For the first time her husband spoke, briefly and to the point. "Good friend to Lizzie here. We paid the week's rent owing and buried her. Don't know who, but a month later some boy knocked on the door with an envelope. Every single penny we spent was in that, along with a note. Just said, 'Thank you, a friend of hers.'"

Lizzie nodded. "I didn't want to stay with them after that. May was dead and they'd cheated her. Our business was doing well, so I gave notice to Mr. Joseph and went home. Mr. Joseph took it well enough.

He never knew May was dead, of course, but he gave me a sovereign as well as my wages and said I could have a reference any time I asked." Her laugh was harsh. "He didn't have time even if I'd wanted one. He drowned drunk less than a year later."

"Did that surprise you?"

"No. Drank enough at home, always off at the clubs and coming home staggering, singing, chasing the maids. Not me, he tried once and I told him if he laid a finger on me my husband would see him sorry for it. Besides," her look was thoughtful, "it was only 'cause he was drunk. I was near forty then, and he liked them young."

I asked a few more questions, sufficient to learn the address at which May died, and any other details of those involved. I spent the remainder of the day, including a brief lunch at a cafe, traipsing about the city, talking to people who couldn't recall much of the events so long ago. I turned for home around five p.m. and walked wearily up the stairs to our rooms. Holmes was already there and Mrs. Hudson was bringing up the dinner tray. I flung myself into my chair, ate in gloomy silence and relaxed back at last with a strong whisky and soda, which began to revive me. Holmes addressed me after some time.

"A long day I apprehend, Watson."

"A long day, and not much to show for it. May Percy is dead, and she's been dead for more than two decades. Lizzie Davis identified the body at the time. The woman was passing under another name and Lizzie thought it best to let sleeping dogs lie. She and her husband buried the woman under the name she'd been using, so the Riggstons never knew. I've seen the grave, and talked to a retired constable who was called in when the landlady found her."

"I see. Tell me all you have heard, Watson."

I talked for some time, recounting Lizzie disclosures, my searches, and adding what Lizzie recalled of Mr. Joseph Riggston's smug claims to have cheated May. "What do you think he meant, Holmes? How did he cheat her?"

My friend took a drink, set his glass down, and explained. "I can think of one simple way. You said that Lizzie overheard him say that some investments paid higher than some could guess, and that tells me the most probable method. He'd managed, or most probably his brother had, to successfully gain control over May's inheritance. They'd invested it in a venture that would pay far higher than ordinary bank interest should it succeed. It must have done so, and the amount the Riggstons made was a substantial sum. They may have reinvested that several times in the fifteen years before the girl returned to claim it."

"They may have gambled initially that at her age, without resources, she would never return." He sat back, gray eyes intent. "They were taking a risk, but their gloating suggests that not only did they not lose the money, but on the contrary they made large profits, and repaying her was easy since they merely returned what they would have owed if they had invested it at a percent or two interest."

"What sort of profit would you estimate?" I used that word since my friend disliked being asked to guess. An estimate was a computation with some known factors.

Holmes became intent. "There are many issues to take into account. However, at the time there were a number of ventures in overseas trading, which could produce immense profits for those involved. If they had a substantial amount in such an undertaking they could have doubled the sum invested. Should they have been successful a second time, and then been wise enough to return the original sum to the trust, they could well have walked away with a large profit and no one the wiser." He studied the file.

"They may have had ample money to live well, yet could have seen opportunity after opportunity pass them by, because they had not the additional monies to invest. The death of their aunt provided those monies. They would waste nothing on the child, a child not of their own blood, and to whom, as they would see it, they owed nothing."

His voice hardened. "Their parents' treatment of her set the example. In addition, Eli Gettes may have known how James and Mary cheated that child. He may have aided them, accepting their claim that investing the money was to May's benefit. But by the time he died, he knew she had been defrauded. Her lot had not improved, as he may have initially thought, and then he discovered they kept the true profits."

His eyes became fixed on the file, and I could see he was deep in thought. I said nothing, for I know better than to interrupt my friend at such times, and it was almost ten minutes by the mantelpiece clock before he stirred.

"Watson, if James and Mary and their sons behaved like that to a child in their care, then although she may be dead, others could have reason to hate the family. If you are not yet tired of this case, I would ask that tomorrow you go back to the Riggston house first, talk to the oldest servants, then go on to Riggston Coal, and read through as many more files as you can stomach. Talk to the older workers there, and ask if they know anyone that the Riggston's … took advantage of. Be discreet. Do not use the word cheated, but that is what you are asking."

Assuring my friend that the case yet held all my interest, I agreed and we retired, each to his bed in a spirit of eagerness for what surprises the morrow might hold. Holmes planned to spend the day looking over the police file on May's death, and then inquiring about the older Riggstons. Because as Holmes said: "If we are certain the girl is dead, then the Riggstons have another enemy, and we need to uncover a motive—which may provide us a name."

* * * *

I returned to Holmes after an arduous day with a list of those who had cause to hate the Riggstons. On the way out of the office, however, I met Bradon, who asked after our discoveries. Reluctantly I showed him the list—over a dozen names—and he was both horrified and disgusted.

"Do you know in what ways and of how much my father and grand-father cheated these people?"

I said that in most cases I did.

"Then may I have a copy of the list as soon as you can manage it? I will repay the monetary debts, and others I will repay in whatever fashion seems equitable. You may be able to suggest how I can do this, Doctor. Please, I beg that you help me."

I agreed, thinking much the better of him, and we parted. I arrived home before Holmes and had time to make the promised copy before he returned. Once he was seated, I shared all I had learned and showed him my list. He perused it carefully, looking at the notes I had sometimes made against the names.

"What of these others, those without any reason?"

"Ah, I got those from some of the older workers, as you advised. Of those four," here I indicated the particular names, "they could only say that the family had treated them badly. In most cases they were sacked from their employment without cause or reason: three of them from the business, and one as a servant in the house. Of the other names, most were cheated in some matter of business. Three lost quite large sums."

Holmes indicated one name. "I know him. Let us ask him directly how he was cheated, for if he was, I believe he will admit it in private."

* * * *

He did so; looking at us across his study once we were shown in.

"Yes, James Riggston tricked me." His look was rueful. "I owned a coal mine, inherited from an old friend of my father's. He died after my father but without altering his will, so the mine came to me. I had no idea of the value, nor if it was producing good coal. I asked a man in the area to make inquiries and received information that the mine was all but worked out and had never produced good coal. I asked him to find me a buyer, and he did so."

"James Riggston?"

"Yes. It would have been about five years before his death. He'd been in charge of Riggston Coal for the past decade and knew his business. He offered a reasonable price, saying that he wanted a good mine in that area and such a one would be suitable. I gathered that he believed there to be a good deal more coal yet, of reasonable quality." He stared at us, shame-faced. "I did not tell him that I knew this was not so. His price was lower than for a mine with decent prospects, but higher than it should be for a worked-out mine with poor coal."

"How then were you cheated?" Holmes asked quietly.

"Because, as I discovered in conversation some years later with an acquaintance from that area, the mine was far from worked out, and the coal was of the best quality. The man who valued my property was in Riggston's pocket. Riggston got a prosperous mine for half its value ...." He laughed with half-amused resignation. "Well, the truth is that I tried to sell him something worthless for a profit, and he tricked me. If I'd been honest and shared what I'd been told of the mine, that it was worked-out and worthless, he'd have had a problem."

"Yes," Holmes agreed. "If he'd offered you a fair price you'd have wanted to know why. And if he offered you what it was worth on your information, it was possible you'd have worried about cheating *him*, and gone to see for yourself."

"So he cheated me instead."

Holmes stood, a smile glimmering in his eyes. "Do you know of anyone else who received the same treatment?"

"Malcolm Edgesley," James Riggston's victim said slowly. "Some time after I found out that I'd been cheated, I was talking to Edgesley. I told him a little of it and he said that he'd had a similar experience,"

We set out for Fassington Place, the address given us, and once there we found Malcolm Edgesley at home, entirely willing to speak to us— and still virulent on the subject of James Riggston—with acerbic side comments on the man's ethics and morals.

8

Malcolm Edgesley was a large, elderly man. Looking at him with the eye of a doctor who had seen a number of men of that type, I considered him a good candidate for a heart attack. His behavior, once he knew of whom we were inquiring, didn't dispel that possibility. He opened the door, asked who we were and what we wanted. Upon Holmes explaining, we were all but dragged inside, shoo'd with gestures down the passage to a large room, and settled in plush armchairs. There we were regarded intently for a moment before our host spoke.

"James Riggston," Edgesley informed us, "was a scoundrel, a black-guard, a liar, and a thief. I was briefly in business with him, and am therefore in a position to speak frankly."

Which he did for some time, while Holmes and I sat and listened without interruption.

The story was, according to the still-infuriated man—with so much arm waving that at times I was half-surprised he didn't leave the ground—that he had owned a stretch of land, on the far side of which lay two coal mines. (I have kept the location anonymous, so as not to attract claims of libel.)

By approaching him as the acquaintance of an old friend of Edges-ley's, Riggston tried to buy that strip of land, and on Edgesley's refusal, made him a business proposition. They could go into partnership and develop the land as a short private road that would allow the mines' output to be more easily and quickly transported. I caught Holmes's eye and we both guessed what was coming.

Edgesley had taken advice from their mutual friend, who said it seemed a sound idea, all aspects of the plan had been extensively dis-cussed—verbally—and a contract drawn up. Edgesley signed it.

"I was a young fool! I should have had my lawyer read the contract first, but I knew what it was to say. I skimmed over it and everything was there, so I signed. No problems occurred for more than a year, then Riggston and I disagreed on exactly where the last section of the road was to go. His way passed too close to my country place, in eyeshot—and earshot, too—to make it worse."

He protested, Edgesley told us. Riggston smiled, and said he should read their contract. Right at the bottom, in what he'd thought to be noth-ing more than details of their addresses and other information of that kind, he found a single line saying—in extremely small print—that in case of any dispute, James Riggston, as senior partner in the transaction, should have the final say. And what Riggston said was that the road went where he wanted it to go, and that was that.

"Talked to my lawyer. He said I'd been had, but there was nothing I could do about it. Oh, I've been paid a fair enough price for the land and an ongoing sum for use of the road, but nothing pays me for having my home ruined. When the mines are in full production in summer you can't sleep for the noise of vehicles going past. They have headlights, and when they come over the rise near the house, the lights shine right in the windows." His tone was bitter. "It was my own fault, I know. That makes it worse. I'd give them twice what I was paid for the land if they'd shift that road, but the last time I tried, their lawyer refused. Said it wouldn't pay them. I get a good amount each year as my share, and I'd give up every coin of it tomorrow if they'd move that road."

"When was the last time you approached the Riggstons?" Holmes asked.

"Must be close to twenty years now."

Which would have been when Bradon was still a minor, I thought. His mother would have listened to the lawyer, and naturally the man would advise her not to agree. To him it was a matter of profit, and he'd have ignored the genuine misery I saw on Malcolm Edgesley's face. It wouldn't do to raise false hopes, but it was possible that if we explained the situation to Bradon, he might be prepared to make some accommodation.

"Why do you not sell your house, and buy or build elsewhere?" Holmes inquired with his usual practicality.

Edgesley glared at him. "Because the place is my home. I was born and brought up there, as was m' father, m' grandfather, and *his* father built it. My son inherits, and his son loves the place already." He sat heavily. "I'm worried that the Riggstons may manage to make the road public, and then there'd be traffic on it day and night all year 'round. It'd be insupportable!"

I broke in. "Mr. Edgesley, I know of someone with a similar problem. They planted evergreen trees all along the boundary between their home and the road, while inside the row of trees they added a thick hedge. The combination muted the noise until it was unnoticeable, nor could they see the vehicles. You could try that to ameliorate the problem."

He brightened. "Do you say so? Well, I'll try anything that might work. I'll send a message to my bailiff and get that in hand at once."

It was possible I could persuade Bradon to an agreement, but even if the road remained as a short cut for the mines, the leafy barrier would be a boon to this unhappy man.

* * * *

I talked to Bradon on the matter. He was saddened at this further evidence of his father's underhanded practices, and agreed to add a signed and witnessed clause to the Riggston-Edgesley contract. It stated that the road was to remain in both families' possession and no interest in it was to be disposed of to any other party. Moreover, when the mines no longer produced the road should be closed and the land—on repayment of the original sum paid and no more—should be returned to the possession of the Edgesley family.

Two days later Malcolm Edgesley signed the adjusted contract with tears in his eyes before turning to Holmes and me, who stood as witnesses. "And I thank you heartily, Doctor. Not only for your actions in this, but also my bailiff had mature trees and hedge shrubs transplanted from another part of my land. He added as well a temporary wall between the two rows, and I find the noise much reduced. Your advice was invaluable." He beamed at me, shaking me by the hand so strongly that I winced.

* * * *

Bradon caught up with us as we left the building where the contract was signed, and walked with us a distance. "Have you discovered anything about the one we seek?"

I knew Holmes regretted we had not, but all he said was that this far, there was no more information as to evidence of identity.

"We continue to inquire, Mr. Riggston. We have the list Watson made, and it may be that one of the names upon that will be the person we seek."

"But you do not think so?" Bradon asked shrewdly.

"I do not, but to ignore the possibility would be foolish. We shall check each name, and once we are done then there are other avenues yet. Do not despair. We have also informed Mr. Arthur Riggston of such progress as has been made."

That was true, and the brusque note in reply had castigated us, saying the writer considered no progress to have been made. If that continued, he would cease to fund our investigations.

Bradon grinned. "Yes, I can guess what he said. Don't worry, you may not as yet have uncovered a murderer, but you are producing useful information. Should Uncle Arthur cut you off, I'll take up your payments." He laughed. "I did not expect it, but with all the research Dr. Watson has been doing in the old files, and all the coming and going of you both, one of my senior clerks came to me yesterday and confessed he's been stealing for years. He's repaying all he stole on my agreement not to prosecute, and he left my employment that very hour. He thought that you were looking for him, you see."

Holmes's smile was wintry. "'The wicked flee where no man pursueth,'" he quoted.

"Yes. The amusing thing is that he was clever with the money he stole. I'm to get back the amount he took, but he's made money on that and his family won't starve."

"You could demand that he return his ill-gotten profits as well," I commented.

Bradon looked ill-at-ease. "Oh, well. He has a wife and children, and they are not to blame for his defalcations."

I thought the better of him for that and once he left us I said as much to Holmes, who regarded me calmly.

"My dear Watson, in what way is Riggston to blame that his clerk took a wife and raised a family on money that was not his? In allowing the man to keep the profits, he permits criminal behavior to flourish."

"And you would not condone such a thing?" I asked, permitting a faint tinge of sarcasm to enter my voice.

Holmes inclined his head and said no more. We both well knew that on occasion he had taken the law into his own hands, and that he would do so again if he felt it warranted.

He changed the subject. "How far down your list are we, Watson? And have you found any names to add?"

"Yes," I said thoughtfully. "With all this talk of Edgesley and his family I had an idea. You recall that sad case of the young child left alone by his mother, an act condoned by Reverend Mathews?" Holmes signaled his recall and I continued. "I said the boy could not have been our murderer since he was dead. But even murderers may marry. I returned to peruse the parish registers."

"I see," Holmes commented. "You found that there was a family, and the children were now adults."

I nodded. "The tombstone I saw included only a name, two dates, and no more. I returned to look at the register, remembering that the original event was on the first year of Jarod Wilson's arrival. That, I found, had been over seventeen years before, and adding together the times, the lad of six was confirmed as being twenty-nine when he died. The register listed a marriage, and noted the birth of a son. After which it gave the death of the father as due to pneumonia. But by my calculations the son would now be nineteen."

"And the young are passionate over injustice," my friend agreed. "But, Watson, if the son murdered Reverend Mathews, who killed the Riggstons, their lawyer, and the Pellys? Do you imagine that the murders were each committed by a different person?"

I was somewhat crestfallen. "Not exactly. But I did wonder if it were possible there was more than one killer. If the lawyer's death was natural, the deaths of the Pellys, mother and son, were accidental, and the father's death was personal animus, could not another person with a long-held grudge have murdered the Riggstons?"

Holmes eyed me kindly. "I agree that although the Riggston family appear to have generated sufficient grudges to encourage any number of murders, what motive would you suggest applies to the Pellys, apart from being close-fisted, weak, and dangerous to young women? And the lawyer? We showed, even if there was no concrete proof, that the man was, to my own satisfaction, a victim of foul play." He shook his head. "Watson, Watson. The introduction of three or four murderous individuals rather than the one does not clarify events."

I could only agree when he put it so clearly. "I fear I lost sight of the road we travel, Holmes. You are right. Even if minister and lawyer and two of the Pellys all died natural deaths, we would have to postulate several killers, and that is unlikely."

"It is. However, I agree that it would do no harm to track down the wife and son of the lad whose ill-treatment was condoned by Reverend Mathews. Ask them most particularly if anyone else has inquired about it. If so, question them closely, have them recount the questions this person asked, every word they may have said. Do not forget any reference they may have made to Reverend Mathews, or questions they asked about him. And obtain the best description you are able."

I was baffled as to why, after he had proven the event to be of no importance to our case, I was now to make such inquiries, but I said that I would begin first thing in the morning.

* * * *

Holmes and I shared a nourishing breakfast of buttered toast, bacon and eggs, and several cups of Mrs. Hudson's excellent tea before departing 221B Baker Street at nine a.m. A cab took me to the parish where Jarod Wilson now ministered, and he consulted his meticulous records.

"Ah, here it is. Yes, the boy was Harold Stowe, and his mother was Katy Stowe. No father listed. Ah, as I recall, it is likely that she was uncertain as to his identity, and as no man was prepared to accept responsibility, no name was registered. I was told that Katy died in Brighton and was buried there. Harold died four years after her and was buried here, but in the interim he married and had a son. The son was, I believe, named Harold after his father, the wife had been a Miss Nancy Upton. Upon the death of Harold senior they removed to a small village just outside of London. The son would be almost twenty by now, I think, and I did hear that he married a local girl. I can give you their address at the time."

I accepted the address and made for the station. If I could catch the next train …. I did, and in short order was racing along at the exhilarating speed of some forty miles per hour, arriving swiftly at my destination. I was first off the train, and was soon bowling along a pretty country lane behind an energetic cob. His driver assured me that he knew the place I sought and would have me there in a trice.

He was as good as his word, and when I knocked, a fresh-faced woman opened the door, with a small girl at her side. I asked for Harold Stowe—the son being named after his father—and she smiled.

"He do be out in the fields. How-some-ever he should be home shortly. Do you come in and bide, I can make us a cup of tea and I've scones just out of the old oven."

I could smell them and my stomach rumbled. In what felt like seconds I was seated on a pleasant chintz-covered window-seat with a cup of tea in one hand and a plate of scones beside me, a cat making overtures—cupboard love I knew, I could see her eyes on a scone—and the small girl watching me curiously from the other side of the room. The cottage was not large, but it was clean and well-kept, as was the child. If this was where the son of an unfortunate father had ended up, he had not done so badly for himself, even if he had clearly married young.

Mrs. Stowe bustled about getting a meal on the table for her man, and the child was diverted with a glass of milk as I made inroads on some of the best scones I have ever eaten. I just laid down the empty cup when the door opened and Harold Stowe walked in, bowing his head as he passed the low lintel. He was broad, weather-beaten, and his hands were those of a man who uses them on all manner of crafts. He looked at me, looked at his wife, and waited.

I stood and spoke politely. "Mr. Harold Stowe, I believe? I am Dr. Watson, and I wished to speak to you concerning your father. Your wife was kind enough to invite me in to wait. I hope my visit is not an imposition?"

His voice was less countrified, but the rural suspicion of strangers was still evident.

"What about my father? He's dead, aye, and my mother and his mother, too. There's just me and Nan and Bessie now. Why would you come asking after him?"

I did my best to explain as he ate his way steadily through a plate piled with food. His Nancy had offered some to me and I took a small amount. The lady was an excellent cook as well and I said so, which brought the first smile to Harold's face.

He patted her arm as she passed. "Aye, that's truth. She's a good wife all 'round, and I couldn't have done better." He finished eating, drained his glass, and sat back, before scooping the small girl onto his lap and settling her there. "I dunno what you want of me, Doctor, but I can tell you about my grandmother to start, for my dad told me the stories. She was a whore. From what I heard she were running after the boys by the time she was twelve, and her parents tossed her out two, three years later.

She never knew who fathered my dad, and although he did say as how she were never cruel to him, well, there's cruel and cruel, isn't there?"

"Reverend Wilson told me about the time she went to Brighton," I interposed.

"Aye, I heard all about it from pa. He near died, with no food nor fuel in the house, and she didn't want the neighbors to know she left him so she'd scared him so bad he feared to call for help."

That, I thought, was something Reverend Wilson hadn't known—or if he had, he hadn't mentioned it to me.

"Dad were found in time and that minister, he did give her a telling off. Mum, she went running to old Mathews, and he told her it weren't her fault, like." His face darkened. "It were, but you couldn't tell the minister. A saint they called him, but he wasn't no saint to my dad. Him saying it was all right only made things worse. Year later it would have been, she did the same thing." He grinned. "Dad fooled her that time. He'd been taking money from her purse any time she come home drunk. Aye, he'd coin for fuel and food, so he were all right that time. Then he married and had me. He died when I were a tiddler, but I remember all the stories he told me."

"Your grandmother died?"

"Aye. She'd gone to Brighton, reliving old days, I reckon. Got drunk and walked right under the Brighton coach. Good riddance to her. Mum took me back home afore then, as she had family in the area, they got her work, and I met Nancy. Her family worked in the same place. We were young, but we knew our own minds. Her family sees she's happy and they're not bothered, and I've a good job with a good master. I work for the Reads, a big farm, and I can turn my hand to fixing anything, so they reckon I earn my wages. Nancy worked in their kitchen till we married, and we saved every penny. Put money down on this cottage and reckon to own it in a while."

I honestly praised his industry and that of Nancy. It was unusual for a farm laborer to own his own home, and so I said.

"Aye, it is. But I heard enough from my dad about Lunnon landlords tossing people into the street because they couldn't pay their rent. Didn't want it happening to Nancy and little Bess, so Nan and me agreed. We don't have the cash for extras, but the master said he'll give me more money in a while if I stay steady, and that'll help. We got a garden and fruit trees here, and there's a field went with the cottage. We got an old cow, and I buy poddy lambs. Don't cost us much but the work. Nan raises them, and they're—*sold*." He cast a significant look at small Bess and I understood.

"Or so you say," I murmured.

"Aye. My dad knew too much while he was still her age. I won't have that for her. Now, Doctor, what do you really want to know, eh?"

"Did anyone ever come asking your father about the old minister?"

His gaze went to the carpet as he thought. Then he looked up. "Aye, I do remember one. It'd be years ago now. I weren't but four or so. A slender man asked my mum about the old minister all right, offered her money. Her needing it to come back here, she took his coin and told him all the stories she knew."

"Stories?"

"Aye, you know a parish. They talk, and mum was one that listened. She told him about my dad being left alone the way he was, and the old minister saying his mum couldn't help it and shouldn't be blamed. Told about young Margie and her mum. Margie wasn't but twelve, and a rich man come, asking to have her as his maid. Her mum took money for it, knowing the job wasn't what he had in mind. Her man were angry and beat her, but old minister said for shame. Said Margie's dad didn't know for sure, and something about judging not."

"'Judge not lest ye be judged,'" I said. "It's in the Bible."

"Might be, but what that man did to Margie weren't. Or if it were, it shouldn't have been. Anyways, there was a lot of tales like that. This 'un sat there listening to all she could say, and when she'd run out like, he stood up and gave her the money he'd promised and a bit more, so she cried and blessed him. He thanked her kindly but said he wasn't no angel; that even a bad man could do good once in a while."

For a small boy, he remembered a surprising amount. He'd been sitting under the table the entire time, he said, and knew how important the money was to their escape. Then, too, the children of the poor tend to be sharp-witted out of necessity. He produced a description, which added up to the man being about five foot and six or seven inches in height, wearing a three-piece suit in dark material. He had a stick, and from the description I thought it to be a silver-topped ebony cane, and he smelled of lime.

"How did you know?"

"I didn't. But a while after we come here, I were in the market and they had some for sale. I asked, and stallholder said they were limes. That was how the man smelled."

I returned to Holmes with a full bag of such information and discovered, to my surprise, that he found all of it interesting, right down to the scent of limes.

9

Holmes listened intently and when I was done he pursed his lips and nodded slowly.

"Yes, as I suspected. Someone has been confirming his own suspicions. Not until he has confirmation does he act."

I frowned. "You mean he wanted to be certain that the incident he was aware of was not the only one?"

"Indeed, Watson. A man may err once, and a man intent on meting justice would be wise to see if it was a pattern rather than a single event."

"So he could have been someone from that parish? Maybe Reverend Wilson could give us some possibilities."

Holmes looked thoughtful. "We can return and ask, or better yet, we can quietly find those who have lived there all their lives. Let us find a gossip who knows all the tales, and persuade them to talk."

I laughed. "My dear Holmes, no true gossip must be persuaded. They will talk so long as you will listen."

And it was so. We fell into conversation with a shopkeeper whose family had served his community for three generations, and who could tell us who knew all about the parish and would talk about it.

"Aye, old Missus Spencer is one. Been here her whole life. She don't work now, but her lad and his wife care for her. She were a good mother and her children all chip in sommat. She don't write nor read, so there's times she don't do nothing but sit and hope someone will call. Likes a good gossip she do, and she'd be most willing to see you."

We got her direction and the shopkeeper was right. Mrs. Spencer was eager to talk, and welcomed too the small twist of paper containing tea and paper bag of chocolate biscuits we brought. She knew the stories of Reverend Mathews, and once she was sure we would not reprove her for speaking frankly, she was eagerly forthcoming.

"Aye, he were a fool of a man. Excused everyone their sins and all that did were to make people keep on with them." She spat into the fire. "Take that whore ..." We heard again the tale of a child left to freeze and starve, but from the point of view of a woman who was some years older than his mother and had known her. "A slut she were from the beginning. It were my opinion she knew quite well whose child the boy were, but the man died in an accident right after the lad were sent for."

I smiled at the old expression for conception. She grinned toothlessly back at me, eyes twinkling wickedly, and continued.

"Aye, cut above her family, and a fair amount of money by her standards. He'd have been a good catch, and that'd be one way to do it. He were an honest man. If he believed the child his he'd do the right thing. But he didn't live to be told and if she went to his family asking for sommat she'd have caught cold at it." She looked at us, her old eyes sharp and hard. "Tell you, I do, that girl made enough money to take good care of the boy. Enough to get a girl in to watch him times she were away from home. But she didn't, not her. She'd rather spend the money on fancy dresses and gewgaws while that poor little lad went cold and hungry. Got out he did, soon as he were old enough to get work. A hard worker, and his master thought a lot of him."

She laughed. "Aye, and for all she went looking and found where he were, she didn't get nothing out of him after that. Told her he owed her nothing, he did. And his master tossed her out, said did she come back he'd have the police on her. Came home swearing and cursing them both fit to wake the dead, and I heard it all. I told her that you reap as you sow, and if she'd wanted a better crop she should have sowed more careful." She laughed again. "She cursed me after that, and my lad told her did she say such to me again he'd drop her in the gutter where she belonged. Said I had the right of it, and if she'd been half the mother to her lad that I'd been to them, she'd have had no cause for complaint."

We got her onto other stories—including that of the girl sold at twelve as maid to a wealthy man—and gleaned facts from them. One was that Reverend Mathews had indeed been of the "see no evil, hear no evil, and acknowledge no evil" persuasion. He hadn't merely accepted that people fall into temptation. Over and over he'd condone that fall, even when it was for money and not out of dire circumstances. In consequence, he would hear all about the things that went on, accept them, and do nothing to mitigate evil. That may not have caused an increase in wickedness, but it certainly did nothing to lessen it.

Once she had finished, she suggested another person two doors away to whom we could speak. We went there and the old man added to our store of knowledge. Like Mrs. Spencer, he had not approved the minister's laxity and said so.

We took our leave at last, and once out of earshot I turned angrily to my friend.

"I do not agree with murder, Holmes, but I can understand why anyone who suffered because that man did nothing would subsequently return to wreak vengeance on him."

Holmes remained silent a moment before he replied. "So can I, Watson. I notice too that both men had similar natures."

I looked at him. "Both men?"

He elaborated. "The minister and the lawyer, Watson. The minister not only did not reprove sin, he ignored it. The lawyer ignored illegalities also. He knew his client cheated and tricked those with whom he was in business, and he knew that some of his client's actions were criminal. I believe he suspected worse yet he did nothing, and by his silence and his continued employment, he actively assisted in their crimes."

"To be fair, Holmes," I pointed out. "He was in an invidious position. If he spoke out too openly he would lose the work. Riggston would continue cheating, and Gettes lose a part of his income. And I think that much was not illegal—sharp practice, yes—but not illegal. I'm sure he would see to that."

Holmes regarded me. "I'm sure, too, Watson. Not because he objected to his client breaking the law, but because it is better that neither he nor his client does so. Or if his client does, then that no one can show he knew of it, or assisted in any way. Do you not see? His actions were similar to those of the minister: they may not have actively moved, but they facilitated. By their passivity, they encouraged others to act evilly."

"I think I understand," I said as his meaning became clear. "You believe that the murderer views them as active participants, since not only did they do nothing, they did not speak out either?"

"I do. And so far as I can tell, there is only one point of connection between both."

"The Riggstons," I said triumphantly.

"Yes. We have heard from the lawyer's partner, from the minister's successor, from several in the parish, and the only point of contact between minister and lawyer is the Riggston family. The Pellys, too, had no other element in common, and it must be to the Riggstons that we look. I want you, if you will, Watson, to continue looking through the Riggston Coal files. Go back to the affairs of Bradon's grandfather and grandmother. Look for any mention of Mr. Arthur Riggston senior."

"I shall do so," I promised. "However, could we not go home and have dinner?"

Holmes consented, and after dinner I went to bed, with the thought that I should be up early in the morning. With so many files yet to peruse it would be another long day. Holmes had said he, too, would be gone all day, although I had no idea of his intentions.

* * * *

Long before I was done I was greatly wearied of my task. I carried home, however, two tidbits for my friend, and over a good roast of mutton—with roast potatoes, and gravy, and a sherry trifle to conclude the meal—I unburdened myself to him.

"You were right and I was wrong, Holmes," I confessed. "And I may have uncovered a possible motive and murderer." He eyed me and waited. I drew out my accomplishment a little. "We know," I said, "that James Riggston senior cheated May out of a large sum and used it to his own benefit. If his son knew of that, and I think he did, he may have used it as an example. I found a file that should have been retained at the office of Eli Gettes. It detailed another inheritance of which we, and I think Bradon Riggston, are unaware. Victor Percy had an aunt. She died at a great age and left everything to her nephew. She died when May Percy was about twenty-five, and she would have known nothing of this."

"But by then May was dead and buried by the Davises," Holmes reminded me.

I smiled. "Yes, but Lizzie said she buried her friend under the name she had been using, not as May Percy. The Riggstons never knew, or at least Lizzie never informed them. And—from what the file says—they didn't look for May. Instead, the money was accepted by their lawyer, purporting to act for May, and turned over to James Riggston junior, who immediately invested it as part of the Riggston fortune. So I was wrong. Gettes didn't merely ignore his client's actions, he actively assisted them. It disgusts me, Holmes!"

My anger rose again as I thought of the file's contents. "He helped Riggston steal from that poor girl. They took a large sum bequeathed to her. Yes, I know she was dead by then." I waved away his attempt to speak. "But she may well have made her own will, and the money should have gone to whoever she designated. Perhaps Lizzie Davis, her good friend." I thumped the table. "The Riggston family had falsely enriched themselves by the sum of twelve hundred pounds. Think what such a sum would mean to most people."

I could see that he was thinking. "Watson, this should be brought to the attention of Mr. Bradon Riggston. He has shown himself ready and willing to remedy such wrongs."

"I know," I said, my anger abating somewhat. "But his family in effect stole twelve hundred pounds from *someone*."

"That is true, yet we could bring the matter to his attention. It is possible that Lizzie knows if the girl made a will. If she did not, it may be that the old lady's will named a second heir."

I shook my head. "I checked that, for there was a copy of her will in the file. It was brief, saying only that 'all of which she died possessed should go to her nephew Victor Percy, and if he was deceased, then to his daughter, May.' She probably assumed that May would outlive them." I brightened. "We could suggest to Bradon that he donate the money to some worthy charity."

"That is possible," Holmes agreed. "Now, Watson, you said you found that Riggston did something similar to another person?"

Recalled, I nodded. "Yes. You will not guess who it was."

"Mr. Arthur Riggston, his younger brother," Holmes promptly stated.

I glared. "I wish you would not *do* that, Holmes."

My friend nodded. "I apologise, Watson. However, I know nothing of the details, so enlighten me, if you will."

I sat back, undid a waistcoat button—that had been an excellent meal—and started. "The papers were in another file, but were bundled together with the one on May's second inheritance. From its appearance and position I would guess that it was placed there several decades ago and forgotten. I believe it was a duplicate, so its absence was never noticed."

"It is likely that Riggston junior held copies that Gettes did not know about. Perhaps to use as a means of keeping him in line," Holmes commented.

"Yes," I agreed. "Now, this file concerned Mr. Arthur Riggston senior, godfather to your client. Miss Janet Riggston, sister to Mr. James Riggston senior, left her estate to her nephew Arthur. And," I added irritably, "I wish that if maiden aunts insist upon leaving money to family members they take more care where their wills are kept. However that may be, her estate consisted of funds on deposit, shares in several prosperous businesses, cash in a bank account, and an amount of valuable jewelry."

Here I grinned at the memory of some of the papers that accompanied the file. "It seems that although Janet Riggston did not marry, she was not solitary. She must have been something of a beauty in her time, since there was a list appended to her will—I believe in her handwriting—detailing not only the jewelry pieces, but where and how and from whom they had been obtained." I cleared my throat. "The entire estate, once her house was sold, came to more than five thousand pounds, without the jewelry, which is still, I believe, held in a safe at the business."

Holmes looked at me. "You think my client may have a hint of that, and set me to discover it? Once we had proof, he could demand the monies peculated, recover the jewelry, and live on in murderous luxury?"

"Yes," I said firmly.

My friend considered that. "I do not think Arthur Riggston that type, although any man may murder if the motive be sufficient," he said. "Yet I would describe him as indolent, not one to hold such a grudge as would lead him to kill again and again, nor apt at dissembling should he do so. He was genuinely concerned that his godfather died naturally, and should you bring your discovery to his attention, I am of the opinion that he would at once approach his nephew and ask for his inheritance to be restored to him. Do you see him as a man who would murder so many, merely to reveal something he already knew? And if he did *not* know it, why then would he kill those who offended him?"

That was comprehensive, and thinking it over, I must admit that my own opinion of the man matched that of my friend. Besides, and I had not properly reflected on it before, if he knew, he had only to approach his nephew since there would be proof obtainable. If he did not know, why would he be ....

I sighed. "Yes. Yet should we not be certain?"

Holmes inclined his head. "You are right. I will make inquiries myself with Gettes's partner, show the file to Riggston, and then speak to my client. His demeanor at the revelation should be sufficient to show if he knew of his brother's theft. If I judge that he knew nothing, you agree that it is unlikely he is responsible for the deaths?"

I did. Holmes is an excellent judge of character, and even if he had been wrong initially over Arthur Riggston's knowledge or involvement, I knew that when he spoke to the man, being by then on guard against deceit, he would see the truth.

* * * *

All fell out as I expected. Holmes went to the cellar with me the following morning and took the file to Bradon Riggston, who was both horrified and resigned.

"How many more events such as this are likely to be uncovered?" he asked wearily. "In the end, my mother and I neither liked nor trusted my father, but it is distressing to discover that he was prepared to cheat strangers and family alike." I cleared my throat and he turned to me. "Oh, dear Lord, this isn't the only time, is it?"

"No," I said, producing the other file and placing it before him. "Your grandfather cheated May Percy of one inheritance, and your father then cheated her of another. She is dead, but there may be a will."

Bradon dropped into his chair and read in silence for some time before looking up. "What am I to do? I can restore Uncle Arthur's inheritance quite easily. His aunt left everything to him, and these papers give the amount. I know the jewelry is still in the family safe here, for I have seen it." His look was bitter. "It is listed in the safe records as being family property descended from my great-grandmother. The record says that it is not to be sold; rather it may be used as security for a loan if required, or a single piece sold at great need within the family, or by the firm. That, too, can be returned to Arthur. But what am I to do about May's second inheritance?"

I diffidently put forward my suggestion that it could be given to charity.

"And if someone comes forward who can prove she inherited from the girl?"

"You could create a temporary trust," Holmes offered. "Place that amount in a trust into which the interest accrues. Should an inheritor appear, the trust can be dissolved and the monies handed over once proofs are established. The fact that you placed the inheritance in a trust indicates that you acted honorably."

Bradon sat thinking before raising his head. "That seems a good idea." He reread a portion of the papers. "I do not at all like that our lawyer acted with my father in these swindles. Have you found anything at all that suggests Grosett knew of this trickery, too?"

I assured him that I had not, neither in his own files, nor in those I read at the lawyers' offices. I pointed out that these two files (detailing the theft practiced by his father upon the two people named) had been held at his firm, perhaps so that Grosett should know nothing of his elder partner's machinations. I thought Grosett an honest man and, when Bradon looked hopefully at my friend, Holmes inclined his head in agreement. Bradon cheered up.

"Good, then I can inform him and he can take the necessary actions. I will put all in train as quickly as may be. Er, would you care to inform my uncle of your discoveries while I call in Grosett?"

We agreed and left at once for Mr. Arthur's address, where we were eagerly received. I watched the man keenly as I revealed how his eldest brother had cheated him. Holmes's client listened with his mouth gradually opening in outrage until my denouement, in which I said that his nephew promised to immediately reimburse all that was taken. He was as shocked and revolted by his father's perfidy as we, and summoned his lawyer at once to make all right. I saw no evidence or indeed suggestion that Arthur suspected his brother or nephew of any ill-doing, and I accepted that my suspicions of him were wrong.

Once I was done with our disclosure, I allowed Arthur Riggston to give vent in a series of spluttered imprecations. After several minutes of fulminating he fell silent, and abruptly smiled.

"Bless Great-Aunt Janet. I know why she did that, for my godfather told me of her. In the family, he was the only one who remained on good terms with her for much of her early life. Yes." He turned to me. "She was a great beauty in her day. She never wished to marry, saying that to take a husband was to take an owner, and she intended to live her life in freedom. She was shrewd, and invested the money she inherited from her father, playing her lovers and other men against each other, and learning in what new prospects her inheritance could best be placed. When her looks faded she retired to a small village, taking on a long lease the small manor house. Over the years she became something of a beloved institution."

He studied the papers again. "I see how James was able to do this. She died at a great age the week before my godfather. He would not have known of her death, nor would she have known of his. I learned of her death only three or four years afterwards. I do not remember asking about her estate or who might have inherited, as I was engaged for some time after my godfather's death in sorting out his estate. I never met Janet, although my godfather told me many tales of her."

He shrugged. "Tell Bradon there need be no haste in this matter. Send me the jewelry and the rest of the estate may wait on a favorable time—so long as it be within a year," he added cautiously.

Holmes and I took our leave, and as we reached the pavement I spoke in a low voice. "He never asked how much she left. For that reason, I cannot think him a killer."

"Nor I, Watson. I looked into his finances yesterday, and he does well. He is not a man to live opulently, and he has more than sufficient. He is one who prefers not to marry, comfortable in his own society and enjoying that of his friends so long as he can return home and shut the door. I spoke to some of his companions and they said that he goes to *their* homes, to restaurants to share meals with them, or to such amusements as the opera or theatre, but they do not spend time in his home more than once a year, and not always that."

He hailed a cab and his comments resumed once we were seated. "I investigated also the finances of the Riggston family and their firm. It was always possible that Bradon knew one day he would be obliged to return monies to which he had no right, and what better to prevent that than by the deaths of those who might demand recompense or uncover the truth. I was able to verify that Riggston Coal is prosperous, and the amount Bradon will repay his uncle is nothing compared to its assets and reserves. Bradon's personal fortune is moderate, yet even did he repay the amounts owing from that rather than from the firm's holdings, it could be done without hardship."

I murmured that for some men the amounts would still be something they would not wish to lose. I was, however, merely playing Devil's advocate and Holmes knew it. The cab halted outside our address, we alighted, paid the driver, and once in our own rooms continued the conversation over dinner.

"You have omitted to note another possibility," Holmes announced. I stared and Holmes dropped his bombshell. "Joseph Riggston had a son."

I thought back. Joseph Riggston died unmarried at thirty-five. I supposed it possible that he had an illegitimate son, but without a will specifically leaving his estate to the boy, he would not inherit. And Joseph could not have done so surely, else we would have found some record of it. I asked for details.

"Joseph had a maid."

I gave Holmes a disapproving look, which Holmes acknowledged.

"Yes, I agree. She was fifteen, and when she was found in that condition, he sent her to live with some of her family outside London. On her production of a son, he settled money on them both, on the condition that he was not asked for more, and that they were not in any way to regard themselves as his heirs. After which he seems to have cut the connection, with neither side dissenting."

"Would his brother know of this?"

"Undoubtedly. What he may not have known was that the woman later married and her son, who was then nine, took the name of his stepfather, a Mr. Scott Marsden, the village schoolmaster. He saw to it that, with the money settled on him, the boy continued his education and became a business secretary. The young man's name is Jack Marsden. He is twenty-five, and is currently Bradon's personal assistant."

10

I stared at my friend. I found my voice after the information sank in. I had seen the young man in question. He did not resemble the Riggston family, being fair and snub-nosed.

"Holmes, are you certain?" I added questioningly.

"I am. I went to the community where he was raised." His look became introspective. "A pleasant place, and one day I may retire to such a village." He shrugged off that possibility and returned to the subject. "I talked to his mother, who admitted that her son has never been told who his father was. She preferred to pass there as a widow whose husband had married a little beneath him, and who died shortly after their marriage. His family was happy to see her living elsewhere."

Holmes smiled a little. "She explained that people do love scandal, so it's wise to provide them with a talking point that is believable. With that tale, most locals sympathized with her, accepted that she'd been respectably wed, and turned their indignation on her husband's family. She refused to mention his family name so that, she explained, her pension would not be endangered. When she did marry she told her husband the truth, who found all faults to be on her seducer's side, and who never blamed a young girl taken advantage of by an employer."

"Nor do I," I exclaimed angrily. "I have seen sufficient of society to know that such things happen. Joseph Riggston should have thought shame to himself. He was a man in his thirties. The girl was fifteen and under his roof; it was his duty to protect her, not to take advantage of her."

"It was because she was under his roof that he could treat her so," Holmes said. "None of the staff would dare reprove him for fear of losing their employment, and the girl was in similar position. I agree that his actions were shameful, but the man is dead and we cannot change the past. Now his mother swears to me that Jack was never told the name of his mother's seducer, nor does she wish him to know. If he is told that, he must also discover the circumstances of his birth. I want you, Watson, if you will, to return to Riggston Coal, and fall into conversation with this boy."

"But Holmes," I said. "If he is twenty-five, he can hardly be responsible for any of the deaths. Why, the last one occurred a full nine years ago, when the boy was sixteen. It is inconceivable that he could convince David Pelly to drink with him in a matter of business."

"No, no, Watson. I do not suspect the boy—nor his step-father," he added, apparently anticipating my next suggestion. "Yet ..." His expression became thoughtful. "It is interesting that the person who may have killed James the younger and David Pelly appears to be a young man. Those deaths were seven years apart, but the same description holds: that of a young man." He fell into introspection while I busied myself sorting through some of my medical files that had fallen into confusion.

Once my friend resurfaced from his thoughts, I asked him the question that was on my mind. "Holmes, if you do not suspect young Marsden, why then am I to talk with him?"

"It is possible that the killer has spoken with him," was my friend's alarming reply.

"What? Why? How would they know of him?" I protested.

"Consider, Watson," I was reminded. "The possible murderer went to Reverend Mathews's church and asked about him. He went to the lawyer's home as well."

"How do you .... Oh, I see. The murderer could not have killed Gettes so efficiently had he not known all about Gettes's environs, such as which was his study window, and what he feared." I contemplated that. "You know, Holmes, this person, whoever he is, knows a good deal too much about everything. How is that?"

"I do not yet know, but I shall discover it," he assured me. "It may be that he developed an informant, someone with a grudge against the family who was within the household and happy to divulge anything they knew if they were well paid. Jack Marsden is one such possibility. I want to know if anyone approached him on such matters, what he said, and a description of the person."

"You think it likely?" Frankly I did not, and was surprised that my friend did.

"Not that someone approached him several years ago, no, Watson. What use would he be until he was working for the Riggstons? I fear, however, that this person could have befriended Marsden recently. We cannot be certain that the murderer's depredations are over and done with, and if that is so, he could be seeking information of other members of the Riggston or Pelly families."

I started in my chair. Such a thought had never occurred to me and I was alarmed. Most of the family members seemed to be liars, cheats, and abusers of those less fortunate—or less on their guard. But I liked Bradon Riggston, Mr. Allan Pelly and his family, and I had liked, too, what I had seen of Jack Marsden. I did not wish to see them drown or take poison "accidentally." Another fatal carriage crash might be unlikely, but the new automobiles, replacing many a good horse, could equally be made to crash, perhaps even more so since they did not have the sense of most horses and must be controlled at all times. Nor was a hard shove into a river less likely to be effective now than it had been.

"I will go as soon as I can," I promised my friend. "I had not thought of such a possibility. I shall do what I can, and you? Where will you be?"

"I have some business to transact elsewhere. I will see you when both our day's work is done." And with that he took himself off to bed. I piled the dinner dishes on the tray and left them for Mrs. Hudson to collect before betaking myself to a night's repose also. Holmes trusted me, and I would be worthy of that. Were any information to be had, I would have it.

* * * *

I went to Riggston Coal as soon as I had risen, completed my ablutions and breakfasted, arriving there, to my pleasure, even as Jack Marsden did. We walked up the steps together, he offering any assistance I should require, and I took advantage so far as to ask him to sit and talk with me, if he were not too busy just now. On his assurance that he could spare the time we made for his office, sat down, he called for a pot of tea and we settled to gossip.

I led him to talk of his mother and family and learned that he loved his mother, that most of her family were, while uneducated, no fools, and had always been kind to him, and that he was fond of his step-father.

I sighed silently. None of that was helpful. Having talked of his step-father, he moved on to a subject akin and which brought me to closer attention.

"I wish I had known my father. My mother only ever speaks of him as Joseph. Never once has she revealed his family." He sighed. "I can't help but wish I had known him, and that I might know his family."

I saw my opportunity. "Perhaps they keep watch over you. Has any person ever asked you about your mother's family perhaps, or even about the Riggstons? As your employers they could be of interest. You have worked here for some time, have you not?"

That led him to tell me how good Mr. Bradon had always been to him. "He took me on when I was eighteen and without experience. My step-father knew a man who knew Mr. Bradon and recommended me. Mr. Bradon hired me, since his previous man had retired, and he told me that, after dealing with his father's assistant, he thought it better to catch an educated man young and train him, rather than to have to cope with one trained by another. I tell you, Doctor, he is good to his employees, meticulous in his business affairs, and a fine, honest, generous man."

"He is not yet married," I stated in a bland tone.

Jack Marsden flushed. "That is easily explained. He was engaged in his youth to a girl he loved. She died of consumption, and I think that until recently he still mourned her. Of late he has ... well, perhaps the term should be 'noticed,' a young lady whose family are allied with the Riggstons. But I believe that he is reluctant to declare any interest as yet."

I have no idea why a mental picture of Gwenyth Pelly came to me. I blurted out her name.

Marsden stared. "How could you know that?" he demanded.

I dissembled, commented that in Holmes's case we met many people, and that it was Riggston business and not to be discussed. He accepted that reluctantly.

"Mr. Bradon would not like there to be talk about her," he muttered. And he was only finally placated when I swore that there was none. It was merely the circumstances of my having met the lady, her brother and parents, and knowing that their business often ran together with that of Riggston Coal that had caused me to leap to a conclusion. I would reveal nothing of that to anyone. Once he was calm again I went back to the topic of his father's family.

"And has someone ever asked about them?" I repeated.

His brow wrinkled and I saw that there was something he was debating. I said nothing but sat there, my gaze on him expectantly until he made up his mind and began.

"Not quite as you suggest, but there is Russell Goodwin. I encountered him first when I recently joined this business. He met me in a pub and we fell into conversation. Thereafter I chanced upon him several times a year, always quite late of an evening. He is a listener, you know the sort?"

I did. They did as I had done here, fixed their whole attention on their target, and by their attitude, encouraged the revelation of all kinds of personal opinions and information. If the listener were skillful, their target would tell much that was private, including events and circumstances that applied not only to themselves, but also to family matters, business affairs, and even friends. Usually such listeners fell into two clear types: those who were genuinely interested in their fellow man, and those who used what they heard to make a profit.

"Could any of what you said be used against this business?" I questioned.

The response was terse. "No."

"And do you continue to meet Mr. Goodwin?"

My having unequivocally accepted his earlier answer, he was more disposed to elaborate. "As I said, I met him several times a year. Of course," he added, "I have no reason to suppose that he had not been about before I entered the firm. He knew others who were often present, and was spoken to by name."

"Of what did you speak?"

"All sorts of topics. Twice he gave me good tips on a horse. They won, and I did well." I knew what Holmes would say about that. It was a way of paying Marsden, while not allowing him to feel compromised by an open transaction.

"Good tips. Did he say how he knew? What horses were they?"

"He said he knew the owner. I can't recall the name of the first horse, but I think second was Halloween Day, or some such."

"Do you still see him about?"

"No, the last time we met he said he was going abroad and might not return. A relative had died and left him a good property, and he could do worse than to settle down." Marsden smiled, an expression that made him seem years younger. "He said he would miss me; that I had been a pleasant companion and an interesting conversationalist."

I detected some pride on his part in that comment of Goodwin's, and I was unsurprised. No one dislikes such a compliment. He dug in his waistcoat pocket and produced a small item.

"He gave me this before he left. He said it was to bring me luck, and maybe it's done so. Leastways I've had no bad luck since, and I carry it in memory of one I liked."

He exhibited what he had received. It was a tiny rabbit carved in ivory, with a silver four leaved clover on its head. The clover was pierced and bore a small ring so that the item could be worn, if desired, as a charm on a fob chain, or displayed in some other similar way. It was a pretty trifle. He handed it to me and I looked more closely, thinking that the clover could become detached and the rabbit figure lost.

On inspection I saw that this had been provided for. The back of the rabbit's head had been carved into a slot, with a section of the ivory left across it. The lowest leaf was in two parts, which had been inserted, squeezed together under that bar, and soldered together after that. I had seen such pocket pieces before; this was well-made and would have cost several pounds. Not something that one would give a chance acquaintance.

"That is beautiful," I said honestly. "Mr. Goodwin must have esteemed you very much to give you it."

Marsden took the item back and stowed it carefully in his pocket again. "I believe that he did, Doctor. It is not such a thing I would ever be ashamed to show."

And therein, I saw, was the trap. Mr. Goodwin—whoever he was—was clever. He offered no money to the boy, yet he had instead shown worldly knowledge and implied wealthy friends when he saw to it that Jack won money on two horses. He had strewed the occasional deft compliment, not praising anything that would make his companion uncomfortable, but admiring his interesting conversation. What man does not wish to think himself a fascinating talker?

And, in parting, Mr. Goodwin presented a token of friendship. Something that Jack had acknowledged he would not be ashamed to show others. But it did more. It suggested to anyone who saw it that the boy had been esteemed and valued as a friend. Without thinking upon the matter, Jack understood that, and would be disinclined to ever think or speak ill of the man who had given him that gift—and that acknowledgement.

"Tell me, can you describe your friend? He must have had money; did he dress well?"

Marsden looked abashed. "To tell you the truth, Doctor, for all that I regarded him as a friend, I can tell you little. We met always at the bar ..."—here he named the hotel and I began to understand. "You may know it."

I did, and I could guess also why it had been chosen.

"Then you will know that it is rather dark, and one does not see a companion clearly if one has retired to a booth as we always did. Mr. Goodwin wore dark suits of a good cut, and obviously bespoke. He said that he was subject to colds and wore always a silk scarf about his neck and throat."

"He wore a hat, I suppose? But did he not remove that once inside?"

"On the contrary, he tended to pull that down over his brow when he talked, nor did he ever put it aside. I thought it a nervous habit, so I said nothing."

I did not. A *useful* habit perhaps.

"He had a fine watch on a gold chain, and a fob of the same sort as the one he gave me." I gained a description of that: an ivory cat curled asleep, the ring in that being inserted in the same way—through a small slot in the creature's shoulders.

"His face?"

"Well, he has dark hair, I think, but his hat hid that. His eyebrows were black. He was short, no more than five foot seven. His skin was pale and he was clean-shaven. His hands were quite small but with long fingers. He wore a ring on his right little finger, a signet with twined initials, but I never made out what they were." He hesitated. "Really, Dr. Watson, I must admit that if I passed my friend in the street after two years, and in the daylight, I might not recognize him. It is strange to know someone so well, to tell them all your fears and triumphs, to hear such in return, and still to think you might not know them. I am ashamed."

"Of what else did he talk? Did he speak of his own family, of himself, or where he lived, or did he mention his circumstances?"

He had. I stored up all that was said, while something within me bade me believe none of it.

I shifted the talk to other things, but before I departed and left Jack to his work, I ascertained that their last meeting had been almost two years ago and concluded that by then Marsden had either provided what information was desired, or outlived his usefulness—or both. Not that I thought too harshly of Mr. Goodwin, for he left his presumed victim happy and with more confidence in himself. I hoped Holmes and I would do nothing to destroy that.

I lunched in a small cafe and chose not to return to Riggston Coal. Instead, I sought out the bar where Marsden met his friend and drew the bartender aside. I went there with Holmes on a number of occasions, and the man knew me. He was a big man, brawny and of sound commonsense, with a noticing eye.

"Do you know Jack Marsden?" He nodded. "From around five years back and up to two years ago he often came here and talked with a man." I described Mr. Goodwin. "Do you remember that man?"

He did, but for all that he noticed most customers he recalled little of Goodwin. "Nothing to him, see. Average, nothing that stood out. A bit short maybe, but not fat, not over-thin, well-dressed but not so as you'd notice, good material, well-cut. Maybe, as you suggest, it were bespoke, but not the sort of fashion you remember, just up to date but a bit conservative. Didn't wear much jewelry that I recall, nothing flashy anyways. No, I never saw an ivory cat, I do remember that he gave young Marsden a pocket-piece, but that were a rabbit, I think."

And so it went. He was able to point out other customers who talked to Goodwin—they too could tell me nothing of any use. I obtained a variety of comments, all of which added up to: "We knew him to greet when he came in. Nice fellow. Knowledgeable, good company." And from the middle-aged man I questioned last: "He came in two or three times a week before he met young Marsden. No, only a month or so before that happened. After that he talked mostly with the lad. I watched them and there wasn't anything in his manner that made me think the lad was at risk, so I said nothing. I could tell Marsden wasn't that sort, and he'd have shied off fast enough if that man made suggestions. I never saw any sign of it, no."

Having mined all I could, I departed. I had a mysterious man who frequented a place where he could meet his quarry. Marsden talked, Goodwin listened, but what was he hoping to hear? What was of such value that he unobtrusively paid his companion and left him with a valuable gift?

I reached home and found my friend had not yet returned. He came in an hour later, weary as I could see from his slight stoop, and chilled from an evening that had turned colder. I stirred up the fire, placed a drink in his hand, called down the stairs for dinner to be served, and let him alone until he had eaten.

Then I recounted my own adventures, finishing with the question I had asked myself on the way home.

"Why, Holmes? Why did he befriend Marsden, and what was he told that was worthwhile?"

I provided Holmes with another drink, and my friend began to explain.

11

Holmes had obviously had a long day, and even with his iron strength, he was a trifle weary. He drank and set the glass down carefully, leaning back in his seat and lighting his favorite pipe.

"Mr. Goodwin is careful, Watson. Look at everything he has done thus far. If not for Arthur Riggston's suspicions, no one would ever guess murder. And on what were Arthur's suspicious based? There was no proof, no suggestion that the deaths had been anything but accident, misadventure, or suicide. His argument was one of statistics: in one family and amongst those allied to them, there were too many accidents."

He looked at me. "That was all he could tell me when he first consulted me. He tried to convince himself he was wrong, that there was no proof of his misgivings, no motives for any of the deaths, and yet, Watson, and yet for all that, he did not believe it. He could not say why, and he could show no evidence. He could only repeat that he had doubts. His much-loved godfather was dangerously ill and he feared his godfather would be—or already was—the next victim. I never discount such a belief, for a person often sees miniscule clues they do not consciously recognize, but unconsciously add these clues together.

"I set out to discover if there was foundation to his fears, and at length I came to the conclusion that, although wrong about his godfather, he was right about other deaths he listed."

I nodded. "But is there yet any proof, any evidence at all?"

"No, and therein lies my difficulty. I believe that James Riggston and his wife were murdered. That his sons, James and Joseph, died by the same hand, that all three of the Pelly family were slain, and along with them a lawyer and a minister who assisted or condoned crimes. Nine deaths, and I have no facts to take to the police, nothing that is even a little convincing. The murderer is clever, ruthless, and utterly determined. He is also careful to harm only those who, in his mind, deserve their fate. All those killed have injured others—either by their actions or by their failure to act."

He brooded briefly before continuing. "And that is why Jack Marsden was approached and cultivated. Somehow, Mr. Goodwin knew that Riggston employed him. I am certain that Marsden was sought out for one reason alone: for Mr. Goodwin to determine if Bradon Riggston followed in the footsteps of his father and grandfather. Was he as crooked and untrustworthy as the men of earlier generations? Once Mr. Goodwin found that he was not, he stepped back into the shadows from whence he came. I spent all day making other inquiries on this possibility. I found that a Mr. Sands was asking about Allan Pelly's family."

I threw back my head and laughed. "Mr. Sands. The Goodwin Sands have killed many a ship and crew. The man has a sense of humor, black though it may be."

"In a choice of names, maybe," Holmes agreed. "His killings are not so amusing. I admit he is careful as to his victims, however. As with Goodwin, Mr. Sands spent weeks cultivating a man who works for the Pelly Sack Company. He was as happy to talk to me about Allen Pelly as he was to talk about him to Sands. He says—and said to Mr. Sands—that the owner is a good man and honest. When he took over the firm eleven years ago, he discovered that some of the workers had been harshly treated, and he quietly made reparation."

"What did he do?"

"Some he re-employed, and for others who were now too old, he investigated the circumstances of their dismissal closely. Where there had been a manifest injustice, he saw to it that they received a small pension. Mark this, Watson. He was not legally required to do so. He acted out of motives of fairness and a wish that those wrongly treated by a man who bore the Pelly name should be requited. The man to whom I spoke was adamant. Allan Pelly is a good employer, an honest and honorable man. Mr. Sands received the same information, and it is clear he believed it. Allan Pelly and his family have suffered no accidents. We also know that someone asked about the minister within that parish, establishing the harm he had done."

"So," I said thoughtfully. "Mr. Goodwin Sands makes certain it is the guilty he punishes and not the innocent."

"Yes, but this gives me pause." He leaned forward to catch my gaze. "Earlier I took steps, just as soon as I heard of Mr. Goodwin. Inquiries were made about the places where David Pelly lived with his wife and son. Questions were asked where the Riggstons lived. And I went again to the home of Eli Gettes and asked around and about the neighborhood myself. No one had ever asked specifically about those who died. Do you see, Watson? He knew about them already, about the crimes they had committed. And I think that he knew of the minister, too; he merely wished to ascertain if the crime of which he knew was the only one, or if there had been others. He found that there had been—and acted."

"In other words, he knew of some crimes and had no need to verify those," I said slowly, thinking it out. "In another case he knew of one error, but wished to see if it was a pattern, and he found that it was. But he knew nothing of the final Pelly and Riggston generations and wanted to see if they were as bad as their predecessors. He discovered they were not and stepped back. But what does it mean?"

"That he was one of those harmed by those who died ..." Holmes frowned. "... and that can only be if he was one of the Riggston circle at some time." He relit his pipe, which had gone out as he talked. "Gettes worked for the Riggstons, and the Pellys were never his clients. David Pelly and his family never lived in Reverend Mathews's parish. But everyone who died was associated with the Riggstons in some way. We have someone who considers themselves grievously injured by both families and by two men who served the Riggstons. The minister's was a sin of omission, and the lawyer's one of commission, I believe. The second was certainly at the behest of the Riggstons, but what of the omission? Did the Riggstons connive at that?"

I frowned. "It could be, Holmes. You have a moderately wealthy family in a parish where the majority of the parishioners are lower middle class or working class, and many are not well off. The minister is a man disinclined to acknowledge the evils that men do. If it were forcibly drawn to his attention that one of the Riggstons was committing crimes, would he not ignore it? I think he would. He had a pattern of blaming the person injured, and that was unlikely to change when the person complained about was his richest and most powerful parishioner."

Holmes eyed me approvingly. "Well done, Watson. That is how I see it, and I am glad to find that your opinion runs with mine."

"Do you know anything else of the killer?" I asked.

"Beyond that he is average in appearance, almost certainly now above fifty, moderately wealthy, and is unmarried, nothing," Holmes said with a glimmer of amusement.

I stared. "How …?"

"Come, come, my friend. We heard from several witnesses that he is difficult to describe because there is nothing whatsoever unusual about him. His crimes began thirty-three years ago. If he was twenty then, he would now be fifty-three. Even had he begun his murderous career at sixteen, he would now be forty-nine. He could be older still, possibly fifty-seven or eight. His wealth is evident from his good quality clothing and modest jewelry, which is yet valuable. He comes and goes as he will, for which reason I also believe him not to be married, as a wife would ask questions."

His voice sharpened. "And there is one other thing. He is a man who does not put his hand to the plough only to turn back. His first victims died more than thirty years ago. His next, ten years after that. Eli Gettes died a few months later. Five years elapsed before James the younger died, and another year until the minister was gone. Four more years go by before Florence Pelly and her son drown, and four years after that her husband appears to take poison. Deaths come again and again, but so far apart that none suspect. Yet in all that time he holds to his purpose. Those who hurt him so terribly shall pay for it. So horrific are his memories that he even checks to see if he should act against the heirs, although he does not know them and they have done him no harm. A man who holds such a grudge for so long is not one to be taken lightly, Watson."

A comment with which I was in full agreement, and I said so. "But what can we do? You are positive the nine deaths were murder, yet there is no proof. As yet you can point to no man. I will aid you in any way I can, you know that. Only tell me what is it that I should do?"

"Talk to Jack Marsden's family. Seek out each of them. Discuss general things such as livestock and crops, but—where you can and without making it noticeable—talk about their neighbors."

I sat up. "Their neighbors? You suspect a neighbor? Why, Holmes?"

"The killer may have made a mistake. How would anyone learn that Jack Marsden was hired on with Riggston, if they had not heard directly?"

I settled back. "Why should Mr. Goodwin not have decided to investigate Bradon and gone to watch the business, selecting a young man of gullible appearance who was leaving at the end of the day's employment, and following him to the bar where he often spent an evening?"

"Because he already knew too much of the boy. Do you not remember what Marsden said? That Mr. Goodwin talked of things that interested him. The man never made a false step. No, I believe that before ever he approached the lad he knew of him and his family and interests. I tell you it fits, Watson. Mr. Goodwin is a man who prepares, and he never moves until he knows what path he will tread. Go and speak with the family. If family members live alone, seek them out and allow them to gossip. You can do this?"

I nodded. "I can and will, Holmes," I said resolutely. "I will put up at a local inn and not leave until I can recount the details of every neighbor. Trust me."

"I do, Watson."

I retired that night with a feeling of warmth. I would uncover the truth for Holmes. I would find who had told Mr. Goodwin of Jack Marsden, and I would return with that name to my friend who trusted me—even if it took me a full month.

* * * *

The next morning I took a cab to Riggston Coal and told Jack I would call upon his parents. He scrawled a letter to his mother and I was pleased, thinking that would assure me a welcome.

I took my doctor's bag—people trust a doctor and are more inclined to speak freely—and a valise containing clothing, a couple books I intended to read all year, along with paper, ink, envelopes, and other minor items. My trusty revolver resided in my pocket. The man whose trail I followed had murdered nine people thus far. I had no desire to be the tenth.

I put up at the Bells and Motley in Shen Green and called upon Jack Marsden's parents. Holmes said that I could tell a portion of the truth and that I did.

I handed them Jack's letter and waited patiently until they read it. I said Jack appeared well and happy, and then I assumed a grave manner.

"I must ask you to say nothing of what I am about to tell you, not to anyone."

Mrs. Marsden nodded, eyes bright with excited interest, while her schoolmaster husband sat silent.

"A Mr. Arthur Riggston said that in his opinion, his uncle Joseph Riggston was murdered, despite his death being declared accidental. To that end he has hired my colleague Mr. Sherlock Holmes to investigate the matter, and if he finds any proof of this, the case will be forwarded to the police."

Mrs. Marsden spoke falteringly. "Mr. Joseph, do you mean …?"

"I mean," I clarified for her, "the brother of James Riggston." I saw her relax, and her husband's glance at her was one of affection and understanding.

Mrs. Marsden looked at me. "My husband knows of my connection to the Riggston family." She straightened slightly. "Ask me whatever you wish. But," she looked doubtful. "Why should Mr. Arthur think Mr. Joseph was murdered?"

I hinted at debts, a wild crowd, and that cheating at cards could have been involved.

The schoolmaster snorted and spoke. "I'd believe all of that. The current man seems to be decent enough, but the previous generations were rogues and scoundrels, wrong 'uns, every man of them."

"How do you know that?" I was intrigued that he should speak so decidedly.

In the end it was merely that he knew of his wife's seduction. "Not that I'd call it seduction when the girl is trapped in a room and given no choice." And what she had told him of the family. "Pack of rascals, thieves, tricksters, and liars. If this Joseph cheated his friends out of their money I wouldn't be surprised."

I received a number of stories about the Riggstons, obviously gleaned from his wife's reminiscences. I can say that they bore out some of what Holmes and I had already heard elsewhere, but with the more intimate slant from a girl who had been close to one of the participants and had heard some of the events at firsthand.

"Did you ever hear of a girl called May?" it occurred to me to ask.

Mrs. Marsden flushed a bright, painful red, cast her gaze down, and my attention immediately focused on her. Her husband looked steadily at her and took her hand.

"My dear, if you know something of this girl, tell the doctor. It can be nothing he has not heard before."

She faltered, but began her tale as he continued to encourage her. It was a pitiful story, although it was true it was one I had heard at other times and in other places. Joseph told her about it, some months into his use of her, by way of a warning. And also, I thought, because it excited him to recall the events. I hid my disgust lest she think it was directed at her, and listened as Mrs. Marsden explained.

"His father started it. The girl was no relative so he said that it was all right. She was eleven when it began. Joseph and his brother used the girl as a convenient scapegoat. They blamed her for all their mischief and watched their mother beat her. Their mother always believed them."

She flushed more deeply still. "Joseph said that James began it some time later, he being a year older than Joseph. He took the girl into their room, where he used her, saying what was good enough for his father was good enough for his sons. He demanded Joseph do so as well, and when he could not at first, laughed at him. Joseph managed some weeks later, and then he said that Joseph had proven himself a true Riggston. They took where and what they willed, and none should refuse them."

I reflected that they had indeed, and they had died for it.

"Joseph told me that May lived with them nearly five years, and was prey during that time of all three men. Being Riggstons, as Joseph bragged, they took what they wanted and would not permit her to deny them. He told me I should do well to learn from her. He was yet angry that at fifteen she vanished, and they heard nothing more of her until she returned to demand an inheritance that Joseph's father had taken and they had no choice but to give up." She shivered. "He laughed at that for some reason, saying she was still the loser, though she did not know it."

Her story thereafter ran in familiar paths; however, I permitted it to play out in case there should be anything I had not yet heard. And all the time she spoke, her husband's face was hardening into lines of rage and abhorrence. When she fell silent, he spoke to me through clenched teeth.

"What do you know of this?"

"Little enough," I said honestly. "Holmes suspected that the father might well have done as your lady says, and we know he attempted to cheat the girl of an inheritance, although she regained a good part of it. I did not know the sons followed him in his lusts, and later they did take a second inheritance the girl should have received. Mr. Bradon Riggston now has that in trust should she ever be found to have made a will."

The schoolmaster was on that in a pounce. "Then you know she is dead, else you would be seeking her and not a will?"

"Yes, she fled the Riggston house and only returned to obtain her inheritance, as your wife says, and vanished again lest they follow her. She retained a friend who was a maid in the Riggston house, a woman who later married, and she told us of May's death. I have seen her grave, and am in no doubt. But it could be that she made a will, and if so, then the money she later inherited should go to her heirs, did she have any." I looked a question at them.

Mrs. Marsden shook her head. "Joseph never said anything of that. If he had I would tell you of it. I am sorry, Dr. Watson."

"And no one ever came asking of Bradon Riggston or of any of his family?"

Mrs. Marsden appeared puzzled. "No one that I can recall. Why do you ask?"

I hinted darkly of blackmail, of threats to the Riggstons, and mentioned that some unknown man had questioned others about the family. The lady assured me that no one of that description had come, and even the schoolmaster confirmed that. I turned the conversation into talk of her village and those who lived here then. She was happy to talk of her good friends and family, most of who lived no great distance from the village.

"All but Aunt Alice. She wed a farmer, and while he is dead now she still lives in the old farmhouse. Their son built another near her, where he lives with his family. 'Tis a good distance from the village, but she likes it there with her family and has no intentions to move."

I got Aunt Alice's direction and determined to see her as soon as I could. I would have to take a dogcart since there was no automobile for hire in such a rural retreat. I added to my list the names and directions of others of her kin who lived nearby. And with that completed, I then, as delicately as possible, asked the lady how much of her history was known to her family.

"What name did you take on your return?"

She appeared surprised. "My own. I have always refused to speak of his family."

I hid my annoyance. It was as Holmes had heard, but that would make it difficult to ask about the Riggstons. Then I bethought me of another possibility. "But your family knew you worked for the Riggstons?"

"Yes. I was there for more than three years, and my family told friends I had a good job as a maid in London. They spoke of the Riggstons and their business, so people knew." She looked at me. "None ever thought that a Riggston might have been my husband. I was always careful to say that it was not so, were I asked. I let them believe I met my husband in the Riggston house though, and all accept that."

I smiled at her. "Thank you, Mrs. Marsden. So you will not mind if I explain to some of your relatives that someone who wishes your former employers ill may be asking about them?"

"I see no reason why you should not ask," she said slowly. "So long as you are careful what you say."

I saw her fear and alleviated it at once.

"I will be cautious, I swear. But Mr. Arthur Riggston is adamant that we investigate, and worries that his godfather, the man whose namesake he was and who died only a year ago, may also not have died a natural death. In turn I ask that you do not speak of that to anyone save your own family."

We parted with mutual promises of silence and I returned to the inn, where I discovered that I could have a pony and trap the next day. I lunched on bread, cheese, and cider at the inn, and during the afternoon I strolled about the village. It was a typical village of its kind, and in the course of my wanderings I called upon Mrs. Marsden's sister and a niece and asked them about strange men calling to talk of her employers. Neither had ever received such visitors but delayed me, talking about others of their family, and again I was told of Aunt Alice and her remote situation.

I was also, to my somewhat sour amusement, told sufficient to make it clear to me that no matter what Mrs. Marsden and her husband believed, the family, at least, had come to certain conclusions as to Jack's father. Others in the village might be confused as to the timeline of the girl's seduction and her son's birth, but I was given to understand that there were few in the family who did not guess that one of her employers was responsible.

"Put up at the inn, he did. Innkeeper he said he signed the register as Mr. Joseph Riggston of Lunnon," said the niece.

"Aye," the sister chimed in. "Talked to banker after that. Next thing us hears is that her husband's family be giving her an allowance. Never stopped it neither, that's how they've a good house."

I kept my mouth shut. I knew about the allowance. Joseph Riggston had settled a good sum on the girl he'd assaulted once he discovered that she bore him a son, and she'd been sensible enough both to be sure that it was secured to her permanently, and to live on the interest. On her death, the capital would be inherited by her son, as was only right in my opinion.

The sister continued spiteful. "Spoiled she was. Dad said as how she were youngest and now he had a bit more money she should get an education. Lot of good it did her. Still, he won't hear a word against her. His little poppet, and don't you try to tell him different. Of course, now she's married to schoolmaster dad thinks it's all his doing, step up for us, one of his girls wed to an educated man."

I made my excuses and left the house. The sister had some cause for complaint, but it was a long time ago and surely she should have forgiven and forgotten. But then, that was families: stand together against outsiders, but fight like rats within the family, often doing more damage than any foreigner was like to do.

I ate a fair dinner once back at the inn, went to bed early, and rose with the sun to enjoy a breakfast of poached eggs and a fine mutton chop, all washed down with a pot of tea. Once I was done and came down again from washing, I found that the pony and trap were waiting at the side door. I retained several slices of the toast from breakfast, one of which I fed the beast, which reacted favorably. With good relations established, I climbed the step, seated myself comfortably, and set off.

The road wound slowly uphill, but nowhere was the gradient so steep as to inconvenience the pony, which trotted briskly along while I enjoyed the sunshine. It was a mild day, warm but not too warm, with a light wandering breeze, and the sight of green fields and grazing livestock on either side of the road made for a pleasant journey. It took more than an hour before the pony turned into a side road to the left. There the road was steeper and he fell back into a walk, waiting, ears twitching back to see if I would object. I had no wish to travel at greater speed, so spoke kindly to him and saw the ears prick forward again.

Another half hour passed before I saw the house that had been described to me. He pulled up by the back door and I dismounted, tying the halter rope to a convenient ring in the wall. He could reach the water trough, and there was shade. I removed his bridle, and took from the trap a light wooden tub into which I poured a small bait of oats and chaff. He set to and I mounted the steps, rang the doorbell, and stood waiting.

The woman who answered the door was clearly one of Mrs. Marsden's family and looked an older version of that lady. I introduced myself, spoke of Jack and his mother, of his employers, and of some questions I would like to ask if she would be so generous as to permit that. In turn I found that she was Alice Miller, that any friend of her family was welcome in her house, and that I should come in at once and not stand there on the doorstep.

After that, the ensuing conversation was pleasant and I was in no haste to ask my questions. She talked of her late husband, the farm, her son and his family, and the weekly market at Shen Green. I commented that hers was an isolated life and she laughed.

"Don't believe all you see, Doctor. The road you came by isn't the main road. That goes other side of the hill, and there's more places over there. By road you'd walk or drive miles, surely, but as the crow flies, I've neighbors only the other side of the hill."

I asked about them. "Ah, there's the widow Batesley." Her eyes twinkled. "Not the sort of widow as my niece, mind you. Her husband were a farmer like me, and when he died she sold all but a couple of acres and lives in the old farmhouse, same as I do." She became sidetracked when her grandson appeared at the door and must be given something to eat and drink. It was some little time before she resumed.

"Ah, yes, then there's the schoolmaster's ma and da. They've a cottage near where the roads met other side of the hill."

Her grandson, a lively lad of seventeen or so, having finished his simple meal, chose to enter the conversation.

"Grandma, you're forgetting Branstow."

"Oh, aye, so I am. Yes." And to me: "There's quite an estate over the hill. It's back a ways from the road and they don't have much to do with any in the village, so we do tend to forget about it."

The boy grinned. "You may. I've talked to them a time or two. One of her visitors, he rides and I've seen him along the boundary over there." He pointed. "Talked to me a few times, he has. I mind telling him all about Jack and the good job he got in Lunnon. Real interested he was, and asked me about Jack and them as had taken him on."

I asked for a description of this attentive person, and I had much to do to prevent shouting at the reply. If this were not Mr. Goodwin, I would eat my hat.

12

I returned to London bursting with my news, all of it. Holmes was home when I arrived and I began almost before I was inside the door.

"I found Mr. Goodwin! He regularly visits an estate called Branstow, near where the Marsdens live. It belongs to a Mrs. Rogers, with whom he seems to be a long-time friend. It's usefully secluded and I found out about it accidentally, as they don't have much to do with local people and they're hardly ever seen, but they know Mrs. Rogers by sight. No one in the village knows about Goodwin, but I was talking to Mrs. Marsden's Aunt Alice up in the hills above the village and her grandson came in and mentioned he'd talked to Goodwin." I finally paused for breath.

Holmes eyed me. "Sit down, Watson. If you take an extra minute or two to compose yourself, it will cause no problem."

I sat near the fire, for the day was drawing in and it was becoming chilly again. "I could find no one who'd been asked about the Riggstons. Then, while I was talking to Mrs. Miller—that's Aunt Alice—her grandson walked in and overheard me. He piped up at once to say that he'd talked to a gentleman on the Branstow Estate some time back. He remembered it because he'd just heard about his cousin Jack getting a job in a London company. The man fell into conversation with him and he told him all about Jack's good fortune. He said his new friend seemed interested and they talked about London for some time. At my request he described this person. I tell you, Holmes, it was Goodwin to the life. And what is more, he still visits there." I gave the boy's description precisely as he had given it to me, and Holmes nodded at each point.

"The mysterious Mr. Goodwin Sands. Yes. It appears that it could be he. What did you find out about the estate and Mrs. Rogers? Of what age is she? How did she come to own the place?"

Baffled as to what these facts might have to do with Goodwin, I yet could answer as the Millers, grandmother and grandson, talked about it for some time.

"Not a great deal is known of her. The Rogers family has owned the estate for many generations. The land is not greatly profitable, and from what they said I suspect it pays its way and no more. However, it is generally known that Mr. Rogers had considerable investments and was wealthy. He preferred, however, to live no more than comfortably and as a recluse at Branstow. The lady first appeared some forty years ago, as a girl. Rogers said she was his wife and no one ever had reason to doubt it, though at the time he was a man in his fifties."

I smiled. "Rogers's heir was generally disliked. He died—of disappointment, it was rumored—nearly twenty years after Mrs. Rogers arrived and a year before the husband." I looked into the flames. "She sounds like a true eccentric. Her servants do not go to the village inn, and from what the Millers said, it sounds as if the lady runs some sort of school. They think she accepts orphans, houses them, educates them, and finds them a good job once they are old enough. She is often away in London, but she has a competent deputy, and while she spends almost no time in the village—if they see her twice a year it is more than usual—still she buys all the supplies the village can provide, so that they are grateful."

"What does the village know of Goodwin?"

"Nothing," I said succinctly. "He never inquired about the Riggstons or the Marsdens there. Only the Miller lad met him a couple of times and saw him several other times. Always around dusk, he said. He thinks that the man likes to ride out in the cool of the evenings when he is visiting."

"Mrs. Rogers, did any describe her?"

"Mrs. Miller and her grandson both. She is in her late fifties now. She is not 'heavy-breasted' perhaps, but quite reasonably endowed, is some five foot and four or five inches, slim-hipped, and energetic. She is an excellent rider, using side-saddle, and is rarely seen without a veil. Always a black one, in mourning still for her husband, it is believed."

"They were so devoted?"

I nodded. "They say she adored him and he her. He died almost twenty years ago, and while the Millers suspect that Goodwin is her lover, they do not know for certain. It may be that he is rather a relative. At least he visited when the old man was alive, and had he been the lady's lover one might have expected some protest." I snorted. "This is not the Regency; there are fewer complaisant husbands about these days."

"But dueling is less common," Holmes pointed out, with the glimmer of a smile. I was bewildered and looked the question. "I merely meant that customs change, Watson. In those days, a cuckolded husband had an obvious remedy. Nowadays he must go to court and have his business bruited abroad to all and sundry. Little may be kept private."

"Yes, that is true, although Mr. Goodwin seems to manage it."

Holmes stared at me thoughtfully. "Yes, he does, doesn't he?" He fell into a vacant-eyed contemplation, and I went to find Mrs. Hudson and seek our dinner.

* * * *

Holmes remained silent the remainder of the evening. The next day he was gone before I rose and returned late that evening looking, if possible, still more abstracted. He wore a good suit, and I surmised he had been in the merchant areas of the city. A dozen times on the day after that the door-knocker sounded, and a number of his irregulars arrived bearing information, departing with further instructions. I could not make out what he was about. He must be hunting Mr. Goodwin, my information sparking the frenzy, but what I said I could not guess. I resigned myself to wait. Holmes never spoke before he was ready.

That readiness came five days after I returned from seeing the Marsdens and producing my information on Goodwin. Holmes bounded out to join me at the breakfast table, ate heartily, and poured himself a second cup of tea.

"You have been most patient, Watson. And I am now in a position to reveal events that took place a very long time ago. May Percy departed the Riggston house and obtained herself part-time employment almost immediately. Yes," in response to my look. "I know it sounds difficult, but what employment would be open to a girl not yet sixteen? One," he added significantly, "who appeared both more educated than she was, and two or three years younger."

I stared. "You mean she became a ...."

"Yes. I found the small, select house that employed her. The place is long gone, but one or two recalled it. One remembered May, and for a small donation was willing to talk. When May started at the house she retained her own name, but the woman who ran the house persuaded her to change it. May then called herself Lucy Locket." I laughed involuntarily and a glimmer of amusement showed in my friend's eyes. "Quite so. A year after that, she changed her name again, to Lucy Strange, and yes, that was the name on her tombstone."

"But you say she worked part-time, Holmes. Why did the place allow it?"

"She brought in clients and cash and, as I am given to understand, she bargained with the madam. May—or Lucy—was not a common street girl. She rented two rooms from the house. She gave them a percentage of her earnings, and made it abundantly clear that should they cause her trouble or attempt to control her, she had friends. In effect she was a tenant, not an employee, and there is no doubt that she made them money—and herself more."

"And part time?" I asked. That had to be the strangest thing I had ever heard.

"She worked only five days a week, for on Mondays and Thursdays she was not available. Where she went on those days, or what she did, no one could tell me. However, she had a bank account. I traced the branch she used, and when she came to deposit money she dressed as a lady, appeared some years older, and they thought she had a small business, possibly a millinery. I was granted a glimpse of the old records. They surprised even me, Watson. She deposited over a hundred pounds a year without drawing against it, and that continued from the time she was sixteen until she was twenty-five. By which time she had almost a thousand pounds on deposit."

I gasped. That was an enormous sum. Now and again over the years I had women in her profession as patients, and I knew those who catered to perverse tastes could earn better than most would guess—although they did not always live long lives.

Holmes nodded. "May Percy had courage, sense, and an iron determination. She left the house at eighteen and disappeared, although she continued to bank a similar sum each year. I cannot find her direction until seven years later, when she turned twenty-five and retained a lawyer who went on her behalf to the Riggstons and demanded May's inheritance. The girl was cheated of the profits James Riggston made from her money, but she regained the capital. That went into her bank account, the entire sum was then withdrawn in cash, and the account closed. Her trail vanishes again briefly, and she then reappears, dead in a boarding house in a different part of the city from where she had been employed."

"As Lucy Strange," I commented.

"Yes."

"And the money?"

"No one knew that she had any, so far as I can discover. She paid a week's rent when she arrived there, and was never seen to come or go until her death was discovered. Lizzie and her husband claimed the body and paid for her burial. I questioned Lizzie again and all she could tell me was that the envelope she received contained a shilling or two more than the funeral and stone had cost, but she thought that could have been so that payment could be made in notes."

"Then the money disappeared," I concluded, wondering who had found it. "Did you discover if the girl made a will?"

Holmes frowned. "I did not. As for the lawyer who assisted her to recover her inheritance from the Riggstons, I know his name. He died some time ago, his office was cleared, and closed files and other confidential papers were burned by a colleague. If it was he who held her will, it was not found. The man had no close kin and no family of his own, his clerk is also dead. I am told neither were sociable, and although they were good at their work, they never gossiped."

"So that is it," I stated. "We know about May, what about Mr. Goodwin?"

"Ah, we'll talk of that tomorrow, Watson. In the morning we shall go to the village and from there we shall hire that pony and trap again and call upon the gentleman."

I retired that night with a pleasurable sense of anticipation. It was likely that soon we could be face to face with the killer of nine people, and I resolved to clean and reload my revolver with great care before we set out.

* * * *

The morning was extremely busy. I rose a little before Holmes, did as I had planned the night before, and had barely replaced the weapon in my valise before Holmes and breakfast arrived simultaneously. We ate in silence as I flicked through the newspaper, Holmes deep in a recent treatise on the varieties and composition of American chewing gum.

We boarded the train around mid-morning, conversed idly at intervals over the ride, and stepped down at the Shen Green Halt. It was a short walk to the Bells and Motley where we spent the night, and immediately after breakfast we stepped into the pony trap and began to drive to Branstow. We had excellent directions to the gatehouse, but also the warning that few were ever granted admittance, and that coming without invitation would almost certainly guarantee our being turned away.

This would have been so, save for Holmes's request on our arrival. We arrived at the scrolled iron gates and a crusty old retainer stared at us through them—I will not attempt to reproduce his all but impenetrable accent. Briefly it was demanded of us who we were, what—or whom— we wanted, and that we should go away because he didn't open the gates to anyone unless they was invited and he hadn't been told of anyone, no, he hadn't, and he'd take his oath on that.

Holmes stepped down from the pony trap, approached the old man, and handed him a card. "Take this to Mrs. Rogers." He returned to the trap and seated himself, with the air of a man prepared to wait.

The old man studied him, turned the card over in his fingers, and shouted. A boy came from the gatehouse and, taking the card, set off at a run down the drive, rounding a bend and disappearing behind the trees that lined it.

He was back in ten minutes or so, muttered something to the old man who scowled, but responded by marching to the wide iron gates and swinging one open so we could drive through. The drive was long, with two sharp bends. Holmes surveyed the second bend and commented, "This place may be older than I thought, Watson. Such a road could have been constructed to deny an enemy swiftness of access." But I had looked ahead to see what he had not.

"Holmes, at the door."

A man stood there. He paused for a moment before turning on his heel and re-entering the house. I would have hurried the pony but my friend touched my arm.

"He will wait for us. He will wish to hear what we can say of his friend's life, and he needs to know if we can injure her in any fashion."

He did wait. When we entered the main hall he was standing by a door to the left. I glimpsed a motionless figure dressed in black on the landing above us and suspected it was Mrs. Rogers. Goodwin indicated we should follow, and I lost sight of the other figure. Heavy curtains covered the parlor windows. In the dim light, Goodwin lounged towards the mantelpiece, waved us to seats, and spoke.

"You asked for Mr. Goodwin. I am he."

Holmes nodded. "You befriended Jack Marsden. He told you of his employer, and Bradon Riggston did not die. You asked of a Mr. Allan Pelly, and he too did not die."

The lounging figure was motionless. Finally he spoke. "Of what do you accuse me, Mr. Holmes? That those of whom I inquire do not die? There is no crime in that, I think."

"Those of whom you did *not* inquire *did* die," Holmes said quietly. Raised brows were the response and my friend continued. "James and his wife Mary, his two sons, Mr. David Pelly, his wife and son, a certain lawyer and a minister—of whom you inquired."

"Ah, I seem to recall some of those deaths. They were accidents."

"Were they? They were believed to be, certainly. Yet the police could take an interest in so many deaths."

"I do not think so. They are over-worked, they could find no benefit in reopening old cases that are without witnesses and without evidence of any kind. No, I do not believe the police would accept such a proposition."

"That might be so. Would you care to hear a story, Mr. Goodwin?"

"That would be amusing."

Holmes nodded. "It is intriguing. It begins thus. A small child loved her father, and came to love her step-mother. But her father died, as did her step-mother five years later. Discarded by her step-father, she was handed over, like unwanted baggage, to her step-mother's brother. He stole her money, abused her in all the ways that one in power can contrive, and allowed his sons to do so as well. She escaped shortly before she was sixteen and took up the trade to which they had accustomed her. Yet she was a girl of strength, courage, and iron determination. She took employment on terms that allowed her some freedom and which were financially advantageous, so that she prospered."

Goodwin straightened slightly as if surprised, then leaned back against the mantelpiece again.

Holmes continued. "When she was too old to make large sums any longer in a specialized area of employment, she changed her name and moved to a hotel, where she became private secretary to a middle-aged man. He esteemed her for her common sense and her ability to sniff out both opportunities and frauds. Somewhere during that time she did him a great favor, and he loved her for it."

"She saved his life," said the figure in the gloom.

"Yes, it would be a favor of that magnitude. So he brought her back to his estate and married her. That is, so he claimed, and so those around him believed."

"He did. Under her true name, in a tiny obscure hamlet some distance from here. She has her marriage lines, and therefore she inherited."

"To the fury of Mr. Rogers's original heir," Holmes commented. "He must have feared there would be a child to displace him further." There was no reply and he carried on. "But after she was free of her oppressors, the girl remembered all her injustices. Once she secured employment with her benefactor, she journeyed to see those who first ill-treated her.

When she departed, those tyrants were dead. A year later she was able to recover her stolen inheritance, although a friend later told her she was cheated of the profits her money had made and which should have come to her. Still, she would have accepted that until another of those who had abused her brought himself to her attention."

"He boasted of things he had done to her," came a voice from the shadows.

"And she decided that both brothers were better gone, and so they were. It was not difficult. A quick thrust of her hand between his shoulder-blades, and with the other, a pleasant drink together while he settled up what he owed." I saw a head nod agreement. "A lawyer connived at the theft of her property, leaving her defenseless, when he should have ensured she had resources. And the minister who ignored her plight?"

"She told him what was happening. He said she lied, that her kind guardian was a good and godly man, that his wife was a member of the parish and cared for the poor. The sons were honest boys, and she was mistaken. She answered that it was impossible to misunderstand rape if one were the victim. And he said sternly that she should pray for her soul, which was surely extremely wicked."

And for the first time I looked more generously upon Mr. Goodwin. He knew May's history. He had heard how her pleas for help were ignored, and of the harm she had suffered. Such things do go on. I am a doctor and I know, and yet: nine deaths?

"And the Pellys?" Holmes asked, even as I recalled them.

"Florence Pelly swore upon her Bible that if anything happened to her dearest friend and May needed a home, she would find one with the Pellys. David Pelly agreed, until he found that he would not benefit as much as he hoped. Florence could have prevailed had she stood firm, but she too decided that having another's child in her home would be 'inconvenient.' It was discussed with May's stepfather and she heard all that was said. They casually discarded a child, leaving her prey to beasts, because she would be a little work and time. Florence ignored the sacred oath she had given, ignored, too, that her dearest friend had trusted her to keep her word."

"So Florence's son died?"

"He misused the daughter of their housekeeper. The girl kept silent because he swore he would have her mother turned off as a thief."

I looked at Holmes. That we had not uncovered, although I could well believe it.

"And Florence Pelly?"

"Her death was unintended."

"I see," Holmes said softly. "She was to live, to mourn her son every day of her life, and perhaps in time understand what she had done to May and regret her actions."

A head nodded.

"And David Pelly was more to blame. He rejected the child and refused her a home. He said the payment was not enough, though it would have recompensed him well beyond the cost of her food and clothes and education. A greedy man, happy to toss aside his wife's oath and a child, because the girl did not bring more money with her."

Again the nod.

"May had her revenge on those who brutalized her, who starved, beat, and raped her. Those who gave her into their hands, to them she provided justice, as she saw it. And she had no wish to kill the innocent. She used you to make certain that the minister was guilty of others' pain, as well as hers, and to be certain too that later generations of the Pellys and Riggstons were innocent. Still, I think she felt a balance should be made between those deaths and her life." He stared at the figure.

"May married Mr. Rogers and he died, but before then she set up a school for orphaned girls. Around fifteen or sixteen of them currently, so I hear. They are cared for, educated, and they are found good employment. They go on to marry and have their own families. And they never forget May, or what she did for them. If I were to take this to the police, well, as you say, all of the deaths were counted as accidents, or perhaps suicide or misadventure. And the school has been established for many years, and a number of those girls have husbands in high places. Should anyone attack May Rogers, they would fly to her defense. Where is the evidence, anyway?"

His voice developed a musing tone. "May Rogers is no longer that brutalized child. For three years she studied with a private tutor, and she learned well. Besides, it is possible that justice has indeed been done and the wicked punished. Will May live for many years more and her works prosper, Mr. Goodwin?"

"She may live a while, and her works do prosper," came the quiet reply. "Yet she can never forget those years when she dwelled in hatred, terror, and grief. She can trust no one completely and with all her heart— or *with* her heart—for she cannot love any truly, save her animals. She is fond of many, she will spare no effort to aid her friends or those in need, yet she is hollow, eaten out from within, and that she knows. With that knowledge she lives and, in the end, with it she shall die."

I almost wept at the words. They were acceptance of what had been done to a child, and of wounds that could never be healed. In that moment

I believed that what May Percy had done could indeed be accounted justice. Holmes stood, and I followed suit.

"Then it is possible that evil was punished," he said. "I see no need for my returning here—unless I hear of another death." He moved towards the door, the figure of Mr. Goodwin preceding us. In the hall I saw again the woman staring down. Goodwin glanced upwards, then spoke.

"The school's manager. She does good work. She was my first orphan."

Homes nodded. Her words sank in and I stared as May Percy moved into a shaft of light. I could see the truth, yet 'Mr. Goodwin' overlaid her still. The disguise she had donned when needed and kept with her, her alter ego who killed, who rendered justice, and could do and say and go where a woman could not.

I managed words. "Lizzie? She saw you dead?"

May Percy nodded. "She saw a friend from the house where I worked. We were strongly similar in looks. My friend was dying and I rented a room for her under my house name when her own place threw her out. I took another room and dressed as Mr. Goodwin. I nursed my friend, fed and bathed her, and when she died I dressed her in my clothes and sent Lizzie a message so my friend should be buried decently, as she had wished. And Lizzie was not wrong. I *am* dead, Doctor. I have been dead for a long time. I merely walk and talk because there are those who need me still."

I walked to the door, stepped into the trap and gathered up the reins. And wordlessly I spent the rest of the day in travel, returning with Holmes to our rooms. He had allowed a murderer to go free, yet was any sentence the law might give harsher than the hollowness May Rogers had described and accepted? I thought not, and so did Holmes, else he would not have withheld his hand. I was content to leave it to him.

* * * *

A week later a letter came for Holmes. In it was a—apparently—faded handwritten will that disposed of the monies held by the Riggston family for May Percy, the beneficiaries being Elizabeth Davis and her husband John. Holmes gave it to Bradon without comment, save to give his word that it was genuine. On his assurance it was enacted, and Lizzie wept for a loved friend who showed she too had cared. We never saw May again. Nor did any others of the Riggston or Pelly families die mysteriously. Arthur Riggston spoke privately to Holmes, and while I do not know what was said, I believe he paid and asked nothing further of my friend.

As for Holmes and me, there was an epidemic of influenza in a nearby area and I was busy for days on end. Holmes was gone a while during that period and returned with a new commission in Brighton, in which a medical friend of mine had been already involved. And thus we embarked on an investigation in which many elderly ladies, a brave girl, a dead canary, foolish decisions, and a number of firemen jostled for attention. It was a fascinating case, and I will relate it to you, my readers, when I have time to write.

THIS AWFUL FIRE

PROLOGUE BY JOHN WATSON, M.D.

I decided to write this account last year at the request of the son of one of those involved, it being almost a decade since the tragedy of which I write. However I had had that task in mind before, since upon the death of a certain person I discovered that she had left me her diary from the time of the fire, as well as a slim bundle of letters.

The lady in question had carefully cut from the letters any heading and the signatures, although in most cases I could guess from whom they had come. However her actions and the fact of the diary being anonymous meant no one could use them as proof to bring suit, which may have been her reason for so doing. Therefore, I too will not identify the writers. Instead I shall be omniscient, as if I had been present and seen all that occurred as it happened, based on those letters and the diary. This I have done so that readers might see the events in their minds, without prejudice or bias, and just as those involved reported it to the very elderly lady who subsequently trusted her documents to me.

1

The house was filling with smoke. It stung the eyes of the sturdy young woman moving through the light shifting haze and she wiped them with the water-soaked handkerchief she held to her mouth. The four suites on this ground floor were fewer that the number upstairs, but would be easier of access. She opened the door to the dining room, shut it behind her and walked quickly to the tiny hall that served as entrance to two of them. She opened the door to the first, walked through the outer room into the bedroom and shook the occupant.

"Get up; please get up, Mrs. Maylon, Mrs. Maylon, wake *up*!"

The elderly woman stirred, and then sat up. "What, what's the matter, dear? Am I late for breakfast?"

"No," Darna Rosewarne hesitated before giving a truthful reply. But she knew Mrs. Maylon to be sensible and not a woman to panic. "No, but you must dress as fast as you can and be ready to leave this house as soon as I return. There's a fire."

That was sufficient warning without giving the woman a heart attack. Mrs. Maylon met the brown eyes regarding her steadily and nodded.

"Go and get Amelie, my dear. I'll be ready. If you have problems with her, come and get me. She does listen to me sometimes."

Amelie Hartsford was French by birth and upbringing, a feather-headed woman with a temperament that demanded she exclaim and flutter over any event. Flora Maylon had never been sure if Amelie was as silly as she seemed—or if it was a facade behind which she watched a world designed for her amusement. She was a pleasant companion however, and heretofore it had never been important. Now, however, it could be life or death as to how sensible Amelie could be. She hoped all that fluttering was merely her friend's way of amusing herself.

Darna opened the door to the Frenchwoman's room quietly. She walked across to the wide bed and spoke in a low voice. "Please wake up, Mrs. Hartsford."

The woman addressed stirred sleepily, producing a sort of querying whine. Darna spoke again even as it occurred to her that perhaps getting clothing ready first would speed up the process. She turned, opened the wardrobe door and took out a warm woollen dress and a magnificent fur coat. Underwear from a drawer followed them, laid out on the bed, comfortable shoes were placed where their owner could step into them, and she turned back to the drowsing woman.

"Wake up," her voice was sterner. "You must wake up, get dressed and come with me. Now!"

A pair of brown eyes flew open to regard her with alarm. "What is it?" The gaze went to the small silver clock on the bedside table. "What? It is barely six of the clock. I do not rise before ten. Go away and let me sleep." The mop of tousled blond hair burrowed back into the pillow.

Darna closed a firm hand on the plump white shoulder. "Get up. Get up and dress, there's no time to waste."

Amelie Hartsford finally heard the note of alarm and sat up. "I do not rise at this hour, me. Go away and ..."

Time was passing and Darna knew the fire was spreading. "Get up, get dressed, and stop arguing. The house is on fire. I don't have time to spend persuading you, get dressed and come along to the next bedroom or I swear I'll leave you to burn."

She ignored the shriek of horror, the bulging eyes, and the fluttering hands. The woman had been here only a year and had not yet signed for the next; it was as well, for she was not sure that she wanted to retain this tenant. She exited and dived through the first suite's bedroom door to see if Mrs. Maylon was ready. She was. Flora sat quietly in her wheelchair, her Sunday-best clothing her spare body, her good woollen coat with the rabbit-fur collar pulled about her shoulders, and in her lap her handbag bulging with what Darna guessed would be all her smaller, more portable, valuables.

"I'm ready, dear. What about Amelie?"

"In a flap. But I'm not waiting. I'll get you to the door and come back for her." Mrs. Maylon could get herself out of the house once the long corridor to the front door was traversed. The old woman's lungs weren't in good condition and Darna would take her to cleaner air before the old lady exerted herself. Darna seized the wheelchair and whisked them out of the bedroom, through the tiny hallway and into the dining room. She opened the door to meet a gust of smoke and heat.

"Oh, my dear," Mrs. Maylon said quietly. "I didn't realize it was so bad."

It wasn't, Darna thought, not yet, but it would be genuinely bad very soon and worse still soon after. She thrust the damp handkerchief into her mouth and breathed through that, trying to keep her inhalations slow. She took a firm grip on the chair handles, lined it up with the corridor, and started forward at a trot. It seemed long minutes until she reached the front door and pushed the chair over the threshold. There she hesitated.

Flora Maylon's hand closed over her wrist. "I'm safe from here, girl. I can wheel myself over to the arbor and wait there out of the wind. Go and save anyone else. And here." She thrust a long scarf into Darna's hand. "This will do better than your handkerchief."

She released Darna and, clamping her glove-clad hands on the large wheels, she began to roll her chair in the direction of the arbor. Darna took a deep breath and coughed vigorously, caught her breath, and hurried back into the house again. She thrust the handkerchief into her pocket and reached for the small vase of roses in the hallway. She poured its contents over the scarf, tied that across her mouth and started back.

If she knew Amelie Hartsford she'd still be flapping about; she had time to help the other residents on the ground floor to safety. She passed the dining-room door and the staircase to the upper floor, continuing up the corridor to two single doors, side by side. She hammered on the first, and receiving no reply, she turned the handle—it was bolted.

Darna said a word she'd learned from her father's groom. Violet Stacy was an unpleasant, obstinate woman, liked by no one, including her attentive family, and she had been told over and over not to bolt her door. Unfortunately there'd been a bolt on the door when Violet Stacy became a resident three years earlier. All attempts to remove it with her permission had failed. Violet, as she often said, knew her own mind, and her privacy was important. No matter how often staff promised never to enter without first knocking and then waiting permission to come in, she insisted on retaining the bolt.

It didn't help that Violet was somewhat deaf. Everyone save Violet realized the danger of a bolted door. Violet was in good health for her age, apparently considered herself invincible, and was convinced that everyone else was merely trying to make her life difficult. After a recent meeting with her solicitor, Darna decided that she would simply wait until Violet was out for the day and remove the bolt, leaving her to face a *fait accompli* on her return. Unfortunately, an opportunity had not arisen in the three days since that meeting. Now it could be too late.

Darna hammered and yelled again. No answer was the reply. Next door was Mrs. Collins, and while in her eighties, she was as practical as Flora and more agile. Darna opened her door. The bed was empty, and in the small parlor, a scattering of items lay across the carpet and the door to the wall safe hung open. The young woman heaved a sigh of relief. Mrs. Collins must have heard her original shouts of "fire" and dressed, gathered her portable valuables, and departed via the nearby back door. It was as well, for flames appeared at the window, and she could feel the rising heat.

She took several breaths, shut the door, and headed back to Mrs. Hartsford's commodious suite where she found the lady now talking to herself as she fussed about. Darna sized up the situation. Amelie had managed to don her underclothing, though her dress, coat, and shoes still waited, and she had gathered a stack of items on the bed, none of obvious value, but all things she apparently wished to save. There was no time to rescue three portraits, one a very large oil painting, two pastels, a small trunk of clothing, two Chinese vases, and a second fur coat. All that was missing, Darna thought, was a partridge in a pear tree and that was probably in the large bag the idiot had just added to her gleanings.

Darna reached for the dress. "Put this on, and *hurry!*"

"My stays. I cannot emerge from my boudoir without stays. It is not *convenable*."

Darna grabbed her shoulder.

"Never mind your stays. Get into this dress and do it now."

"No, no ..."

Darna's grip tightened. "*Get into your dress!*"

Snivelling, Amelie obeyed and Darna wrapped the magnificent fur coat about her, kneeling to slip on her shoes. Not the ones Amelie had planned to wear—high-heeled, with diamante buckles— in which she would turn her ankle the minute she crossed the grass to safety. Darna wet the scarf again in the bedside jug, tied it carefully across her mouth, and with Amelie decently clad and shod, took the woman's handbag in one hand and Amelie's wrist in the other and practically dragged the lady out of her bedroom, down the length of the dining room, and opened the door into the long passage.

Amelie screamed in genuine terror. "No, no, you are trying to kill me. I knew you never liked me. I won't go out into that, I won't ..." She dissolved into French, from which Darna could only distinguish Amelie's firm resolve not to advance a single step, and her reiteration that Darna was a would-be assassin. There was something about being of good family, and not accustomed to such treatment, thrown in as good measure.

Darna jerked her forward, slammed the dining-room door behind them. She renewed her grip on the hysterical woman and marched into the thickening smoke. If they stayed here they'd die. The windows in the house were all high, even on the ground floor, too high for an old woman to climb through. Darna could escape, but this woman couldn't, and she would not leave the dithering fool to burn, no matter what she had threatened. The smoke had thickened considerably in the last five minutes and it was almost impossible to see across the width of the corridor, but she couldn't lose her way.

Amelie had stopped that ear-piercing shrieking—thank heavens for that, Darna thought vaguely—now the woman coughed, choking, sobbing, and coughing again between spluttered complaints. Darna moved down the corridor, Amelie reeling beside her, until at last she saw the outer door. Amelie shrieked and lunged for the exit, grabbing her handbag from Darna and reeling out into the clear cold morning air before she turned to fix venomous eyes on her savior.

"Murderer! Assassin! I will report you to the *gendarmes*. I will lay charges. I will have you punished, you'll see, you ..." She stopped in astonishment as Darna vanished back inside. "Ah good, you suicide yourself, you are remorse. I will forgive you perhaps." She turned to look about her, spied Flora Maylon and headed across the lawn to join her, regretting as she did so that she was not wearing her best shoes. Who could look well wearing shoes with no heels or style?

Inside the house Darna had returned to hammer again on Violet's door. No reply remained her answer and the heat increased. Crackling sounded behind the door. She shouted a final time and accepted that if anyone was still inside, they were past saving. All she could do now was to make her way out of the house. She groped her way back down the corridor and as she passed the bottom of the staircase she paused. Had that been a faint cry? The fire's roar was loud in her ears but she thought she heard the sound again. The upper floor had housed another eight residents; were some still trapped inside?

Darna shuddered. Tiny pinpoints of pain blazed abruptly across her shoulders as sparks penetrated her dress and she yelped before making up her mind. If someone needed her, how could she leave anyone to die? She started up the stairs. Halfway up she bent double, coughing, unable to advance, or even to take a decent breath. Beneath her the stairs shook, juddering, and ... they dropped downwards slightly! Without conscious thought Darna descended the stairs where clearer air beckoned. She emerged from the heat and smoke to find chaos all about her. People dashed to and fro, women called out names, a fire engine pulled up in the wide driveway while the harnessed horses snorted and plunged, and two policemen in uniform called contradictory questions and orders to nobody in particular.

Darna took half a dozen quick steps to a watering can half-filled with clean water, and soaked the scarf yet again. Then, with that clamped firmly over her mouth, she poured the remainder of the water over her back and shoulders and plunged into the house again. The fire seemed to be worst at the far end of the house near the kitchen. Jars of preserved fruit exploded in the pantry. The flames had apparently travelled upwards, and the smoke rolled and roiled like a living thing on the upper portion of the stairs.

She gathered all her resolution and started to climb the staircase. When she reached halfway she staggered, almost falling as the staircase swayed. The fire must have run along the underside of the floor and burned the staircase supports. The staircase swayed again and she leapt toward the lower landing. She landed hard, dropping to one knee but forcing herself up again. Behind her the staircase crashed down, collapsing inwards. The fire roared louder, the heat, the smoke increased and she reeled down the corridor, one hand trailing along the wall for direction, no longer thinking, merely an animal desperate to escape.

She did. An open doorway loomed and with her last strength she stepped past the threshold, stumbled onto the grass and dropped to the ground. Coughing again she gasped for breath, removing the scarf. A man appeared out of the smoke and addressed her sternly.

"You can't sit here, miss. It isn't safe. Move along."

She looked up, her voice a hoarse whisper. "There may still be someone upstairs. I couldn't get to them. Do you know? Is everyone safe?"

She half-turned to look at the blazing building and his objections to blasted nosy bystanders died in a shocked gasp. Her dress had small holes burned in a spray that extended almost to her waist and to the point of both shoulders. Through the holes reddened flesh could be seen. His gaze lifted to the burning house, and his voice was almost reverent.

"Were you in there, miss?"

"I helped two people from the ground floor," Darna said, her voice a monotone. "It's Mrs. Stacy I'm worried about. She bolted her door and I couldn't make her hear me. Please, can someone check?"

He shook his head. The fire had grown in intensity and even the firemen wouldn't take that chance. Someone should look after this woman. He glanced around the confusion and his gaze lit on a man whom he recognized as the local doctor. Leaving the lady sitting slumped on the grass he made his way over to him.

"Doctor? That woman over there," he pointed. "I think she was in the house. She's burned across the back, looks like sparks landed on her. Can you tend to her?"

The doctor looked where he pointed and exclaimed, "Miss Rosewarne! Good heavens." He trotted across the grass and stooped to speak to the slumped figure. Satisfied that he'd done what he should, his informant disappeared into the crowd—and out of the story.

Darna became conscious of a voice that urged her to her feet, and then encouraged her to walk. Obediently she walked. She dimly recognized the voice and knew she must obey, that it was important. Eons later she lay down on what felt like a comfortable bed. Someone washed her face and hands, then removed her dress and she whimpered with the pain. A woman's voice said that it was ruined anyway, that they should cut the material. There was the slight pull of scissors slicing through the fabric and then colder air was cooling the pain.

Barely conscious she obeyed, doing what they asked of her, but all the time under that cooperation there was the knowledge that there was something more she should do. Or had she done that? Could she really rest now?

Gentle hands dressed her in a nightdress, a glass was tilted to her lips and she drank. Foul-tasting stuff, but she was coaxed until it was gone and she drank cold milk to wash away the taste. The hands laid her down, her head against a feather-pillow, the drug stole up on her and slowly, peacefully, Darna Rosewarne drifted into a deep restful sleep.

Over her head Doctor Edwin Blascourt and Darna's ex-nurse—now her housekeeper—Mary Whittle, looked at each other, and turned in mutual agreement for the bedroom door. Once out of the room, the door shut silently behind them, Mary spoke.

"Do they know if anyone is dead?"

"We do not know exactly but," he hesitated, "you must prepare yourself and your mistress for the news that some will have died, Miss

Whittle. Of the twelve women residents and six staff, at least one woman of the four living on the ground floor is not accounted for. Of the eight residents on the upper floor, I know for certain of no more than three who have been saved."

Mary Whittle stared at him. "Six? You think that half may be dead? What about the staff? How many managed to flee? Of course," she considered. "They live in the staff cottage. Who would have been on duty last night?"

"Only two, I believe, the matron and her assistant, and I am sure both escaped."

"Did you see them?"

Doctor Blascourt nodded. "I saw Miss Halpen out on the driveway, she was fully dressed," he frowned. "It is strange, but she carried a small case. Maybe her possessions or some equipment. And Matron Dean I saw outside, comforting one of the women."

Mary Whittle glanced back at the door behind which her sleeping mistress lay. "She will be devastated. They need to find out what caused this awful fire."

That, I thought as I re-read my last sentence, was very true.

2

I was sitting with Holmes, both of us engrossed in crosswords, when my visitor was announced. I had known Edwin Blascourt since our days together at medical school, when I was completing a refresher course and he was in training to follow his father into practice. I was pleased to see him. I knew that for the past seven years he had been working in Ampthill with his father, and his practice had—with the recent death of his father, and the death also of the elderly doctor in the next town of Flitwick—now spread to encompass both areas. He was extremely busy, and whatever brought him to London must be of importance.

"My dear Blascourt, come in, come in. Here, sit down and what can I offer? Whiskey and soda suit you?"

"Thank you, Watson." He accepted the glass while still standing and drank half off at a single gulp. He obviously was not here to renew old friendships. I introduced him to Holmes and urged Blascourt again to sit down, which he finally did. Normally the most abstemious of men, he emptied the glass with a second gulp and I quietly refilled it before sitting down as well, fixing my gaze on him expectantly.

He smiled. "Yes, there is a problem, and yes, I am here to ask your advice, if this will not put you out in any way." He looked across at Holmes who sat regarding him. "Six people have died, the inquest claims it to have been either accidental or carelessness on the part of staff, and I believe neither suggestion."

My friend stiffened just a little and I turned to him. "You know of what he speaks, do you not?"

"I do. Some nine months ago there was a deadly fire at Flitwick in which six women died. There was considerable outcry since all of them were women of the middle-class, all had devoted families, and they were reasonably well-to-do. The inquest was, I believe, some four weeks ago. However while the reports in local newspapers were voluminous, most were so sensationalized I would be interested to hear what really occurred from a witness." He sat back in his chair.

Blascourt hesitated before beginning. "On April the 26th last year, fire broke out in a residential home for elderly ladies. The building is more than a hundred years old, the wood, after an unusually hot summer was extremely dry, and the building burned ferociously. Four of the women lived on the ground floor. Of those, three escaped the fire, one using common sense, and the other two with the aid of the young woman who owned the building. At great risk to her own life, I should add."

I perceived that here could be the motive behind his approach to us and nodded for him to continue. He described the actions of that woman—a clearer description of which began this exposition—then moved on to indicate the system that had prevailed, as well as what had occurred on the upper floor.

"Upstairs there were eight residents living with two night staff. The two staff, Matron Dean and Miss Halpen, escaped the fire along with three of the residents from the upper floor, while a fourth escaped on her own. However, the remaining four women on that floor perished, and as all five dead were from local families, the grief and anger in my area are considerable."

"And at such times," Holmes said quietly, "people seek someone to blame."

"Exactly so, sir. The truth is that neither the firemen nor the police could find any reason why the fire broke out. Therefore, and I say to you that it is the most ridiculous verdict I have ever heard, the jury brought it in at the inquest that the fire was deemed to be misadventure, possibly caused by some failing in care by a member of the staff, and that Miss Rosewarne, who owns the property, should have supervised them to a greater extent."

His face twisted into a terrifying scowl. "She does *not* supervise them. That is the duty of Matron Dean, a very experienced nurse of excellent qualifications who, together with her assistant, lived in the building, while Miss Rosewarne lived in a cottage in the grounds, some quarter mile from the main house. She merely owns the estate and I see no way in which she should have been held responsible. But things have come to such a pass after that verdict that urchins spit at her in the street and call her names."

He was all but panting in his indignation and I refilled his glass, adding considerably more soda this time.

Holmes studied him. "You say that the verdict was ridiculous, Doctor Blascourt. In what way precisely?"

"Why, that if they could not ascertain how the fire began, how could they say the staff must have been careless? And if they could not be sure that any of the staff were to blame, how could they say that Miss Rosewarne should have supervised them more closely? If no staff member caused the fire, how would her closer supervision have saved anyone?"

Holmes nodded, his expression thoughtful. "That is true and very logical. Was there no indication of how the fire began?"

"No, sir, there was not. At least, none whom those that investigated it could uncover. The theory put forward at the inquest was that a coal had fallen from a fire and set the floor alight. From there it spread to the suites, and then to engulf the upper floor."

"In which room do they believe the fire began?" I asked

"There is a small office on the ground floor beside the suite of one of the victims. A fire normally burns there since any of the staff may use it as it contains various necessary items, and also as a way of disposing of confidential papers. However, because there had been a short spell of unseasonably warm weather for the two days previous, the fire had not been lit. Furthermore, it has a large fire-screen before it, which is only moved aside when the fire is tended, and then put back immediately." His brow wrinkled as he paused. "Yet there is no doubt that the fire started in that room, and I cannot imagine how it could have happened."

Holmes nodded. "The jury believed then that there *had* been a fire burning there that day, and that a member of the staff had not replaced the screen. That the staff had lied about it, fearing to be blamed?"

"Yes, sir. That has been made very plain to all of the staff by those in the town, and several have resigned. Fortunately, of the residents who survived, three decided to live in a large cottage adjacent to the destroyed building. Nor has all of the staff left Darna's employment. Both the Matron and her assistant stayed, as did the housemaid. Those first two have certain requirements that could not easily be satisfied elsewhere. The housemaid is an orphan and has no one to whom she could go, and I think that she fears to leave a well-paying job where she has also comfortable accommodation."

He hesitated. "I have no wish to offend, Mr. Holmes. And I know Doctor Watson will assist me in any case." I nodded. "However I would feel easier in my mind if you could look into this matter with him. I have discussed this both with Miss Rosewarne and with two of the families of those who died, they have agreed to defray your expenses and pay you a consultation fee, as well as an additional amount should you be able to prove how the fire came about and name anyone who was responsible. Such proof being a charge laid or police acknowledgment of either solution."

Holmes nodded slowly. "I cannot give you an opinion on this, Doctor, without seeing the building. Does it still stand?"

"For another few days, yes, it does. However it was badly damaged by the fire, particularly in the upper floor where the flames spread to almost every section. In the past four weeks since the inquest Miss Rosewarne has twice discovered local boys clambering about on beams that were partially burned through and she has decided that it is too dangerous to permit the building to remain standing. Its destruction and the leveling of the ground to become a garden will therefore begin in eight days."

Holmes stood. "Then there may be no time to lose. Go back to your practice, Doctor. Watson and I shall pack tonight and take a train to Flitwick in the morning."

A great smile of relief spread over my young friend's face. "You will find it an easy journey, sir. The line runs along the outskirts of both towns, and if you take the mid-morning train I can inform Miss Rosewarne. She will have a pony trap waiting for you and any luggage you may have brought. As well there is a decent inn at Flitwick that is no more than a five minute walk from her estate."

"Can she put such a trap at our disposal, perhaps? It would facilitate our inquiries."

"I will arrange it. Thank you, sir. Thank you, Watson." And with that he wrung our hands, hurried from the room and down the stairs into the street, where we soon heard him shouting for a cab.

I turned to my friend. "I must call Tolcomb, who will be happy to locum for me. For how long do you think that I should pack?"

I received in return a grave look. "Perhaps as much as two weeks, Watson. I did not say so to Doctor Blascourt, but it has come to my attention that Miss Rosewarne may be in greater danger than from the taunts of small boys. I was talking to Harrison and Lestrade the day before yesterday and both talked of this fire. It seems that their colleagues are determined to fix the blame on the lady, and with that coronial verdict, they may be able to arrest her. It is unlikely that she would be convicted, yet feelings run high, and it is not impossible."

I absorbed that information. "*Do* you think her to have been at fault?" I questioned.

"I dislike theorizing ahead of the data, as you know, yet I think it unlikely. As your friend said, if they cannot discover how the fire occurred, how then can they say who may have been responsible, or even if any person was. No, it is a pretty little problem and it will not be easy to uncover the truth."

I tilted my head in query and Holmes regarded me. "Do you not see, Watson? The fire was nine months ago, and at the time the scene was trampled by locals and officials in their scores. The site has suffered the weather since, as well as the depredations of boys searching for clues, or for small items as souvenirs, and it is possible minor valuables may have been overlooked. Officials will have returned a number of times, digging in the rubble, and clambering about the safer portions of the building. Now it is decided to raze the edifice and it is probable that in advance of that action, various workmen have toured. Our investigation will be on the heels of all those who have gone previously, and what clues do you imagine may be left to us?"

I was crestfallen and showed it. Holmes eyed me kindly. "Do not despair. It may be that we can yet come at the truth. Some item they have disregarded as irrelevant may spring to the eye. We might still vindicate the lady and restore her to the town's good graces." A slight smile turned up the corners of his lips. "We may also restore her to your friend, whom I think to be interested in her."

I agreed with that summation. I, too, had noticed how Blascourt's voice seemed to linger over her name. I could understand why he was so eager to see her exonerated. It would do a rising doctor no good at all to wed a woman locally notorious as the inadvertent murderer of five elderly women, some well-known and well-liked. Blascourt was not a greedy man, but from the sound of it Miss Rosewarne had money, and of Blascourt it could be honestly said that while he would not marry for money, he would be careful to marry where money was. I packed my case, put my medical bag beside it, laid out my clothing, and went early to bed.

* * * *

I was up at seven the next morning, as was Holmes. By nine we had completed our ablutions, dressed, eaten a hearty breakfast, and set out for the train station. The train that passed through Flitwick then Ampthill was on time and we were bowling through outer London by ten. I enjoyed our journey, for the rocking motion of a train is soothing and very conducive to thought. I asked Mrs. Hudson to make a packet of sandwiches, and we picnicked in comfort. Soon after that we arrived on the outskirts of Flitwick, and when we alighted we were accosted by an elderly man, inquiring if we were Mr. Holmes and Doctor Watson. We acknowledged it.

"Ah, then do you come with me, sirs. I've the pony and trap waiting right outside the station." He called to a man standing nearby to bring our bags, and in minutes we were ensconced in a comfortable pony-trap with our bags beside us. Our driver clucked to the pony, which started off down the road at a slow trot, and once we had cleared the immediate buildings he spoke again.

"I'm to take you to the Dog and Pheasant, sirs, wait while you send up your baggage and write your names in the book, then I'm to take you to Miss Darna, if you please."

I looked at Holmes, who nodded. "We are happy with that," I said. And our driver wasted no time. We pulled up outside the inn, a lad collected our bags and carried them upstairs while we signed the hotel register, and once we had discovered the direction of our rooms, we descended the stairs and entered the pony-trap again. Doctor Blascourt had spoken the truth. The inn and the Rosewarne estate were close enough to walk from inn to estate outskirts in five minutes, but the drive to the house was as long as that again and I was glad we should have the use of a trap.

We rounded a bend in the long avenue and my gaze sought out the location of the fire. It was a sorry sight. The ground floor had mostly survived, but with the spread of the flames the upper floor had been almost fully engaged and all that remained was exposed and partly burned beams, some of the partitions, and the blackened floors or portions of them, in several rooms. I saw to my interest that there had been a fire escape. It was unusual, but not unheard of, and I thought that Miss Rosewarne's family was sensibly farsighted in the matter.

We drew up at the front door of a cottage—as its owners would have described it. I estimated it to have two or three suites, rather than mere bedrooms, and it had probably been conceived as a guest cottage, or perhaps for the longer stay of an elderly relative who wished for quiet surroundings, along with the attendance of her maids. Closer to the ruined building were two other cottages, one of similar size and type, and the other smaller. The building where we halted was some distance from the main house, and I recalled Blascourt said it was a quarter mile between the two. I looked back to where the ruin was hidden by a screen of trees. Yes, it would be that far certainly and perhaps a little further. My attention was returned to the immediate vicinity by the sound of a voice.

"Mr. Holmes? Doctor Watson? I am so glad you are here. Please, come inside."

That first meeting with Darna Rosewarne impressed me. She was a slender woman of around five and a half feet in height, and her hair was that shade of dark brown that verges on black but which in sunlight shows chestnut glints. It was fine but thick, had a wave that indicated a tendency to frizz should it become wet, and was neatly confined by a green ribbon. From the newspaper accounts I knew her to be twenty-seven, but she looked several years younger, and her dress was a somber dark brown that did not at all suit her slightly olive complexion.

She was not pretty, for her nose was of no distinction, her mouth a little small, and her eyebrows too thick for fashion, while she wore no cosmetics, not even face powder. However, she was composed, spoke as a lady, and her smile when it came, transformed her face to that of a woman whose acquaintance anyone would be happy to make. We followed her into the cottage and she ushered us into a pleasant sunlit parlor. We sat where she indicated, and accepted food and tea from the trolley that was brought in by a woman in her fifties. I saw at once they were on familiar and affectionate terms, although not related, and guessed the older woman to be a long-time servant, licensed to friendship by years of devoted service.

"This is Mary—Mrs. Whittle," Miss Rosewarne told us. "She was my nurse when I was a child and stayed on to look after me after my parents died from influenza and I came to live here with my grandfather. Now she is housekeeper, and I could not do without her. She can tell you much about the events of that day."

Holmes placed his cup and plate on the trolley, sat back and considered. "I understand that you gave the alarm, Miss Rosewarne, and that you then entered the building in an attempt to save some of the residents. Will you tell me how that began?"

A small shiver passed over her body. "I was asleep. I was awoken by my cat, which cried and cried until I got up and dressed before feeding her. I thought that she was merely hungry, but it may have been that she smelled that smoke. I did not mind being up early, for there were things I intended to do in the herb garden once I had breakfasted and so it was fortunate that I dressed in older clothing and wearing stout boots. I decided once I had fed Freyni that I would walk over to the main house before breakfast to speak to the matron, and I set out."

Another shiver shook her. "I was close to the line of trees that screens my cottage from the main house when I saw smoke. I thought that someone must be burning rubbish and thought no more of it until I passed through the trees and I could see the house. It was awful; the whole end was ablaze, smoke thickening even as I stood there. I screamed, I then shouted "fire!" a number of times as loudly as I could to alert the staff in the cottage and those in the burning building, and as I shouted I ran to the main entrance. The door was not locked and I entered. I knew the four residents on the ground floor and I was determined to get them out safely." She paused.

Holmes spoke. "You need not describe your actions further. We have heard of them from Doctor Blascourt and they reflect great credit upon you."

"Yes," I agreed. "You behaved with great bravery."

She looked me in the eye. "I did not. Bravery is feeling fear and acting despite it. I felt no fear, only the greatest urgency. My whole mind was bent on reaching all the residents that I could and bringing them from the building. I would have dragged them if necessary. Indeed, I was quite brutal to Mrs. Hartsford and she left after the fire because of it. Nor could I save Violet Stacy."

"You saved two lives," Holmes intervened. "You would have saved two more had one not already escaped, and the other taken such ill-advised actions as made her survival impossible. You did well."

His measured evaluation of her actions calmed her and she nodded. "I would wish to have done more. But you are right; I should be content that I did the best I could."

"Yes." He looked across to where Mary Whittle sat silently, bright eyes watching everyone and taking in each word. "Mrs. Whittle, will you describe what you saw and heard?"

"I woke when Miss Darna screamed. Then I heard her cry 'fire' and I dressed as fast as I could. I ran outside thinking that the cottage was on fire, but I could see no sign though I searched inside and out. I could not see Miss Darna either, and for some time I searched for her. I eventually saw smoke coming from behind the trees and I ran that way. I saw the main house afire and I was stunned. There were people all about. I found Mrs. Maylon and asked her if she had seen Miss Darna. She said Miss Darna had got her and that Frenchwoman out. I looked and looked but couldn't find Miss Darna anywhere. Then the doctor called me and she was there on the ground, her clothing burned. Poor thing, she coughed and coughed, and it wasn't fitting." Her tone was pure indignation.

"Not for a lady like that. I got her to her feet and back to her home and the doctor and I undressed her and put her to bed. Her poor back was all burned in patches." Her tone became venomous. "That Frenchwoman, I was glad to see the back of her, her and her screeching that Miss Darna had threatened her. Saved her life she did. A common woman, I always thought, and we can do without her here. And there wasn't an ounce of gratitude in her." After I untangled all the pronouns, I agreed that the Frenchwoman had not appeared in a pleasant light.

"Her! Miss Darna only did what she must to get her out of the place before she burned. But no, it was 'she threatened me, she hit me.'"

I gave Miss Rosewarne a querying glance and she smiled ruefully. "When first I entered her room I could not rouse her, for she is a heavy sleeper, and I took her by the shoulder. I also threatened that if she did not dress and come with me, I would leave her to burn. It was Mrs. Maylon, you see. She is in a wheelchair much of the time. Mrs. Hartsford was well able to walk, but Mrs. Maylon required my assistance. I took Mrs. Maylon out, and then went back for Mrs. Hartsford only to find that she had not even dressed. Instead she was stacking items on her bed as if I could summon servants to carry them out for her. I'm afraid that they burned and she does not forgive me for their loss."

I was disgusted. Darna Rosewarne had risked her life to save the ungrateful woman and all Mrs. Hartsford could do was bemoan her possessions. Anyone with sense would be glad they lived. It was clear that here was a resident without any sense; it was probably as well for everyone that she had packed what remained of any possessions and departed. I asked about that, only to be answered by Mrs. Whittle.

"Departed from here, aye. She took a cottage on the outskirts of Flitwick and there she stays, causing trouble, spreading rumors and calling Miss Darna all sorts. It's my opinion that half the wicked gossip in Flitwick was started by that woman, and her supposedly a Christian. I think shame to her, I do really."

We asked questions and now and again I made notes. Finally the two women grew weary and Holmes rose to leave. I joined him, and we took our leave politely and departed, temporary owners now of the pony and trap, with the assurance that the beast would be well cared for at the inn. We reached that place in time to leave the equipage in the good hands of the ostler, return to our rooms, bathe, dress in clean clothing, and sit down to a good dinner. I hoped to pass a pleasantly quiet night and planned to continue our search for the truth once I woke and we were on our way again.

3

It was a cool, clear morning with little wind and the pony strode out eagerly as we drove into the town to find Mrs. Hartsford. That we did without difficulty, and a more malicious woman I hope never to find. At the last she even hinted that Miss Darna had set the fire herself to kill everyone, and that she, Mrs. Hartsford had been fortunate as well as clever to escape.

I would have spoken sharply on the subject of slander, libel, and her own conceit, but for a look from my friend. Once we were clear of that den of spite and malice, he said, "You waste your time, Watson. Such a woman would never agree she was anything but the victim and heroine of her own tale. What we must do is discover how the fire began, and in that way exonerate the one she blames."

A suggestion with which I agreed most heartily.

So it was that we returned to the pony-trap and drove out to the Rosewarne estate. Miss Darna had told everyone there to answer our questions honestly and fully. If we wanted help, it was to be given. Initially we needed none. At Holmes's direction I drove directly to the ruins of the main house, dismounted, tethered the pony and placed a bucket of water by him, and we walked slowly around the ruins. It was a sorry sight, the blacked beams stark against the pale sky, the breeze ruffling the ashes of lives lost. We walked as close to the building as possible and I stirred the debris with my boot.

I saw a glint and reached into the cinders, moving a charred length of wood, to discover a small, delicate gold watch made as a broach. There was some blackening, the case was warped from the heat, and I doubted that it would ever work again, but once I had wiped away the soot the engraved script across the back was clear.

To Louise from her husband,
Love forever, Vincent.

I held it out to Holmes. "Wasn't this one of the women who escaped?"

He nodded. "Interesting. Yes. Louise Collins had the suite next to Violet Stacy. When Miss Darna went to check on her she found her rooms empty. Yet I would have thought a watch such as this would be the one thing she would be certain to take with her when she fled. However, it will open her door to us once we know where she now lives."

I was delighted. For once I was ahead of him, as I had chatted to the girl dusting the hall before I went into breakfast, Holmes coming down a little later. "She resides here still. She is one of those who stayed, and she and Mrs. Maylon and one of the others are all living in that cottage over there." I pointed.

Holmes's attention fixed upon it. "Then let us go and talk to her, Watson, before she leaves or anything befalls her. There are a few questions to which I would like answers, and with the watch to restore to her she may be more inclined to answer."

In which he was not wrong. Our knock at the door was answered by the lady herself, who was happy to welcome us inside, invite us into her own suite, and received her watch with soft cries of joy.

"Oh, thank you, thank you. I can hardly believe that you found it. It was my own entire fault. It was pinned to one of my coats, and when I ran from the house I wore another one. Oh, I am so happy to see it, and what a mercy that it wasn't found by one of those horrid boys."

"Horrid boys?" I questioned.

Mrs. Collins seemed to come back to herself and looked distressed. "Yes, but never mind them. Please, sit down. You will have tea?"

No woman is more settled than one who can dispense hospitality, so we agreed, and waited as she tugged gently at a bell rope. A maid arrived, was instructed to bring tea and biscuits, and vanished briefly, to return with a tea trolley containing a silver tea service and charming rose-painted china. Three plates held a fine assortment of biscuits and we accepted cups of tea and plates with biscuits. Once we were settled comfortably in matching armchairs, Mrs. Collins looked at us.

"How can I help you, gentlemen? Miss Darna tells me that you are investigating the fire. Even had you not brought my dear Vincent's gift back to me I would be happy to help. Ask me any question you wish and I shall do my best to answer."

She did so, and we began to form a picture of the fire from her point of view. She had been asleep but something woke her, what she did not know, but it was somewhere about one in the morning. She had lain there, drowsing a while before sliding back into a sounder sleep, to wake again around half past five.

"I do not always fall asleep again so easily at that hour, for the old need less sleep I think, and I was lying there for some time trying to decide if I should get up and make myself a cup of tea. I had the equipment at hand, you see. Oh, no," in reply to Holmes's query. "The staff would not have been in the kitchen yet, they begin work at six ...."

* * * *

Here too, I felt that an excerpt from the diary and letters would best serve my readers. It goes towards explaining some of the anomalies that at the time puzzled me—although not Holmes.

Louise Collins lay in her bed. It was pleasant to lie relaxed, warm and comfortable while debating if she should get up and make her own tea, or if she should wait half an hour and ring the bell for an early breakfast in bed. At her age it was nice to be waited on. The bedroom fire was almost out, but the small kettle would have boiling water. Her only sorrow was that Vincent hadn't lived to be with her. Dear Vincent. He'd been such a gawky young man, so diffident at approaching her to make friends when they were nine. But once he knew her, and she knew him, it had been as if that relationship had been there for years, not months. He'd been a friend of her only brother, poor Francis. Her brother had died young, unmarried too, so that the family name ran out and she inherited everything.

Was that smoke she could smell? Odd. She glanced at the small silver carriage clock on her bedside table—a gift for her eightieth birthday from her grand-daughter. Only twenty minutes to six, cook must have arrived early and lit the range. But smoke from that didn't normally travel this far. It wasn't the first morning she had lain here and listened to the house wake around her. Something made her uneasy and she decided that she may as well rise, since she wasn't going back to sleep. She got out of bed and put on her clothing. The smell of smoke seemed to be getting stronger.

Louise Collins might be all of eighty-seven but she had never been slow-witted, and all her life she'd had occasional premonitions. She'd learned as a girl to listen to them, as had her husband and her two children. They didn't come often, but when her instincts told her something emphatically, it was a good idea to heed them. She was a kind, often generous person, but when push came to shove, she was a survivor. Then she'd save those she loved. Genuine friends came next, but after that she held no responsibility for anyone else, they could take care of themselves. It wasn't an opinion she shared with others, but it was a precept she followed.

She wandered into her other room, opened the small safe and dumped all of her jewels into a large handbag. It wasn't her usual smaller one, but it would do. Into that also went the cash she always kept by her, her silver hairbrush, mirror, and comb—inherited from her father's mother—the little clock, and a number of photographs and other mementos she wouldn't want to lose. She picked up her hand-warmer, placed that safely in her pocket and went to the fireplace where she poured out boiling water. A wisp of smoke curled past her window.

Mrs. Collins looked at the smoke, went quietly to her wardrobe, and picked out her silver fox-fur coat, a matching scarf and the stylish little fur hat. She sat to don good-quality shoes, nearly new but comfortably broken in for wearing and safely low heeled. She dropped the linen drawstring bag containing her greatest treasures into her most capacious coat pocket, picked up her best gloves—white doeskin with silver fur around the cuffs—and going to her outer door she touched the handle. Cold metal. Good. She opened the door a few inches and looked out. A thin haze of smoke drifted by. Her instincts shouted at her and she wasted no time in walking quietly thirty feet up the corridor, opening the small side door there to the outer world and departing the house. Outside there was more smoke and against the building she saw bright hungry flames flicker by the outside wall of Violet's suite.

Violet Stacy was a thoroughly unpleasant woman; if she died it would be no more than her due. Why, she'd heard Violet viciously abusing her daughter only the previous week. Did she have a duty to warn Violet? She thought not, for the woman was not a friend, she was no relation. If she knew Violet her door would be bolted and the woman was as deaf as a post, so any time spent on her would be useless. No, there was no onus upon Louise to exert herself. There were more flames, and… Was that smoke wreathing the inside of Violet's window?

That decided her. She took a firm grip on her bulging handbag, drew the fur coat around her against the early morning chill and walked silently over the grass to the arbor. She sat quietly on the long cushioned seat and listened while she debated ethics in the growing light. Should she attempt to give the alarm? Darna spent every penny she received on keeping her old home from falling down. She'd be better off without it, and there was no one inside Louise liked much except Mrs. Maylon—the smoke was thickening steadily—and maybe she should warn Flora …

Miss Darna walked out from the line of trees between her cottage and the main house, carrying a basket. She froze, screamed once, and ran shouting towards the house, dropping the basket and vanishing around the corner. No doubt she entered the building. Well, Louise had left her door ajar, and the girl would know at a glance that one inhabitant was out and safe. Darna would get Flora out safely, and probably that idiot Frenchwoman, too—it was fortunate she wasn't typical of the French, but someone like her gave them all a bad name. The flames were slowly engulfing the upper floor now, with figures emerging from the smoke wreathing the fire escape.

And what had been in that basket Darna dropped? Louise Collins went to see, to find … Oh good, she hadn't breakfasted yet. She returned to the arbor and sat to eat the fruit, eyes busy. Her eyesight had always been long. She had spectacles for reading, that was all, and the arbor was only seventy or eighty yards from the house. The time must be all of six now, she'd heard the church bell; chime the half hour after five some time ago. No one noticed her, but she could see everything, and very interesting it was as the hours passed.

* * * *

"I heard Darna scream," Louise Collins said quietly. "I saw smoke outside my window so I got up and dressed. I left the house and went to the arbor. Darna brought Flora out, then went back inside while I went over to Flora and helped to her the arbor where we waited out of the way. She was shivering, so I loaned her my hand-warmer." She looked at us. "It was terrible, and I'm glad there were no more than the five deaths. Everyone could have died, including Darna."

Holmes nodded. "Indeed, that is very true, Mrs. Collins. Tell me, what do you think might have been the cause of your first waking? What type of sound might wake you?"

Louise pondered that while she finished her cup of tea. "Anything that is unfamiliar to me. It could have been a sort of bump."

"As if someone had knocked into something solid?"

"Yes, but it wasn't a *sharp* sound, you see? If someone kicks a piece of lighter furniture or knocks into it and it rocks back, you get a sharper noise. This was dull."

"Ah, that may be useful. Thank you, Mrs. Collins." He rose to go and I followed suit.

"It is I who should be thanking you, gentlemen, for my lovely watch had been there all this time and I'm so happy to have it returned."

"The horrid boys!" I exclaimed, remembering her earlier words. "Did you see them?"

"I did. They were digging about inside the house, climbing up that fire escape—and it so dangerous—walking along the beams like tight-rope walkers. I called a man who works here and he chased them off. If they'd fallen they could have broken their backs—or their silly young necks."

Holmes nodded. "Boys can take very foolish risks. If you see them again I hope you will tell Miss Darna so they can be warned away."

Mrs. Collins smiled. "I have done so and they were told. I haven't seen them since."

We took our leave, and once we were back by the pony-trap Holmes spoke quietly. "I think she told us all she knows, Watson, but I believe she lied or omitted things at several points."

"How do you know?" I asked.

"The hand-warmer, Watson."

I recalled her casual mention of that. "She loaned it to the crippled woman because she was shivering."

"And how did she come to have a hand-warmer with her? She didn't mention that, and from the doctor I was told that of all who escaped, Mrs. Collins was the only one who got all of her valuables out.

"Consider the situation, Watson. She is woken by Miss Darna's scream, then her shouts of 'fire.' The building was already burning by Mrs. Stacy's window when Miss Darna saw it. Yet in the next five minutes Louise Collins has time to dress, gather a large bag full of jewelry, framed photos, silverware and other items, and does she then leave? No, instead she goes to her fire, takes up the kettle and fills a hand-warmer since the morning is chilly. Only with that accomplished does she stroll out of the blazing building."

"Miss Darna never saw her?"

"Because, so Mrs. Collins says, she crossed to the arbor while Miss Darna was inside and before she came out with Flora Maylon in the wheelchair. In my opinion, Mrs. Collins was there certainly, but she had been so for some time before Miss Darna gave the alarm."

"That nice woman? You think she saw the fire, gave no alarm, but instead got herself and all her valuables out, then sat watching events from inside the arbor?"

"I do, Watson. I think as you say, that she is a nice woman—most of the time. I also think that she has a very strong sense of self-preservation and a cold logic when it is important to be rational. Consider the circumstances. She is almost ninety, she is healthy, as physically fit as a woman of that age is likely to be—you observed that she required no walking stick—but it is unlikely that she can shout loudly or run. If she left her rooms and went to find help, there was the probability that all of her possessions would burn before she was able to get back to save them."

He frowned. "And who does she tell? If she goes to Miss Darna, it could take her some time to walk that far and longer still to walk back, since she will be tiring. Upstairs were the staff and eight residents, all of them fitter than she, which is why they were housed on the upper floor. If she goes up the stairs to wake one of the staff in residence—always supposing that they do not yet know of the fire—then she must climb and descend a long flight of stairs. In either case all her possessions would have been lost and as well, had she chosen to alert the staff, there is a strong chance that if the fire had spread, she could have been trapped, as others were."

I admitted the logic of that, but I still felt Mrs. Collins should have done something to help, and said so.

"She did, Watson. She dressed herself warmly, she got herself and her valuables out of the burning building, she stayed out of the way of the firemen and police, she succored Mrs. Maylon, and she can swear that Miss Darna not only came upon the fire well after the building was alight, but also that Miss Darna risked her life twice over by going into it to bring out residents."

I was contrary. "Just because she saw Miss Darna then doesn't mean that the woman wasn't there before that. What about the bump that woke Mrs. Collins earlier?"

Holmes eyed me. "Whoever or whatever that may have been, it was not Miss Darna. Newspaper reports, contrary as ever, between accusing her of being somehow responsible for the fire, have also complained that she was with friends at one a.m. They had been to see a play in Ampthill, returned to the friends' home for a very late supper, and their driver—the friends are modern—drove Miss Darna home in their automobile, waiting until she was safely within her home before he departed. Her nurse opened the door, and Mrs. Whittle is adamant that upon her arrival at half past one her employer went straight to bed and did not wake until shortly before six, when she decided to walk over to the main house before breakfast, with fruit from her kitchen garden for the residents."

"Mrs. Collins probably got to that first," I said sourly.

"Eating discarded fruit would not make her culpable of anything, Watson."

I still believed that she should have done more, but ... I changed the subject.

The pony trotted briskly toward our inn, and once there and the animal relinquished into the care of an employee, we ascended the stairs to our rooms and met in the small adjoining sitting room. On the way up I asked for our dinner to be brought, and it arrived just as we sat down. We found it a good meal, not lavish but well cooked, with a broth to begin, a sound main course of mutton, and with an excellent cheese-board to finish. We drank apple cider made locally, and went to bed at last after a long discussion of our discoveries to date, and after deciding what information we must seek out the next day, and from whom.

* * * *

We were out of the inn by nine and in Ampthill by train before ten. There we interviewed Miss Darna's friends, who began by being indignant over newspaper reports.

"It's monstrous. Why would they believe Darna started a fire that would burn down her home? She loved the place. If it had been mine I'd have pulled it down, but not her; she spent every penny she had keeping it up."

Holmes, by delicate questioning, got the story of the Rosewarne family and their estate.

It had been purchased by an impoverished son of a noble family who had decided that trade was better than starvation. His family, Cornish in origin, disowned him, but James Rosewarne turned out to have a sharp eye for a bargain and prospered in London. In his later years he had been offered this estate, which had fallen into disrepair since the last owner had lived long on little, done few repairs, lost the servants one by one from inability to pay, and died at last without heirs.

James had purchased the place for what was then a considerable bargain and year by year brought it back into heart. It was, however, the old story: his son had gone into business with him and done well also, the grand-son had been given a good education, married well, and his sons had been pleasant, good-natured, and hard-working—and also less apt to trade or intelligence. One had died quite young from diphtheria, the other had married, and he and his wife had died three years ago, a month before the grandfather, with Miss Darna inheriting the estate and what little money remained from both generations.

"It wasn't in bad condition, but it takes a lot of money spent on it every year, and her family's income had dwindled. It was her idea to use the main house as a residence for women who did not wish to have a house of their own any longer. The twelve suites were let by the year at a reasonable rental, staff service and meals provided."

I heard details and agreed that the residents would have been very comfortable.

"My wife and I visited Darna quite regularly and it was a snug situation for the residents so far as we ever saw. She had a good class of people there, all comfortably off, and mostly sensible and pleasant - all but that Mrs. Hartsford. She was the acquaintance of a friend and poor Darna had been prevailed upon to let her lease the suite on a one-year agreement. It was up six weeks before the fire and Darna didn't want her to stay, but the woman refused to move and it would have taken legal action to get her out."

I briefly toyed with the idea that Miss Darna had set the fire to remove Mrs. Hartsford. However, Miss Darna wouldn't burn her home to be rid of one inconvenient tenant.

Holmes poked down conversational byways, finding no more than that Miss Darna had been very well liked until the fire, and that Mrs. Hartsford's venomous gossip would perhaps wear off in a while. People were getting tired of her histrionics and her increasingly wilder claims. As the friends said …

"Some have starting saying that Darna risked her life getting the woman out of the fire, so it's ungrateful to say such things. And Mrs. Whittle spoke up on market day last in Flitwick." He grinned, and his wife smiled. They did not particularize but I gathered that Mary Whittle had been very clear about tattletales and gossips and how much credence *she* would put in anything Amelie Hartsford said. On the other hand, some of the bereaved families still accepted what the woman said and the police were being hard pressed to take action against Miss Darna. Thus far they had not done so, but her friends feared they might for no other reason than to gain a temporary silence.

"And if they do that, it's the sort of thing that keeps rumors alive forever, you know the way it is."

We did, and agreed that any action by the police would be precipitant, and we could only hope that none was taken. We caught the train back to Flitwick and, back at the inn, enjoyed bread and cheese for lunch, and more of the apple cider, before taking out the pony-trap again. We drove at a placid walk over to the estate and as we rounded the final bend in the avenue to the main house I pulled the pony up sharply.

"Holmes!"

"I see them."

I set the pony in motion again, intently watching the events unfolding before me. A police vehicle stood before Miss Darna's cottage, a constable—probably the driver—waited by it, while three men were on the doorstep. They were arguing with Mary Whittle and one man attempted to thrust past her. She said something, was pushed aside by the same man, lost her balance and fell heavily, apparently unconscious, in the doorway. Holmes and I abandoned the pony and trap and raced towards the scene. The three at the doorway turned to face us while the constable stepped into our path with an upheld hand.

4

I paused in front of him while Holmes brushed past and continued towards the cottage.

"I'm a doctor, and that woman is injured. If you impede my care of her I shall make a complaint to the National Medical Council. I shall also make a complaint to your superiors."

His broad face fell and he moved out of my way. I hastened after my friend, thanking providence I had my medical bag with me, and on this occasion I feared I might have need of it. I reached Holmes who was on one knee checking Mrs. Whittle's pulse. He looked up.

"She appears to have struck her head, no doubt as a result of the brutal shove she received."

One of the men grunted in protest while Holmes continued. "In an older woman such a head injury could be serious. Please examine her carefully, doctor."

I assumed a deeply serious mien and dropped to my knees. On examination I found sufficient to make me angry. The woman had indeed suffered a head injury, although not quite as grave as Holmes and I were suggesting, but bleeding sluggishly none-the-less and I expected her to have a severe headache.

"She must be got to bed at once," I said decisively. "I can care for the head wound, but she requires watching. Should she take a turn for the worse, she may need to be transported to hospital. I am tempted to do that now, for if her condition worsens, she may be too ill to be moved later."

I glared up at the three men. "I do not know who you are, but my friend and I observed your attack on this lady. Should she die from it I will have you taken up for murder. By what right do you attempt to force your way into a private home and strike down the innocent servant who prevents it?"

One of the three men stepped forward officiously. "I am Superintendent Bartholomew Goodbody, and I am here to search this house."

"Your warrant?" Holmes asked.

"Eh? Ah, yes, well, I have no need of one. I am Superintendent Barthol …"

"I heard you the first time," Holmes cut in, speaking severely. "It does not matter if you are the Chief Constable, a warrant is required to forcibly enter any private dwelling. Merely being a police officer gives you neither the right to enter where you will, nor to assault a household servant who protests your invasion. Both my colleague and I witnessed your aggression against an elderly lady who now lies unconscious, and who may be seriously injured. I suggest you leave immediately. I will be speaking to your Chief Constable about this and discussing if we should take the matter further."

Very chapfallen they departed, while Holmes assisted me to carry Mrs. Whittle into the house and shut the door behind us. Once inside I spoke in a low voice.

"They're gone, Mary, you can stand up now." Mrs. Whittle, placed on her feet and held steady for a moment, was then able to stand and regarded us with amusement.

"Thank you both. Oh." Her hand went to her forehead. "I have such a headache."

I hastened to support her into the kitchen where I drew a glass of water and added a headache remedy, offering it to her. She sat down carefully in one of the straight wooden chairs, took the glass and drank its contents down, before going straight to the point.

"They said they were determined to search the place. That man expected to find something to show that Miss Darna caused that fire. I couldn't abide the thought of them digging through her things, and I said they must wait until she returned from the village. He said they were the police and didn't have to wait. He intended to come in and search this very minute and I must stand back."

Holmes nodded. "Did they say why they would believe Miss Rosewarne to be responsible?"

Mrs. Whittle all but spat in her outrage. "That French ... woman! The superintendent said she'd lost everything, poor lady, and he was real sorry for her. Miss Darna wouldn't pay when Mrs. Hartsford came here a few days back and demanded money. She said she'd lost everything and it was my lady's fault, and in the town that woman's been saying she'd have her money or my lady'll suffer." She snorted. "I reckon she's trying it on too brown, claiming to have lost all sorts of valuables I know she never had, and it ain't as if she weren't going to be paid anyways."

I noticed that her polite accents were slipping in her rage, and the countrywoman showing through. Holmes was faster in hearing something else.

"So she was insured?"

"Aye, she were. She thinks nobody knows, but I do."

"Tell me, Mrs. Whittle, who were her friends in the main house?"

Mrs. Whittle thought. The lines of strain vanished from her face as the remedy I had given worked and her headache eased.

"That Miss Reeves, her that's stayed on here with Mrs. Maylon and Mrs. Collins. Nice lady, but she listens to anyone that talks firm, you know the sort." She looked up at Holmes. "They say as is most pleasing to the listener, and they believe it too if they're told it a few times. That Hartsford woman flattered her until Miss Reeves thought her a great friend and would do all sorts of small things for her."

Holmes nodded. "Not a strong personality. What can you tell us about Miss Reeves?"

"She's just turned seventy, been here five years now, she's healthy enough. She were a private tutor to a family, taught all their younger children in two generations of them. She had whole lines of pictures, sketches like, of them along her walls. She never stops wailing about losing all those *and* the fur coat the family gave her. She has a pension from the family, and I will say for them, one or the other comes to see her every Christmas and on her birthday to bring her a small present."

She nodded to herself. "Aye, I think they're fond enough of her, but more the way you like an old dog: it's never done a wrong thing, you had it a long time and liking it's a sort of habit. It's my opinion the family gave her the pension so she *would* retire, as they'd run out of children for her to teach, and being with them so long she'd know all sorts of bits and pieces they mightn't want talked about. I do know they persuaded her to come here to Flitwick when all her life she lived in Ampthill."

She took in a breath. "They didn't have to worry. She doesn't talk about them save for tales about Master George and Miss Hetty and others, all about how smart and nice-looking they were and funny things they said, nothing to hurt. She's a mouse, never raises her voice, and if she ever laid a hand on a child in anger I'd be knocked down with a feather. All *her* so-called valuables was stuff that a family with money would throw away for being out of fashion, with them they'd give it to her as presents and she'd think herself lucky. Rest of it were cheap souvenirs from places she went with them. You know the kind of thing?" She looked at us.

Holmes and I nodded.

"She's a decent sort, don't get me wrong. Walks down to the nearest school half a day a week and teaches the smallest ones for the afternoon. She won't take any money for it, neither. She says her pension's generous and she don't want for nothing. But now and again she tutors some older child as is having a hard time learning. She's good with that, she don't lose her temper or get impatient. Some of them comes back to see her, and I think they honestly like her. She'll take money for teaching *them*, but never has more than one or two of them at a time."

I could imagine the lady. A brown mouse, timid, shy with adults, but children would trust her. For most people she'd engender a careless trust, and a mild liking. People wouldn't be unpleasant to her, unless they were the sort of bully who thrived on her kind, and should they do so before others, there would always be someone to step in on her behalf. Thus she would believe that people were kind, really, and that even bullies would repent in time. Sometimes a woman like that can be dangerous. They refuse to see what was in front of their eyes, and they can be surprisingly obstinate.

Once I was certain all my patient had received was a knock on the head, and that her apparent unconsciousness had been a way to send the police packing, we left her to the ministrations of Miss Darna, who had arrived back from her shopping. There was much exclaiming and anger over what had happened, but we disengaged ourselves and once back at the pony-trap—the pony was found peacefully grazing at the back of the cottage—Holmes spoke thoughtfully.

"Drive to the main cottage, Watson. I think we may be able to stop this persecution of Miss Darna, and if I'm correct I may have ammunition with which to do so once we've talked to Miss Reeves."

That we did. The lady was home, and Holmes, invited to share tea and cake with her, accepted at once for us both. He mentioned the excellence of both tea and comestibles, congratulated her on her good taste, and by degrees drifted into talking of poor Mrs. Hartsford. How unfortunate that she should lose so many charming and valuable items. How fortunate that she was insured. Of course, insurance companies were remarkably unpleasant about paying out. They were very happy to accept your money but far less eager to part with it.

"Oh, I do so agree. Dear Amelie is devastated at her losses, so many lovely things as she had. And the unpleasant way in which Miss Rosewarne behaved, actually threatening to burn her, I could barely believe it, and then to refuse to aid Amelie when she was left with nothing, it was unconscionable. If I had not already paid for this year I might have removed to be with Amelie, as she does so need support in her time of trial. Indeed, could I have afforded to do so I would already have gone to her."

Holmes patiently brought the subject back to insurance companies and we heard of their wickedness, how they would apply arcane formulas to payment so that something worth a great deal to its owner was valued—and paid for by the company—at far less than its real worth. Her words now and again seemed as if she quoted, and we could guess whose words they really were.

"It is iniquitous! That's why ..." She broke off abruptly, and Holmes in a low smooth voice finished her words.

"Why you and Mrs. Hartsford decided to redress the balance, most sensible of you. That way she would not be cheated as they intended. *Your* plan I expect?"

Miss Reeves's thin cheeks showed faint color. "I am not so clever, Mr. Holmes. No, it was dear Amelie's idea, but," she added with some pride. "I helped. I have—I had—some lovely things. A silver tea service, porcelain, and some good jewelry."

"And you let her borrow them," Holmes agreed. "That's what a good friend would do. And of course she would not claim them to be hers, merely allow the company's agent to see them in her suite, and if he was foolish enough to believe everything to be hers and list them on his policy, well, then it merely balanced their plans to cheat your friend if should a time come."

"Exactly." Miss Reeves breathed. "I saw no harm in it. Dear Amelie explained it all to me. She made no claims, told no lies, and after all, it was only fair."

Holmes disengaged us from our credulous hostess shortly thereafter. Once out of the cottage we mounted into the trap and I grinned cheerfully at my friend.

"So that's how it's done? All smoke and mirrors with borrowed valuables, and the insurance company falls for it."

Holmes frowned. "No, Watson. I know insurance agents and their companies as Miss Reeves does not. Amelie Hartsford would have to sign a list of her possessions with a printed clause on the form saying that they were her property before the company agreed insurance. She did not mention that to Miss Reeves, who would have been shocked." His eyes twinkled at me. "That sort of woman is more horrified by a lie than by the thought of cheating an insurance company. And if we can gain verification of that lie, I think that she will repudiate Mrs. Hartsford with speed."

"That would be well," I said seriously. "I dislike the idea of Miss Darna having in her household a woman whose best friend is the sworn enemy of her hostess."

"Nor I, Watson. It is clear to me that Mrs. Hartsford has gathered supporters. Some will continue supporting her even if they learn the truth, others, those who are more honest and clear-sighted, will not. We must endeavor to find the truth."

Which was our next undertaking. We arranged the assistance of a lad at the inn who drove us to the train station—returning to the inn with pony and trap to await our return on an agreed train—while we embarked on a trip to Ampthill, where Mrs. Hartsford's insurance company had its offices.

There Holmes was known and the file was placed before us. Holmes at once took out from that the list of insured items and together we read it. During our conversation with Miss Reeves she had particularized several of her possessions lost in the fire. Putting that together with what had been said about her loan of some items we could make a fair guess which of her items were listed as being the insured possessions of Mrs. Hartsford. More interesting still, the list had been clearly signed by Mrs. Hartsford—below a section of print in which she swore, promised, and avowed, that everything listed herein was her personal property.

"May I have a copy made of this list?" Holmes asked. Making a copy would not take more than half-an-hour, and while we waited we were provided with something to drink. Soon we had a copy of the list in our hands. They had asked no questions but I saw that the copy had been made on an identical form and a note appeared at the bottom saying that the original had been signed by the company's client and in the presence of a witness.

Holmes nodded to the manager. "Thank you, that is most satisfactory." The man's gaze met ours, but he said nothing ushering us out. Once in the open air again I spoke thoughtfully.

"He suspects something."

"He does," Holmes agreed. "However I have done them a service or two over the years and they will leave this in my hands."

We returned to Flitwick by the next train, were met and conveyed to the inn, Holmes vanishing to his room for an hour before dinner. Dinner was excellent, after which we sat talking for some time, followed by a restful night. My last thought was that tomorrow would not be so pleasant.

* * * *

In which I was right. We went first to see Miss Reeves, where we recounted the perfidy of her friend and the betrayal of her trust. We showed her the list and persuading her that we had indeed seen her friend's signature with our own eyes. (Who, I wondered silently, ever saw anything with someone else's eyes?) She wept. Holmes endured it for sufficient time to wring from her a new list, one that detailed the items loaned to her friend. Then leaving her to be comforted by the practical Mrs. Collins, we drove again to the rented home of Mrs. Hartsford.

That lady was a different story. We met with no tears there, only adamant denial. She had not done such a thing. If the list was wrong then it was the fault of the company's agent, for he had misunderstood her. A stupid man, one who did not listen, but perhaps her accent was to blame—*that* became more pronounced on the spot. No? But of course she had not read the list before signing, since she had trusted the man to know his job. Her hands fluttered into the air, her pretty air of feminine helplessness deepened. What would you? She was not a businesswoman. Her husband had done all that sort of thing. She had relied upon him utterly. The English, so used to filling in forms, so understanding of them and the language they used.

Holmes was polite but firm. "Madame, you signed a list claiming valuable possessions that were not, and never had been, yours. We have proof of that. Your signature was witnessed by one who will testify in court, and to the fact that he read you the print on the form, and that verbally you agreed before signing that you both understood what you signed and that all the listed items were your personal property. Because of this the company is not inclined to pay any portion of your claim whatsoever." A statement that produced loud outcry and, finally, tears. "Yes, that is what I said," Holmes said quietly. "However, I have persuaded them to be reasonable." The tears dried as if by magic. "They will pay you what is owed on those possessions that can be shown to have been yours. However, you will also sign a statement saying that you attempted to cheat them, that Miss Reeves did not know what you planned, and that you withdraw all accusations against Miss Rosewarne. Furthermore, as soon as you have your money you will leave this area and not return."

The pretty face twisted into a startling snarl, and I suddenly saw that the lady was not the innocent, helpless, and rather silly woman that she appeared. There was a cunning in her eyes that had not shown before, and the spite and malice of her nature was apparent. "You would ruin me?"

"You planned to do it to others; learn that you are not exempt," my friend said coldly. "You will sign the statement and be safe and paid, or you may refuse, in which case the insurance company has empowered me to immediately lay information before the police. I can be with them inside the hour."

He made as if to leave and she shrieked. "I will sign. Wait, I will sign."

Now I saw what my friend had been doing before dinner the previous evening. He drew an envelope from his pocket and, opening it, produced three sheets of paper covered with his handwriting. "You will sign each one," he said sternly. "Doctor Watson and I will sign as witnesses. One statement shall go to the insurance company, the other to Miss Rosewarne to be held against your continuing your accusations. The third statement merely says that you withdraw all allegations against Miss Rosewarne, that you completely misunderstood the situation and that in reality she saved your life at risk to her own, and that third statement shall go to the police today."

Amelie Hartsford wept, then she broke down completely, pleading through convulsive sobs that she was too distraught to act now, we must return once she had time to consider. Holmes calmly replaced the papers and walked to the door. "As you wish. Watson? How far is it to the nearest police station?"

The lady's pitiful weeping stopped as one turns off a tap and she snarled again. "*Cochon*, I sign. Give me the papers." They were handed over, and she read them meticulously before she signed, even the duplicate that would go to Miss Darna—so much for her ignorance of business—she read, she signed all three, and then all but threw us from the house. As we passed through the front door she screamed a question after us. "When is my money?"

"Inside a week," Holmes informed her, turning to face her. "Were I you, I would be gone in no more than ten days once you have it. Else I may feel it incumbent upon me to show the police the longer statement Miss Darna will shortly receive."

In return we received a look that should have reduced us to ashes before the lady slammed the door.

I climbed into the pony-trap and set our transport in motion. "Whew, Holmes, I can't help but wonder where Hartsford found her, and what *he* was like to have thought her a suitable wife."

"The lady is an efficient actress. Miss Darna never thought her to be more than she seemed. Mrs. Maylon seems never to have suspected either. It took Mrs. Whittle to tell us information of use. And now for the police."

That we did and while I showed nothing of my triumph, keeping a bland expression throughout, it delighted me to see them admit that they now have no reason to suspect Miss Rosewarne of arson, and that she would be left in peace.

"Unless we receive further information against her, of course," the Superintendent said. "You may have persuaded that poor lady to withdraw her complaint, but I don't know that I believe it," With that he left the room in angry strides, his companions looking after him. One turned to me.

"Joe Stokes, Detective Stokes. Don't mind him, sir. He liked the lady, thought her hard-done-by. She comes across as pitiful and a gentlewoman, see? Matt and me, we didn't think it right to be bothering Miss Darna, for she wouldn't do what was claimed, we know that, but he don't come from around here."

I understood their situation and nodded. "He's your superior, and you couldn't refuse to follow him. Don't worry, with this statement in your files he can't cause any trouble."

"Unless someone chooses to make a new complaint," Holmes said as we exited the room. "Mrs. Hartsford dare not appear in the matter, but she still has friends who could be persuaded to cause difficulty. However, we must hope for the best. Now, we shall take this statement to Miss Darna in the morning, and then see the other copy safely into the hands of the company."

Both items were accomplished over the next day, to the delight of the young woman and fervent thanks from the insurance company. She, happy at having her reputation restored to some extent, and they having now to pay out rather less than half the amount originally assessed. With two sufferers satisfied Holmes turned to considering a more full account of the escape of those on the upper floor.

We sought out the two staff that had resided there and, sitting in the pleasant common room in their small cottage, Holmes encouraged them to remember that all they could. The matron's assistant seemed to recall nothing. She stammered, broke off in half-sentences, and stopped altogether after several attempts. Some of their account would undoubtedly be unpleasant and distressing to them, and I was not surprised when—I thought her the more sensible and less emotional of the two—the Matron, Sibyl Dean, touched her companion on the arm to silence her and began her own recollections.

5

She began by looking inquiringly at her assistant, Esther Halpern, who nodded back reluctantly. Matron Dean took a deep breath.

"I must first make a confession. Miss Halpern was not in the main house that night. Her younger sister was ill, and she asked to spend two nights there to care for the children, her sister's husband being away in London. I saw no harm in her absence, however I admit that I allowed her to leave on my own authority and told no one."

Holmes nodded. "I knew she was away, and so will your employer if she ever thinks about it. In her account she noticed Miss Halpern standing in the driveway with a small suitcase. She assumed it contained items which she had saved from the fire. It was not, for she had returned to find the house in flames and did not know what to do."

The matron nodded. "I take responsibility, Mr. Holmes. Once our conversation is over I will go to Miss Rosewarne and admit what I did." She straightened in the chair. "Now, as to what I remember …"

Matron Dean had gone early to bed, she informed us. Everyone else had retired and there was no need for her to remain awake. Miss Darna trusted her to be there when required. It had been a tiring day and she was glad to fall into her bed, and allow herself to swept into dreams of a day out she'd enjoyed as a child. From one dream she moved to another, until they changed. She was at the zoo, something was shrieking, someone was warning her, she was shaken again and again, until, abruptly, she was awake.

"Matron, matron, wake up."

She reached out blindly, caught up the small candlestick by her bed and lit the candle. Bess Touhy stood shivering at her bedside. Matron Dean picked up her bedside clock and looked at the time. It was almost six, but the residents weren't normally up before eight at the earliest.

"Bess, is something wrong?"

"I woke up a short time ago, and I smell smoke." The blind woman's voice had a soft quaver of fear.

Matron Dean sat up and inhaled. Yes, there was a taint on the air. She climbed out of her bed and went to the window. Along the side of the building she could see a red glow. Dear Lord, Bess was right, and the building was on fire! Sibyl Dean had been a nurse for three-quarters of her life. She was trained not to panic, to prioritize. She went to the door and opened it. Smoke drifted past, thickening as she looked. She spoke quietly. She must not alarm anyone more than needs be. There were some who would panic, and panic could kill.

"Bess. Go and wake everyone. Tell them they are to dress quickly, take their handbags, go to the end of the corridor, and wait for me by the fire escape door."

"Should I say there's a fire?"

They'd know that as soon as they opened their doors. Better to be honest. If she told Bess to lie, it would be discovered as soon as they left their suites, and they'd panic the more.

"Yes, tell them there's a small fire down in the kitchen, but we must leave the building to be safe until the fire brigade arrives."

Bess walked confidently out of the room and down the passage. She heard her knocking at the first door, the one by the head of the internal stairs. She heard the door open, and there was a muffled answer, Bess spoke briefly, and could be heard hammering at another door. While she listened to Bess's progress the Matron dressed warmly, stuffed the contents of her handbag into the capacious pockets of her walking-jacket—she might need both hands free—walked out into the corridor and headed for the door at the end , which led onto the fire escape. Thanks be that old Mr. Rosewarne, the present owner's grandfather, had been a pessimist. He'd believed in preparing for the worst, and his cynicism would save lives this morning.

Once at the door, she hesitated. Should she open the door, or would that feed the fire? It was more important her ladies be able to see their way, for in the corridor it was dark still, but with the door open some light would penetrate the gloom. She swung it open and bit back a cry. A smoky haze filled the whole corridor. Bess appeared, walked unerringly to her, slid a hand down the matron's arm, and tugged at her sleeve.

"Some won't come. They're going to wait for the fire brigade or they're packing things they want to bring."

Like Darna Rosewarne, currently downstairs persuading Amelie Hartsford that leaving was more important, the matron was seized with exasperation. She marched back down the corridor, turned the bend that led to the right-side suites, coughed in the smoke and hammered at a door. "This is Matron Dean. Get out here now!" She couldn't make out the reply but it was mutinous. "The building is on fire. Come out and get to the fire escape at once."

No reply. She vacillated. If she entered the room, stood over the woman, made her dress, dragged her to safety, she wasted time she could use in saving others. Under her breath she used words she'd heard her father use, walked to the next door and hammered on the stout wood there. The door opened. Oh, thank heavens for sensible people. The occupant stood there, dressed, handbag over her arm, and walking stick in one hand.

"Come quickly." She led her charge down the corridor to the door and pointed outside. "Go down the fire escape, carefully! Once you're at the ground walk away from the building and wait for me. Do not under any circumstances come back into the building. Do you understand?"

"Yes, matron."

"Then start down now." She patted the thin shoulder. She should give credit where credit was due, as people did better for a few words of praise. "You're a brave, sensible woman, now go and be safe."

A smile lit her charge's lined face at the words, and the thin figure walked towards the stairs leading to the ground. Then Sibyl Dean gathered her courage and walked back into the smoke.

Bess loomed out of the murk, coughing. "I got one more of them ready. Here," her hand took the matron's fingers, leading her confidently. Ahead, a figure waited.

"Come with me. Don't panic, I'll get you out, follow me." The woman obeyed. She saw her to the door, and repeated her instructions. She heard the halting footsteps die away along the old wooden boarding, and a pang of dread hit her. The boarding? Wood burns. If she didn't get out soon herself, she could be trapped. But once again she turned back into the smoke.

Bess approached, her figure wavering. Sibyl Dean coughed, coughed again. Her head swam, and then she couldn't stop coughing. She was doubled over, one hand on a door handle, when Bess reached her.

"I can't get the others to come with me, and Gail isn't answering."

"It's all right, you've done all you can. Get out of the building, Bess. Go now, and leave it to me." The woman disappeared and the matron, eyes streaming from the billowing smoke, coughing shaking her body, turned to the nearest door and beat on it.

"Mrs. Simons, Mrs. Simons? Come out at once." There was no response and she stumbled to another door, the name was different but the message the same: Come now or die. And again, there was no answer. The smoke had become so thick she could no longer see more than a foot or two ahead, but it eddied in the direction of the open door so she followed it, back out into air that was only tainted, not too thick to breathe. She hung on the railing, gasping and choking. Below stood those she'd sent out. The figures wavered, dividing and recombining, four … five … of them? They clustered on the lawn, a small, frightened, group waiting obediently for her; she must go to them.

She turned back to stare into the smoke. She could hear the crackling of flames. Something crashed in the distance and she shivered convulsively. She'd done her best, too, and what would it profit anyone if she died? They'd been warned and they'd chosen not to follow Bess. If they died it was no one's fault but their own. Sick at her decision, but knowing she could do no more, she turned away and started along the fire escape. The iron railing was hot to touch, but she needed to hold on. Anyway, if it hurt, that was her pain to bear. She'd saved half, but behind her three were left to die. As she staggered along the escape and descended the stairs, she mourned those she'd failed to save.

"Three?" I said involuntarily. "But …"

Her tear-filled gaze met mine, guilt clear upon her face. "Yes. I didn't know at the time. It wasn't for hours that I learned she hadn't escaped. I *told* her to get out, but the smoke was so thick I didn't see her go back down the corridor. I couldn't see, I couldn't breathe. But Bess was blind, she didn't need to see and she knew every inch of the building. She went back to try to save her friend, Gail." Tears ran down her face. "They found them in Mrs. Ashworth's bedroom together." Overcome with the memory she sobbed. Miss Halpern put an arm about her and making wordless sounds of consolation.

I did my best. "Dying that way is painless. They wouldn't have felt anything." And half to myself. "Why didn't her friend leave her room?"

The matron looked up and smiled through her tears. "Oh, Mrs. Ashworth was unduly modest, the sort of woman that wouldn't leave her room unless she'd had her wash, donned her corsets, was fully dressed, did the small amount of makeup she allowed herself, and then put on her coat and picked up her handbag. If I know her—and she was a resident for years—she was doing that all the time after Bess knocked on her door and said to leave the building. Bess would have guessed and gone back to hurry her along. Mrs. Ashworth was found lying across the bed. She was ready to leave, all but one shoe. I think she must have sat down to put her shoes on, been overcome and fallen back. Bess found her and tried to get her on her feet. They found Bess lying on the floor by the bed."

She sobbed once, dryly. "I should have gone back. I should have saved them."

Holmes shook his head. "No, all you would have done was to add another death to their numbers. You saved three, to go back would have only meant that three lived and five died on that floor, including yourself."

Her gaze was desperate. "You are certain?"

"I am." His voice was calm, with a quiet certainty.

I saw some of her tension slide away. She had accepted his judgment and it had eased her distress. I leaned towards her. "What happened once you were out of the building? What did you see? Who spoke to you? Did you see Miss Rosewarne or talk to Mrs. Hartsford?"

"Oh, Mrs. Hartsford, yes, she spoke to me, some rigmarole about Miss Rosewarne beating and threatening her to make her leave. I told the silly woman anything that had been done had been to save her. I had no time to listen to that nonsense. I got Mrs. Maylon, Mrs. Collins, and my three to the staff cottage, made them a pot of tea and left them there. The Hartsford woman was coming to join them as I left."

She looked down, absent-mindedly brushing her hand across the soft fabric of the chair. "I found the firemen, and told them there were people still in the building. They said it was now too dangerous to go in, and they were sorry but anyone inside the building would be dead. I saw Miss Halpen coming down the drive towards me and I went to tell her of the fire. Once I had done so I looked back and saw Miss Rosewarne sitting on the lawn by the house. Then I felt faint. I'm told I collapsed."

"Smoke inhalation, most probably," I informed her. "You were breathing that smoke for some time while you rescued those women. It was fortunate you recovered. I have known people to die from it, despite being safe outside."

She nodded, but said nothing. Miss Halpen looked at us. "Could I have saved those we lost?" she asked. "If I'd been there and wakened when the fire started? Could I have saved them?"

I could not tell her the truth—that it was likely. Two women, both of whom knew the building, kept their heads, and had authority the residents would have accepted, might well have saved more. But how could I say that? I shook my head slowly and told her another truth—one that was equally possible.

"I dislike putting it this way, Miss Halpen, but you are older. Those older succumb to smoke inhalation more quickly, and you are lighter of build and shorter in height. The smaller the body-size, the faster the smoke would overcome you. Miss Rosewarne gave me to understand that you lived on the other side of the upper floor?" She agreed.

I met her gaze steadily. "That was where the smoke was thickest and it covered that area first. The suites either side of your room held one resident each. From their positions, they barely even woke, but died from smoke inhalation. That could have been your fate had you been there. No, your absence meant another person saved."

Her fingers twisted together. "You believe that?"

"I do."

Holmes stood. "Go on from now, and do not look back." He spoke as if giving an order, and they accepted the command. We left the cottage and once free of any listeners Holmes pursed his lips. "A sad business, yet some things become clear."

"Not to me," I thought, and inquired what he meant.

"The fire started in the vicinity of the downstairs office that much is certain. Those who died all died from smoke inhalation, none from violence or the flame, for all the bodies are unmarked."

"So it was an accident," I said with satisfaction. "We know the fire could not have been set, as the experts investigated and are sure of that."

"Yet they cannot say how the fire began," Holmes reminded me.

"Oh, well. It's like illnesses, there are times one cannot say what caused it," I assured him. "We can only say that the patient died. Here we have a fire, but no one could wish the residents harm." I laughed at the idea. "Who would wish to hurt a group of harmless old ladies, Holmes? No. The fire was an accident, and while awful, it is—as you said to the women just now—something that must be moved beyond."

"Miss Rosewarne is not of that opinion, nor is Doctor Blascourt."

I was disconcerted. I had overlooked the accusations made against Miss Rosewarne and I admitted it. "Yes. Then we must prove her innocence in some other way since we cannot uncover how the fire started. Should we not talk to others, the firemen perhaps?"

"Let us find out who was on the scene first, apart from those in the main house and cottages."

That turned out to be the neighbor on the south side of the estate. Mrs. Hemble was a widow, a lady only just turned fifty, fit, healthy, and the possessor of a most untypical dog, along with a pleasant, commodious house set in landscaped grounds, with four servants. She often woke before the others and walked with the dog. She also had a number of modern conveniences installed.

"Yes, it was one of those mornings when I woke early. I decided to take Hero for a walk." At the sound of his name the dog roused, saw he was not required, and fell asleep again. He was a mastiff of some type I believed, solid, powerful, and although he appeared amiable, I would not have liked to approach his owner with anything but benign intentions. That mild look would be deceptive in such a case, I was certain.

"We walked along the road for some distance. Hero began snuffling about, and I watched him He turned towards Darna's place and when I looked, I saw smoke. I hurried to where I could see between the trees—there is a gap where you can catch a glimpse of the house. The smoke came from the house and did not look like smoke from an ordinary fire.

I have excellent long-sight, and I walked in a direct line across the grass, between the trees, towards the house."

She frowned. "I did not wish to raise a false alarm, and the fire appeared to be coming from the other side of the building. If I walked to where I could see better it would take me as much as twenty-five minutes whereas, if I went back, I could be home in no more than ten. A fire can move rapidly, and if I waited I could endanger those inside. Hero stared at the smoke and barked. I took that as a suggestion, returned home as quickly as I could, and sent the gardener's boy to the police who said they would call out the fire brigade." She smiled in seeming embarrassment.

"Not wishing to appear vulgarly curious, I remained in my house once I made the call, sending my maid out to inquire. She returned to say that the main house was indeed on fire." She clasped her hands together. "It was awful, gentlemen. I feared that lives could be lost, and I was right. And since then there has been worse yet." He eyes gleamed in what I thought to be vicarious enjoyment. "There is talk that Darna is to blame in some way. One of the residents there accused her of making threats, and it is said that she actually attacked this woman."

"I would not believe all you hear," Holmes said.

"Oh, no, no, of course not. I am merely mentioning what is said. I would not believe it for a moment. Darna Rosewarne is a lady, even if her family was in trade. I have lived next door to her for years and never heard her raise her voice. It is impossible that she would attack a woman so much older. And why?"

"Perhaps," I said dryly, disliking that eager gleam in her eyes, "the woman would not rouse herself when Miss Darna wished to get her out of a burning building and save her life. Perhaps the woman wished to risk her life by gathering heavy, unwieldy, and valueless possessions before sitting by, waiting for a servant to come and carry them out for her. Perhaps her foolish behavior risked the lives of other, more helpless women in the building, who might otherwise be saved by Miss Darna?"

"Oh!" The gleam brightened in her eyes, and the lady drew in a deep breath. "I *see*. That is reasonable, quite understandable, and the woman is French after all. They do so tend to panic."

Giving me an inscrutable look Holmes rose. "If you can tell us nothing more, madam?"

She could not and we left her to ponder my suggestions. I had little doubt that shortly after we were gone she would be with friends, sharing what I had said, while they gossiped and enlarged on what they would now see as information.

Once clear of the house I apologized. "I'm sorry, Holmes, I should not have spoken as I did, but it infuriated me to hear Miss Darna so defamed. You are right, we must find some proof that she could not have been responsible for the fire."

"The trouble, Watson, is not that people are saying she was responsible for the fire, but that they say she was responsible for the servants, and that it was some careless act by one of them that began the fire."

I was downcast. "How could we prove that that did not occur?"

"As yet I do not know. But we must persevere, Watson."

To those ends I went alone to the corner shop near the inn and fell into talk with the proprietor. Such people tend to know much of their customers, and once I had advised him on his lumbago, examined his wife's sore arm, and provided a salve that she immediately declared to have relived much of the pain, he was eager to aid me.

"Aye, Miss Darna had more servants at the main house. After the fire they left their jobs and the district, too. It were the gossip, you see. There was a lot of talk, and they said it weren't nice." He snorted. "Better talk and keep a good job is what I say. I don't know where most of them went since they didn't get mail. But I do know about Bill Lewes. He comes from Harlington, only a couple of miles away. His dad's been ill, see? He do have a shop there and Bill's running it now. Mind you, he made sure to get a reference before he went, in case his dad got well again and took back the business, he *said*."

I obtained Bill Lewes's address and asked two final questions. "Do you know if the police spoke to him?"

"Nay, worked outside, did Bill, never in the house. Why'd he know anything?"

"Do you think he could have been up late that night?"

The proprietor threw back his head and laughed. "I make no doubt he was. Bill Lewes is a poacher and a good one. All of us knew around here. Well, Miss Darna doesn't have shooting on her place so she mightn't care. But there's pheasants, rabbits, hares, partridges and such to be had. Bill, he's good at snaring and I wouldn't take my oath that whatever he had were all got on her land neither."

He leaned closer and lowered his voice. "He used to sell rabbits to the inn, and a few hares and pheasants, an' maybe a partridge or two to some of the gentry when they was having friends to dinner. I always thought that were why he scarpered so fast He didn't want the police asking too many questions, and then that new man, not knowing about him, he thought Bill'd know nothing and didn't chase him."

I returned with that to Holmes, who showed his interest. "And you have his direction, well then, let us go and find this Mr. Lewes. A man who was out and about the estate may have seen or heard something useful."

Bill Lewes—short, stocky, brown hair, gray eyes, and in his early forties as I would have guessed—knew a number of things. Initially none of them appeared to be of use to us until Holmes got him onto the subject of walking about the estate late at night. Not poaching, as Holmes explained carefully, but as a man who did not sleep well, making Bill Lewes understand that we accepted such as his reason and that it could also be used as an innocent explanation at need.

"Ar, that's so, I do like to walk at night," he agreed. "Place is quiet, peaceful like. Nobody sees or hears me, and I sees things, as you say."

"Naturally you'd glance into the main house windows when you pass it," Holmes suggested. "You'd see anyone still awake and moving about there, any of those in the staff cottage, too."

"Ar, I do. Only natural, ain't it?"

"And that night, the night of the fire, was anyone awake in any of the houses?"

He chuckled. "Ar, I saw Miz Darna, she come home with that driver as drives for her friends other side of Flitwick. I looked at the moon and I can tell time from that. She don't usually stay out so late. I sees her through the window making herself a cup o' tea, and I sees her carry a lamp to her room. Couldn't see what she did there, kitchen window curtains is thin and you stand back, you can see thorough them. But rest of the house, all you can see is the light moving about. How-some-ever I'd say she went to bed, 'cos she didn't come back, and light went out. I were gone after that, taking a walk like you say, off down along a bit."

From that I understood that he had been poaching elsewhere.

Holmes nodded. "When did you return home?"

Bill Lewes cogitated. "Reckon it would have been along about four, mebbe a bit later. I'd walked a fair piece and I were tired. I stowed what I'd brought back where I always does and went to bed. I were woken by the fire, and I says to myself, Bill, they ain't going to want you underfoot while there's the police and all running about, so I went back to sleep." He grinned at us. "Got what I had put by that next night and took them to my customers. I worked in the main house, man of all work, that was me. I guessed I wouldn't be wanted with the house being gone and all, so I waited a couple o' days and gave in my notice proper. Told Miss Darna as how dad were ill and I were needed and I could see I didn't have no job here no more. She give me a good reference, and a week's extra pay. She's all right, she is."

"While you were walking on her land," Holmes asked gently. "Did you see or hear anybody else about? Someone who might have been there about the time you were leaving the estate and walking elsewhere. Someone who was being quiet, too?"

Bill Lewes nodded. "Reckon I might have. Would have been around one, or a bit after that. Like I says, I don't have no watch but I'd reckon that to be about the time. I heard someone about, right enough, didn't see nothing, just someone walking quiet. They come past me up the drive to the main house." He grinned, his eyes snapping with mirth. "Thought as how it were that sweetheart of Janet's, I did. But like I say, I didn't see him, just someone walking slow and careful and it's mortal dark under them trees. I couldn't tell you no more if'n you paid me."

6

I caught Holmes's eye and he indicated that I should say nothing. We moved on to speaking of Mr. Lewes's father's shop and discussed that for some minutes before Holmes worked his way back to the person who had been prowling about Rosewarne that night.

"You are a man who knows people, Mr. Lewes. You could see nothing of this person, but you could hear; a man who customarily walks abroad at night learns to perceive through his hearing. Already you know that this person was moving cautiously. Think back: did he move heavily, or was he light of foot? Did he move as if he knew the ground, or more carefully, feeling his way? Did you hear him stumble in the dark, and if so, did he speak?"

Bill Lewes grunted. "Ar, I see what you mean, sir. No, he didn't never trip over nothing. He were light of weight mebbe, now I thinks back. Could be he were young and not so heavy, but being slow an' careful how he put each foot down, aye, now I think back. That could be so."

"So, the trespasser could have been young and even light of weight, but being careful to walk slowly and softly so as to make no sound?"

Lewes nodded slowly.

"Would you say that he was familiar at all with the drive?" asked Holmes.

"I'd guess him to be familiar in a general sort of way with the lay of the land. Like one that's come to the place a few times, mebbe a number of visits, but only in daylight, never at night. He walked easy for the direction that is, not for his footing with it being so dark."

"Ah," Holmes said, and I knew he had something. "Thank you, Mr. Lewes."

We made our farewells and took the train back to Flitwick, Holmes being silent the entire journey. Something that Lewes said had given Holmes cause to reflect and had provided him with a clue. Knowing his desire at such times to be left to think in peace without foolish chatter, I said nothing, but watched the countryside pass by and pondered a few questions of my own. However, it was my friend who broke the silence as we alighted from the train and began the companionable walk back to our inn.

"Watson, it could be dangerous, but tomorrow I intend to walk over what remains of the main house at Rosewarne."

I could not see how walking over the ruins could be dangerous, unless he expected some portion of the upper floor to fall in on us, so I looked at him in query. Holmes nodded in response to my silent question.

"I say dangerous, because I do not propose merely to walk the lower floor, but to ascend the fire escape and traverse the upper floor as well. As you heard earlier, some of the boys from town have been doing this before they were chased away, and it may be that there is evidence remaining to be uncovered there. If that is so it must be found before the building is demolished."

I allowed him to see not only my worry for his safety but also my understanding that he might be correct. "I'll bring my medical bag, Holmes," was all I said.

* * * *

Mid-morning the next day we repaired to the ruins and stood looking up at them. They were a sorry sight, and I feared for my friend. The beams that had been the ceiling for the lower floor were in some places burned almost half-way through. It was true that in several corners the beams were intact, and even a corner of upper flooring remained here and there, where a piece of furniture shielded it from the flames. Once they reached that floor, the flames seem to have mostly travelled sideways rather than upwards from below.

Mostly the furniture that could be seen from the ground was smallish chests of drawers, chests—I saw a small tin trunk—or something similar. The occupants of the rooms would not have had time to retrieve many possessions out of such containers. The beds had fallen through and now formed a part of the rubble, but in two places I saw that they yet remained above us. One of them even retained all its bedding.

"Holmes?" He turned to listen. "Should you find anything personal, would you drop it down to me?"

"If I can, Watson."

I settled myself to watch with trepidation while Holmes climbed the fire escape and circled as much of the building's upper floor as the fire escape allowed. He paused at the area where even patches of the fire escape's boarding had burned or charred and commented on that. The day was clear, windless, and all about us was quiet so that I could hear him without any need for him to raise his voice.

"The fire burned hottest here, Watson. It is directly above the office, which would appear to lend some credence to the firemen's theories."

I glanced at the office. It was a shell, everything within gone, yet oddly enough the outer wall was still intact and I could trace the path of the fire in an inverted triangle, black against the white boards of the building's outer armor. I supposed that would be so since the open fire within the room had been by the inner wall. The fire, if started by a coal there, would have burned directly upwards.

Holmes was moving back along the escape talking to me as he examined the building. "This must have been the room of Bess Touhy, and here, next to her would have been that of Mrs. Simons. I think we should discover the direction of that lady and speak to her, too. Here is the chimney that comes from the office, and the floor there is particularly destroyed towards the centre of the room. Hmmm, interesting."

"What is it, Holmes?"

"It indicates that the fire was not confined within the chimney."

"Of course not," I protested. "If the floor in the office was afire, the flames would hardly have been confined to the chimney."

"That is true," Holmes agreed and I felt a small sense of satisfaction.

He moved on, pausing to look into the devastated suites through their broken gaping windows. I followed him, keeping pace below as he walked around the outside of the building, watching where he stepped, fearful that at any time the escape might give way where fire had weakened it. It did not, and apart from that burned section directly above the office, another charred portion nearby, and a missing area above the kitchen and pantry where it may be supposed that a fire escape was not considered to be required, he successfully circumnavigated almost the entire structure. Back at the head of the stairs he spoke thoughtfully.

"I shall make an attempt to enter the suite there." It was the suite he had identified as having been that of a Mrs. Simons and was one of those where portions of the floor survived. The remaining corner held a low chest of drawers and a partly burned Persian carpet. A pity it had been so spoiled.

Holmes walked slowly out along the beam, testing each foothold and slowly transferring his weight once he was sure the beam would hold. He advanced steadily while below I gazed up, hoping that he would be safe. He reached the chest and moved to stand on a crossbeam that did not bear the chest's weight before stretching across to open a drawer.

"Stand by, Watson,. I will drop the contents, which appear to be remarkably intact."

I received three photo albums, a hand-knitted cardigan lavish with fancy stitches, and a bundle of letters. Holmes opened the next drawer, and added to that a knitted jacket—clearly from the same hand—a large flat case of some sort, a bundle of silk scarves, a quantity of good quality leather gloves, and belts of various materials. The chest, being small, had been placed on a raised stand. I thought that to be it, but Holmes was considering the drawers with an intent glower.

"Ah, yes." He swooped on the drawers and pulled both right out, dropping them as he groped inside the back of the chest. His hand emerged with three slim diaries bound in black leather. He dove again and produced another three. He dropped the six items to me and continued his prowling while I half-opened the case to ascertain its contents. They were a mixture of photographs, sketches, and beneath all of those, a small miniature painting on ivory in a silver case. The painting was of a charmingly attractive girl with a wistful air, bright blue eyes, and auburn curls. An inscription upon the back read 'Esme, from her proud father on the occasion of her eighteenth birthday.'

I resumed watching Holmes as he moved on. At another three suites he found items of possible value or something personal that the owner might with to have returned. These were dropped to me and I placed them safely to one side. At the last he vanished from my sight and I waited nervously until he hailed me.

"Over here, Watson, and stand by."

I did so, to receive, to my astonishment, a flat case, partly open, which contained bank notes. A considerable amount, as I judged. To that he added a jewelry case, locked, and only somewhat singed.

"I shall come down now, Watson. I think we have everything that is of value or use." He did so, stepping nimbly down the fire escape stairs and joining me where I stood with my small heap of salvage.

I smiled at my friend. "It was extraordinarily good of you to take such risks, Holmes. The owners have cause to be deeply grateful to you."

A slight tinge of red showed on his cheekbones. "They will be the means by which we may approach them. No one refuses to answer intrusive questions if the one who asks has done them a signal service."

I refrained from commenting that some of the items had come from the suites of those who had died, and I have never found the dead to be so grateful. Holmes has a kinder heart than he wishes anyone to know, nor does he like reference to such things, so I remained silent, merely gathering up the heap of items and placing them carefully into a large box I had brought with me in hopes of such a bounty.

Usefully, the box was of the type with rope handles so we were easily able to carry it to a secluded corner of the grounds, where Holmes examined the items one by one. The knitted jacket was an attractive garment, originally cream wool—now blackened in places—with a chocolate brown trim and bone buttons, each beautifully carved as a curled and sleeping cat. I groped in the pockets and came up with a small lace handkerchief, half a shoelace, and a card. I turned that over.

"'J. Mortimer Fitzbane, solicitor at law. Wills, conveyances, and contracts.'" I glanced up at my friend. "The lady may have been making a will."

"Possible," was his reply. "Look at this, Watson." He had opened the case with the banknotes. It was of fine leather, and had buttons down the overlapping edge; to fasten the case, one wound a length of attached string around the buttons. The case contained fifty-pound bank notes, which Holmes counted, revealing the sum of five hundred pounds. I stared.

"That is a considerable sum, Holmes. Who had that suite?"

"A Mrs. Clermont. The jewelry case came from the suite next to hers, originally the residence of Mrs. Dumfries. They are the other two ladies who escaped the fire." He drew the jewelry case to him, produced a tiny skeleton key, unlocked the case and lifted the lid displaying a series of small drawers which, when opened in turn, contained various attractive and valuable sets of gold and silver ornaments set with precious stones.

"Holmes, they must be worth a considerable amount. Look: emeralds, rubies, oh, those are just amethysts, but here are opals."

"I wonder," Holmes said thoughtfully. "I wonder if they are insured."

* * * *

Really, there are times when I sigh for human nature. The jewels were indeed insured—falsely, as emeralds and rubies—which falsity my friend had seen at once. The owner hoped they would be either stolen or covered over and lost when the building was razed, since far from being of great value, they were garnets only, and of a value far less than the sum for which they were insured. I had not known before that green garnets existed, but I was later told that not only is it so, but also that they can be more attractive than emeralds, since many are of a brighter, clearer color.

The owner, Mrs. Dumfries, insisted that she had not known what they were. She protested that the man sent to assess the items before issuing the policy had not known either. If that were so, how could she be blamed for her ignorance when a professional could not tell? Whether that was true, there was no way of knowing since the original valuation had taken place more than thirty years ago, and the person in question had been dead for almost nine years. So while the lady received her jewels and could only now reinsure them at the minor sum they were worth, she was also safe from prosecution. The insurance company later complained bitterly to us that at times they had the impression the whole of humanity was out to cheat them. A criticism that, from my own observations over time, I could not entirely deny.

* * * *

Mrs. Clermont, sharing a small house on the other side of Flitwick with her friend Mrs. Dumfries, proved to be an American lady of formidable aspect, and who received her banknotes with equanimity. Holmes asked a question after handing her the case and she stared at him.

"I do not know what business it is of yours, but I *do* keep such sums about me normally, yes. Should I have wished on a whim to shop, to buy some item offered me, I like to have the money available on the instant. No, I do *not* regard it as dangerous. I had a suite on the upper floor, and anyone wishing to reach that would have to pass a number of other such suites, mine being at the far end of the building. I had an excellent lock on the door, and I had other—ah—protection besides." She glared at his next question. "No, nor did I feel in such danger as Violet Stacy. The matron had a key to my suite in case of emergency, unlabeled and secure, but her assistant also knew where to find it."

She smiled, a quite unpleasant look, combining smugness and a sort of threat. "As I said, sir, I have other protection should someone gain entrance to my suite."

Holmes pronounced two short words and her glare intensified.

"Precisely, although I do not understand how it is that you know."

"An impression of it was left. Where I found that you will know."

"I see. This remains none of your business however, and I will bid you both good day."

She swept out of the room and I turned to my friend. "*What* other protection, Holmes?"

"She has a gun. Small, some sort of lady's weapon I should think. In America they are freely for sale. She is American, wealthy, and it is probable that she regularly returns to her country to see friends and family. The shipping label on a partially burned case in her rooms suggests so."

"And it left an impression?"

"Under the pillow corner," he said, adding that he also found a drop of oil of the type used to clean a gun.

I tut-tutted. "Really, Holmes, is that legal? What if she forgets to lock her door and someone does enter? Not necessarily a burglar, but a friend seeking some headache remedy, or to ask her a question. If she shoots them, think of the uproar there would be. And what if they die? Really, I think Miss Darna or the authorities should be informed of this."

Holmes shrugged. "She is rich, Watson, with friends and influence. She has only to apply to the Chief Constable to be given a license, and with that in her hands she may have as many weapons as she wishes."

(Unhappily he was right about that. I mentioned Mrs. Clermont's pistol to Miss Darna, who saw the same pitfalls I had and was horrified that the weapon had been in her house. Knowing too the lady who currently rented Mrs. Clermont and her friend their house, passed the information on to the police. Accosted by them, Mrs. Clermont mentioned a number of powerful friends, applied as Holmes had expected to the Chief Constable, and once some pressure had been applied, received her license. I feel sorry for any burglar, as I have since heard that the lady is an experienced and accurate shot.)

Once we were back at the inn and sitting to eat luncheon, I appealed to Holmes. "Whom else should we see now? What about returning Mrs. Simons's belongings this afternoon? After all, she lives close to the estate."

"And moreover, she would wish to have her diaries returned," Holmes said with a faint smile.

I glanced at him, suddenly suspicious at his tone. "I suppose she would."

"I should," Holmes agreed, "had I spied for years on those with whom I resided, and written down all their actions, follies, peccadilloes, and failings."

"Did she do so?" I was disgusted. "Well, in that case, I am sure she would wish them returned."

"Quite so, Watson, but I think that firstly we shall read them carefully all through. There may be information to be gleaned."

I protested but was overborne, and after we had eaten we retired to the common room between our bedrooms and sat down to do as he suggested.

I admit that I became engrossed as I read. Had the lady turned her energies to writing horrid novels I am certain she would have had great success. The diaries had begun five years earlier when she came to live on the Rosewarne estate. Mrs. Simons was a widow, not wealthy, but well to do enough that she had all she desired—her desires not running to such items as exotic jewelry, several fur coats, or an automobile. However, she was alone in the world, her husband having died shortly before she moved here. They had no children, nor were there other close relatives remaining.

On a number of occasions she had reflected upon her will in the diaries—ah, that explained the lawyer's card—and in the end, a copy included in the diary stated that all she owned would be left to two charities and .... I blinked at the name.

"Holmes, have you seen this?"

He read the passage. "I had not, but while it may provide a motive, the money is, I believe, insufficient to entice most people of the class involved, to murder. Moreover, Mrs. Simons was *not* murdered, and yet could have been with great ease under the circumstances that existed at the time—had the beneficiary known of the will. So I discount that. Either she does not know, or she does not consider murder a reasonable response."

"Do you think we should mention it?"

"To whom, Watson? To Mrs. Simons? And explain that we have been reading her private diaries? To Matron Dean? And tell her that a grateful resident intends to leave her a third portion of all that she possesses? To what end? All you would achieve is embarrassment all around, and perhaps the changing of the will. No, I think it wise to let sleeping dogs lie in this case. Mrs. Simons is entitled to leave any amount she wishes to anyone she deems a suitable recipient, or do you think the matron unworthy?"

I did not.

I continued to read, finding as I progressed that the writer too had known of Mrs. Clermont's gun, and the falsity of Mrs. Dumfries's jewelry. I was then informed of what I had *not* known: that Violet Stacy terrorized her family, that Gail Ashworth borrowed small amounts from some of the residents and if asked for their return insisted blankly she had received nothing, that the writer suspected that Bess Touhy shoplifted now and again to gain small items she needed and could not afford or which she gave to other residents as Christmas or birthday presents (it would take a brave shopkeeper to accost a genteel blind woman if he even suspected) and then, to my startled eyes, that the writer suspected Mrs. Collins had murdered her—Louise Collins's—husband.

"Holmes!"

He looked up and mutely I held out the diary, indicating that accusation with a forefinger. Holmes read it, and while he showed nothing I think that even he was slightly surprised.

"Surely it can't be true?" I protested once he glanced up again. "I mean, if there had been any suspicions the police would have investigated. And what of the children? A beloved father dies under suspicious circumstances and they say nothing? It is inconceivable."

Holmes turned over several pages, seeking, I thought for Mrs. Collins's name again. After a time he frowned. "From Miss Darna's description of the lady's circumstances, Mrs. Collins's husband died ten years ago and she still mourns his death. There were two children, a boy and a girl, both of whom have been married many years, and there are half-grown grandchildren. Mrs. Collins remains on excellent terms with her family and one or the other of them drops in any time they are in the area, with all of them coming to see her at Christmas. It is quite possible the lady is a murderess, but if so, her family know nothing of it. Either that or he was a brute, his family were well rid of him, and all agreed to that."

"You think so?"

"I do not know. I think that we shall hold Mrs. Simons's diaries until we can look into this accusation. We can go now and give Miss Darna the other items to return to their owner, not mentioning the diaries. The owner will not wish to ask about them, I suspect, hoping them destroyed in the fire or as yet undiscovered. In the morning, Watson, we can take the train to London. Mrs. Collins, before she moved here, resided with her husband in Finchley. Let us find any newspaper account of her husband's death, and then we may ask around the neighbors, should the accounts give rise to any questions."

I smiled. "Yes, it is surprising what neighbors hear and remember."

So instead of seeing Mrs. Simons, we spent the afternoon instead with Miss Darna, giving her the possessions and then quietly interrogating her as to what was known about, firstly Mrs. Simons, and secondly about Mrs. Collins. On both she could give us information—some of which shed considerable light on the diaries.

At a soft knock on the door we look up. Louise Collins asked our pardon for interrupting, but she had a question for Miss Darna. After receiving an answer, she continued. "And have you come to any conclusion, Mr. Holmes? Was this awful fire an accident? But how could it have been? I was in and out of the house all that previous day, and I swear that the office fire was never lit. The coroner was sure that the servants were lying, but Mrs. Maylon agrees with me it was never used. We passed the doorway on a number of occasions, that day and the one before, and had the fire been alight on either day we can only swear that we would have seen it. I tell you that the whole thing is incomprehensible to me."

Holmes nodded. "I do not believe that the office fire was lit that day at least," he said firmly. "I am developing a theory, which if it can be proven, will exonerate all here. I shall say nothing as yet, but do not lose hope."

We left the ladies smiling and returned to the inn again for our dinner—an excellent meal of steak, baked potatoes with rich gravy, and side dishes of fresh green peas and baby carrots. The dessert was a mouth-watering apple pie with cream and a jug of hot custard. I made a very good meal before going to bed happily replete and entirely at peace with myself. Also—Holmes had a theory; he said so, and I knew what he meant: he knew the perpetrator now, and waited only for proof with which to convince others.

7

In the morning we left at ten to see Mrs. Simons. We'd been advised not to go earlier as the lady was, by inclination, a late riser, and if we annoyed her by appearing before she had had her breakfast she would be less inclined to speak to us. We knocked on her door at half past that hour and she graciously permitted us entrance.

"Darna said you would be calling at some time today. I apologize, gentlemen, for my dishabille, I have but just risen from the breakfast table."

I gave a slight bow rather than a hearty handshake. "Ah, but you look charming. That shade of rose becomes you."

For which effort I received a sardonic look from my friend and a vague smile of approval from Mrs. Simons.

"If you will seat yourself in my parlor I will go up to change." And taking two paces to a further doorway she called out. "Mavis, morning tea in the parlor at once, two gentleman and myself. The silver service." She smiled at us again and disappeared up a set of stairs to the left side of the hallway.

We went obediently to the parlor, whose open door made the location plain, sat down, and waited.

Holmes regarded me. "Not necessary, perhaps, but the lady did seem to appreciate it."

"I've had patients of her type before. They respond better and have more confidence in a doctor who appears to have had wider experience."

"I see."

I felt that I had struck the right note and was pleased at my acumen. I had long since found that the air of a man who has travelled tends to make some patients more comfortable; they feel that they are dealing with a man who knows what he is about, more so than a doctor who had not merely remained in England, but one who had not stirred from his own county. It is just the suggestion of a man of the world, and they appreciate it.

Mrs. Simons entered, now clad in a lilac gown with a necklace, broach, and bracelet of amethyst and silver. We stood, and I thought though Holmes might sometimes sneer at my failure to observe, that jewelry told me a great deal—as it undoubtedly informed him. The lady was quite wealthy, but chose to wear jewelry that was delicate and inexpensive; items that suited her and that she liked, rather than a more vulgar and expensive look. I saw Holmes indeed appreciated that and it told me another thing. The lady was her own person, slave to no fashion, and would go her own way for all that she seemed rather feather-headed and a trifle lazy in her habit of sleeping late.

She nodded and her words reinforced our impressions. "Gentlemen, you need not introduce yourselves. Darna said that I may repose confidence in you and that I should be frank in my replies. You were initially called in by Dr. Blascourt to discover the truth of the Rosewarne fire, I believe?" Holmes inclined his head. "Yes. And as one of those who survived it, and as one who had lived in the house since it was established, I daresay you have a number of questions for me?"

This time we both nodded. She sat, disposing her gown about her.

We sat as well and Holmes leaned forward. "Tell me how you came to the house, if you will."

"I married young, to an older gentlemen whom I genuinely esteemed," Mrs. Simons said with composure. "He had no great wish for children and nor did I, so we travelled extensively, and even when after twenty years he became less able to enjoy living abroad we still wandered Britain, staying where and as we fancied. He had inherited considerable wealth, and further inherited from two older relatives. We lived as we wished, travelled as we pleased, and enjoyed life until his death twelve years ago."

She looked down and turned her bracelet about her wrist. "My husband died, as I have said. We were in England at the time, staying in London, and I grieved alone. However, staying in the hotel was an elderly man with a young girl, his grand-daughter. They took compassion on me and I was permitted to take the child about the city, thus easing my sorrow while showing some else their first experiences of the places I knew and loved. Despite the fact that I was older than one and younger than the other, we became good friends. I moved to this town when they returned here, staying almost a year before I took up my travels again. We corresponded frequently, and on news of the death of Darna's grandfather I returned to her at once."

She continued to play with the bracelet, turning it around and around. "I was apprised then that there was little money remaining to the family, and that Darna could be forced to sell a portion of the estate to pay the taxes and the urgently needed repairs of the main house. Rather than see this happen I paid the taxes, and gave Darna advice. Together we decided that her removal to one of the two guest cottages would allow the main house to become a place where, when converted to suites, she might lease to women like myself, who could afford to pay for a comfortable home, servants and meals provided."

She looked at us squarely for the first time and I noted that the vague and fluffy appearance concealed two very sharp blue eyes—that were not at *all* vague. I felt a small sense of embarrassment; she was not one to feel the need for the manner I had initially adopted.

She saw that and nodded. "Don't bother about it, Doctor. Now, to continue, I stayed with Darna while she called in an architect, and once we were satisfied with the plans she had the suites prepared. They were empty, you understand. Those who would live there brought their own furniture and ornaments. There were twelve suites, some smaller, some more spacious, and they were leased by the year at an amount accordingly. Darna repaid me simply by providing one of the suites to me without charge, and I can tell you that the loan I had made was in a fair way to being paid back. Another few years would have seen it entirely repaid, and her estate free of other smaller debts besides."

"How long would that have taken?" Holmes asked.

"A further three years."

"So when the police suggest that the lady may have caused the fire as a means of enriching herself, they would be wrong?"

Mrs. Simons snorted. "If they suggest anything of the sort they will answer for it. Yes, I heard that they were considering an arrest. They'd have caught cold at it, did they do so—as I understand they would have, had you two not come upon the scene. However, I have good lawyers and if the police had been so imprudent, they'd have regretted it. But what can you do? I could hardly call upon that idiot of a Superintendent and tell him to take no precipitate action. He'd have thought it some attempt at intimidation and arrested her immediately to show such an attempt had failed."

"That night, can you tell me of your own experiences during the fire?" Holmes requested. "To do so may be distressing, but the more information I have the easier may be the solution."

Mrs. Simons nodded. She sat silent, and we could see that she was returning her memory to the early hours of that day in which she had wakened to the smell of smoke, and the frantic calling of a friend.

* * * *

Esme Simons slept well, but she had always been quick to wake at need and it was so that morning. She heard through her dreams the sudden sound of voices, footsteps, and then a beating on her door. She recognized the voice that called her name as that of Bess Touhy, a pleasant woman who managed very well about the large house despite having been blind for many years. But why would Bess be waking her at this hour? She glanced at the clock as she rolled over; it showed an hour at which she would still have two or three hours of sleep. The voice came again and then the door opened.

"Esme, Esme, are you awake?"

"I am now," was the acerbic reply. Esme Simons never liked to wake early. The response made certain that she not only came fully awake in a breath, but that she was galvanized into action.

"The house is on fire. Get up, get dressed, and get out."

Bess wasn't wasting time on circumlocutions. She'd delivered information and directives in a dozen words and now Esme saw her turn, one hand sliding along the wall, and depart, while seconds later through the open door she heard the delivery of that same recital to the occupant in the next suite down the corridor.

Esme stared at the doorway and saw a wisp of smoke float by. It looked as if Bess's information was correct and the directives sensible. She stood, walked to her wardrobe, selected a warm, comfortable frock that was easy to don, added underwear and shoes and dressed quickly but without the kind of panicky haste that makes fingers fumble at their tasks. She walked to the half-open door, noted the increasing amount of smoke in the corridor. Some minutes yet, but none to waste. She went to her safe and retrieved money and several sets of inexpensive jewelry . No great value, but she would regret its loss.

She looked about her suite; there sat her larger shopping handbag. She picked it up, dropped the money and jewelry inside, as well as other papers from the safe, added the bedside carriage clock—a cherished gift from her husband—the miniature she'd had painted of him soon after their marriage, and which stood on a small gold stand by the clock, and made a final scan of her rooms. There was little that could not be replaced by spending money. She'd be sorry to lose the painting over the fireplace, but she wasn't prepared to risk her life by attempting to drag a four foot by three foot painting the length of the corridor and down a fire escape in the teeth of flames. What was more … yes, she could hear the flames cracking under her floor now.

She moved to the window and opened it sufficiently far to look out. Flames leapt past her face and she drew back swiftly. In that one glance she had seen that the entire wall from the ground up was ablaze. She'd thought to climb out the window and walk along the fire escape, but that was obviously too dangerous. And the fire would have closed off the inside stairs as well. She'd have to go along the corridor and through the door at the end. She seized her good winter coat and scarf from the wardrobe, donned the coat—wool didn't burn as quickly as other materials—and wound her scarf over her nose and mouth. Handbag in hand, she walked steadily out into the smoke-filled passage, turned left, and with one hand on the wall to guide her, Esme Simons made her way to safety.

* * * *

She completed her account and fell silent, waiting for our questions.

"You never saw the matron?" asked Holmes.

"I heard her voice three or perhaps four times while I was dressing and traversing the corridor. The first time she was farther past my suite, the other times she was on the far side. I heard her as I left the house. The house is—or rather was—built in a horseshoe on the upper floor. Both ends meet in a wider section of the corridor at the door to the fire-escape. The suites are placed in a line that curves around and back the other way to that door. There are four on my side: that of the matron, then Bess's, mine, and the fourth suite on that side. Continuing around the bend, that is taken up by service rooms for linen and bedding, a small two-roomed suite used by Miss Halpern, a large room containing minor furniture and supplies for the matron and with a laundry chute between the rooms. The remaining five suites run along the other side of the horseshoe."

It was fortunate no one had thought to try the laundry chute, for they would have landed right in the midst of the worst part of the fire. The chute came out by the foot of the stairs, just across from the office door, and by the time most residents had roused, the stairs had, or were about to, collapse, being eaten out below by the flames.

A question occurred to me. "Who else did you see or hear before you left the house?"

"Bess. She pushed past me as I reached the outer door and I wanted to know why she was still in the building. I said that she should leave." Her eyes glistened with unshed tears. "She said that Gail wasn't answering the door. She was going back to make certain that she was out, and if not, to guide her. She sounded proud. She was the only one who couldn't get lost in the smoke. She'd get Gail out, and any others who had got turned around. That was the last I saw of her."

And it explained where Bess's body had been found, I knew. Gail Ashworth heard the call of fire, awakened, smelled smoke, and begun to dress hastily, however between her terror and the sudden exertion she died from a massive heart attack before she had quite finished dressing. Leaving her, like Cinderella, sans a single shoe. Bess reached her friend, sat on the edge of the bed, thinking perhaps that Gail Ashworth had fainted, and Bess had then been overcome by smoke. She had been found, once the fire was extinguished, slumped on the floor by her friend. The bed had been by the window and on the less-damaged side of the house. Firemen gained access by the fire escape to remove the two bodies. Others from that floor who died had to be disinterred from the ground floor rubble, for the floor had given way, precipitating the bodies into the debris below.

After a thorough examination of the bodies, it looked probable all had died either from a heart attack as had Mrs. Ashworth, or from smoke inhalation. In one case where the medical decision was dubious, the coroner had chosen to give that verdict rather than distress her relatives with the possibility that the woman had been burned alive.

"What do you intend to do now, Mrs. Simons?" I was curious. "Will you stay here?"

She looked pensive. "Darna did consider trying to rebuild the main house and finding new tenants. I have convinced her that it would be a waste. She took in the women because she had that white elephant of a building eating up everything she had. Now that it's gone, she doesn't need tenants. I suggested that she renovate the larger guest cottage as her own home, while retaining, if she wishes, the smaller cottage for the staff. Mrs. Maylon, Mrs. Collins, and Miss Reeves could continue to occupy the other guest cottage, if they wish."

"What are your own plans?" Holmes remarked.

"Oh, Darna and I have discussed that. If she enlarges the cottage in which she and Mary Whittle reside, she will add a separate suite there for me. That way she will be able to complete paying her loan, and still have an income from the other three women. She will require fewer staff, as well."

"And what of Doctor Blascourt?" Holmes inquired.

Esme Simons was briefly silent before she spoke. "He will doubtless make up his own mind, as will Darna." There was an odd note in her voice that I could not identify, although I thought that Holmes could.

"Yes, one last thing before we depart, Mrs. Simons. I presume that you kept a record of the residents for the benefit of Miss Darna. Should any break the law too blatantly she would have warning and could refuse a renewal of their lease, removing them from the estate before the police became involved."

The lady was composed. "I did. I presume if you know that, you found the diaries?" I nodded when she looked at me inquiringly. "I had money in the venture, and had a right to ensure it was not imperiled. I made notes of everything I overheard or saw or that others mentioned to me. It has been the saving of our undertaking on other occasions." There was again that hint of something in her voice.

Holmes sat up and looked at her keenly. "If I mentioned your name to my brother, would he vouch for you?"

Esme Simons laughed but made no reply. Holmes stood and I quickly followed. Mrs. Simons ushered us out, shutting the door behind us with a soft click. Once we were out of earshot I spun on my heel.

"Holmes! You think her to have been some sort of spy for Mycroft?"

His lips curved up in mild amusement. "She and her husband went everywhere, did you not hear her say so? They visited many countries, had a wide circle of acquaintances, friends in diplomatic service, and she is a woman who could make servants like—and trust—her, too. No, not a spy, Watson. I think she and her husband did as she has done here: they listened, noticed, talked to others, and overheard gossip and chatter. They boiled that information into some well-considered suggestions that were passed on to where they would do the most good."

* * * *

I may say that some time after this case was done and we were back in London, Mycroft, when applied to, confirmed Holmes's suspicions. Mrs. Simons and her husband had been two of his most useful people. They did not visit dark and doubtful streets, wave guns at villains, or leap about over walls burgling suspicious houses; they merely listened.

"They were superb at putting two and two together and coming up with a solid piece of information—and still more often with often excellent suggestions as to seven or eight possibilities. They travelled all over Europe and had friends or made them in a host of odd corners of the world. There was that air about them; he played the bluff English gentleman, not too intelligent but always completely trustworthy, protector of his vague, good-hearted wife from those who would take advantage of her kindness. She was just a nice woman, always ready to listen to a sad story and help out if she could—and he would allow it. I may add that between them they could get by in nine languages."

Mycroft grinned. "She was the brains of the pair. He told me once that he was sure she'd married him because of the sort of life he'd offered. 'All those younger men wanting to cosset and keep her safe at home. She was made for what she does, she saw I'd accept that, and that I had a ready-made life of it that was much to her liking for her to step into. She married me for that, we made a great team, and neither of us ever regretted it.'"

Holmes nodded. "Now she practices on the neighbors."

"Maybe she does," Mycroft said seriously. "But if at any time she comes to you with a tale, I'd advise you to listen. She's a very shrewd woman."

I thought it unlikely our paths would ever cross again once this case was done, but Holmes agreed with the suggestion. We went on our way after that, catching a cab back to Baker Street where Holmes sat by the fireplace considering a new monograph, and I went to consult a medical book while considering an old patient with an obscure respiratory problem.

* * * *

But long before that and back at the inn we talked over Mrs. Simon's diaries and revelations. "A spy," I said in some awe. "She and her husband were spies."

"*Not* spies, Watson. They *listened*."

"To international intrigue, to other spies, and no doubt they foiled plots against Britain."

My friend smiled at me. "Maybe they did. Now I have a case of my own to solve."

"Yes, of course. You took a copy of the diary items about the inhabitants of that house. Should we perhaps investigate the backgrounds of those Mrs. Simons flagged as criminal or unpleasant?"

Holmes put his fingers together in a steeple while he considered. "Yes, if you can spare the time?" I nodded. "Well, then. I would like you, if you will, to investigate the accusations that Mrs. Stacy terrorized her family, and that Bess Touhy shoplifted. Both women lived in Ampthill until they removed to the Rosewarne estate, and that should be convenient for you. I intend to investigate the suggestion that Mrs. Collins murdered her husband."

"Yes," I said thoughtfully. "I wondered why they came *here*. Why didn't they stay with their families?"

Holmes looked cynical. "Maybe their families didn't want them. Both women appeared to have sufficient money to live here, and that is one of the inquiries I wish you to make. Delicately, Watson, delicately. But see if you can find out how much money they had. Was there property, valuable jewelry, or other items of significance? Did anyone stand to inherit who was in great and immediate need?"

I met his gaze soberly. "Then you *do* believe that the fire was *not* accidental. It was set, and whoever set it killed five people." I was outraged. "Murder. Did someone set it for money, not caring how many others died in a particularly horrible way? Holmes, find this person, I want to see them in the dock and paying for the lives they took so casually."

His face was serious. "Then go and ask your questions, Watson, while I ask mine elsewhere."

"Ah yes," I said. "I suppose a woman who murders her husband might be callous enough to set a fire, not caring whom it killed. But why?"

"Perhaps she knew of the diaries," Holmes suggested.

"And if she did, she might believe that to destroy both diaries and writer would silence that knowledge. Yes, well, Holmes. I'll catch a morning train for Ampthill, but how am I to introduce myself, how do I explain why and by whose authority I am asking questions?"

Holmes produced five calling cards, each bearing the name of the Metropolitan and Counties Insurance Company. "Use these. Say that you are making inquiries on behalf of the company, you being a semi-retired doctor and related to one of the major shareholders. This shareholder suspects that the fire may have been set by a resident, and finding the police are making no headway, is determined to have certain events checked by his own agent."

"Which events?" I asked.

"That the fire began within the house, and that so many died on the upper floor. By the way, your relation is named Manfred Gilbert."

"And if my taking of his name in vain comes to Mr. Gilbert's ears?"

"It won't. He is in Spain and goes from there to Brussels. He will not return for another five weeks or longer."

I nodded. I was a temporary, acting, unpaid agent of the Insurance Company, related to a far-travelling suspicious and determined shareholder, and as usual, Holmes had the answers while the questions remained mine. I went to bed that night impressing the tale upon my memory and hoping that when the time came I would forget none of it and stumble over nothing—particularly not Mr. Manfred Gilbert, unexpectedly returned from the continent, despite Holmes's assurances.

8

I chose to investigate Mrs. Violet Stacy first. Mrs. Simons had written in her diaries that the woman had abused her family, her daughter in particular, but neither had she spared her grandchildren. Before catching the train to Ampthill, I had a quiet discussion with Louise Collins. Her suite was next door to Mrs. Stacy's and she might have overheard the occasional word. She had certainly done that and more, as she assured me, and she agreed with the summation of Mrs. Stacy's character.

"You wouldn't have thought it to look at her. A nice-looking woman, always neat and well-dressed, politely-spoken to most, always a please and thank-you for her acquaintances. However, I lived next to her and I can tell you, Doctor, that it was far from the truth where her family was concerned. I don't know if she believed that family were owed nothing, or she didn't need to restrain herself around family. But many is the time I saw her daughter leave in tears. Violet apparently thought that because she couldn't hear my guests or myself through the wall, no one could hear her."

"But she was audible?"

Mrs. Collins made a small moue of disgust. "Only too much so. The parlors of our two suites were against each other with the bedrooms on the far sides. That gives us two rooms between the bedrooms, and on her side there was the office, on mine that short hall to the outer side door. For normal conversation, the wall between parlors is quite sufficient. But Violet was moderately deaf. She talked loudly anyhow, and if she was angry she raised her voice to a level where, was I sitting close to the dividing wall, I could hear most of what she said, entirely too *much* of what she said."

"And she was unpleasant to her family?"

"Unpleasant! My dear Doctor, she was a monster. I heard her abuse her daughter, calling her names and accusing her of such things I'm certain were untrue. She referred to her son-in-law as a thief and an adulterer, claiming he had affairs with half of Ampthill—something I do not believe, since I have friends there and there is no gossip of it. And you know people, Doctor. Had he done so there most assuredly would have been gossip. She said that her grandson was a congenital idiot and her granddaughter a whore. She claimed that their house was a den of iniquity and a pigsty. I requested more than once that she lower her voice when entertaining her family. She told me that I shouldn't be listening, and on my pointing out that when her voice was raised I couldn't avoid hearing, she said that in that case I should either go to my bedroom, or take a long walk."

"What did you do?" I asked with interest.

"I wasn't about to change my habits for her. If she wished to bruit her opinions abroad that was her choice. I stayed in my parlor when I wished to be there, and if I had to hear her giving her family what she referred to as a piece of her mind, then I listened shamelessly. Those who do not wish to be overheard can stay silent." She smiled. "Something Violet found impossible to do."

I grinned at her. "How true *do* you think her allegations?"

"I have lived a long time, and I have a reasonable ability to sum up those I meet. I would say that Violet's daughter is an inoffensive woman, that her mother was a bully and a brute, and that if I'd been the daughter,

I couldn't have persuaded my mother to live in another town fast enough. I saw the grandchildren many times, and if Violet's comments on them were true I'd be greatly surprised. As for the son-in-law's character, as I said there was no gossip about him, and had he been half the adulterer she named him, the town would have buzzed over it. I never saw him in person."

"What?" I said in surprise. "He never visited?"

"Not to my knowledge. And if that was how she treated her blood-kin, I can only imagine how she spoke to *him*, so that I was never surprised he didn't want to see her. No, Doctor, she was a termagant and a wholly unpleasant woman so far as her family was concerned. And it wasn't as if they'd get anything out of her."

Mentally I came to attention at that. "Oh? I would have thought her to have had some money to live here."

"She had money," Mrs. Collins informed me. "Not a huge amount, but sufficient to live on comfortably and renew her lease here each year. But if what she shouted at them regularly was true, it was all left to others. They weren't getting a penny piece, she told them, since her daughter had married to disoblige her."

"I see," I said. "Thank you."

Louise Collins smiled. "I'm happy to help. I suppose while you are at Ampthill you'll also visit Bess's family?"

I nodded, wondering what made her leap to that supposition, but she said nothing more and I took my leave.

The train was on time and I was in Ampthill by late morning. I hired a cab to take me to the home of Violet Stacy's family and when greeted, I allowed them the impression that I was making inquiries over the amount of Rosewarne estate's insurance. Once I was sitting with Violet's daughter and son-in law—Mr. and Mrs. Sanderson—I asked the expected questions. Had the servants been careful, what did they know of the fireplace in the office next door to their mother's suite, and other such inquiries until they had relaxed. Then I asked about Violet's opinions of the house and servants.

The grandchildren—Michael and Violet (after her grandmother, I supposed) but addressed as Vee by her family—had joined us and the boy, a lad of some thirteen years, winced. "She said the servants were all thieves and sluts, the owner was a bigger thief and a liar, and she didn't know who was worse." His voice was already deepening, and he was a broad-shouldered lad. In another few years he would be a formidable man, should any dare to cross him.

His mother demurred. "That was only her way of talking, she didn't mean anything by it."

"Oh, didn't she?" said Michael.

His father looked at him and the boy fell silent. Mr. Sanderson turned to me.

"I'll make the situation clear to you, sir. My mother-in law was a spiteful, vicious, evil-minded, backbiting old … woman. She was so unpleasant that anyone, once they came to know her well, ceased at once to have communion with her. She hated me because I courted Amy here." His smile at his wife was both kind and tender. "She forced Amy to stop seeing me, saying that I was only after one thing like all men, and that once I'd had what I wanted I'd be gone. Amy stood out against her for a while, but she was underage and her mother had her way."

He gave me a triumphant stare. "What she never knew was that Amy's friends helped her. We still saw each other in private, and as soon as my girl was of age she packed up everything she wanted, and when her mother was out for an hour at her church, I called and took up Amy and her possessions. We went straight away to the minister and by the time her mother caught up to us we were wed."

"How did she not know the banns had been called?"

His grin stretched from ear to ear. "Special license, and I go to a different church. Our minister knew the circumstances, and he agreed there was no reason we shouldn't marry." He chuckled. "We had all Amy's friends there, too. Old witch tried to take it to court. Said that there was money coming to my girl and she wanted the marriage annulled so's I couldn't get my hands on it. Silly old besom thought that the court would take her word for it. She couldn't show any money *was* coming, apart from whatever she might choose to leave and the court said she could leave that anywhere she wished. So she claimed the marriage should be annulled anyhow," his face darkened. "Said it had never been consummated."

His wife burst out laughing. "She caught cold on that score as well. I'd seen the midwife only three days beforehand and I'd asked her to be in court. I knew my mother. I handed up a certificate the midwife'd written saying that I was, well, you know … and a note with it to say that the writer was in court and could be asked. Judge called her up and spoke privately, then he dismissed mother and her case. Said he'd had inquiries made beforehand and I'd been of an age to wed, that my man had a good job and a decent house for me, and that all spoke well of him. He advised mother to mend her fences else she'd have no family." She giggled. "Went out of the court like a thundercloud, she did, and knowing she'd have to pay her lawyer."

I found that I, too, was smiling. I could see the scene, and I was rapidly coming to the conclusion that everything said of Violet Stacy was true.

"If I may ask, how was it that she moved to Rosewarne and you began visiting her there? It's none of my business, but you make her so vivid to my mind."

They were happily enough to explain.

"Mother was getting on. She was healthy enough, but her deafness was getting worse, and she couldn't keep servants."

That didn't surprise me, I thought.

She continued. "I heard about Rosewarne though a friend of mine whose godmother lived there, a Mrs. Merrimin." I recalled the name as being one of the women that had died on the upper floor. "I heard all about it, how nice it was, how all the residents were friendly, and the food was good. They provided servants, too, so mother wouldn't have to worry."

"And you mentioned it to her?"

The son-in-law guffawed. "No, that's wouldn't have served. Amy let her overhear us talking to someone about the place, and Amy said she couldn't understand how anyone would let family live away like that. When Violet spoke of it to us *we* said it wasn't to be thought of, that it was too far away, and that we couldn't visit more than every now and again. She told us her life was her own, and she'd make her own decisions, thank you very much. We stood out against the idea, so without telling us she sold her house, leased a suite, and moved there, thinking she went against us. We knew all about it from the start, soon as she put the house up for sale, but we kept dropping hints against the idea so she wouldn't change her mind."

Mrs. Sanderson flushed. "I suppose it was wicked, but she was so pleased, thinking she'd put one over on us. She wrote to us once she was settled in saying what she'd done and that we should come to visit every week if we wanted to inherit a penny."

Her husband scowled. "I never went near the old besom, but Amy would go, not for the money, we knew well enough we'd never see that, but Amy would have it that it was her duty. She went every week, and sometimes the children went, too."

The girl, some fifteen years of age, spoke for the first time, her voice passionate. "I wasn't going again. I told mum. The last time I was there grandmother said things about me," the tide of red suffused her neck and face. "She said, she said … anyhow, mum was in tears when we left and cried all night. I said I wasn't ever going to see grandmother again, that she was a wicked old … and none of us loved her." She looked at me.

"No one even *liked* her. I bet she didn't have any friends in that place either." She fell silent.

Amy looked sadly at her. "Dear, she was an old woman. She said things she didn't mean, and we have to forgive her now she's gone."

"Why?" her son asked logically. "She was a cow." His parents drew in shocked breaths. "She *was!*" And turning to his mother. "You didn't hear the last thing she said to me. I'm not repeating it, but it wasn't, well, nobody decent would even *think* such a thing. She hated everyone and everyone hated her. Look at how she treated you, taking you to court and stuff, not leaving you anything. I'm *glad* she's dead and I hope she's in Hell where she belongs. And I wasn't going to see her again, either."

His mother winced. I could see that the lad had told only the truth, and that her sadness was her inability to gainsay it. Mr. Sanderson stood up.

"I apologize for my son. Not that I don't agree with him, but it isn't decent to air dirty linen before visitors. If we've answered all your questions?"

I said that they had, expressed my gratitude for their hospitality, and Mr. Sanderson seeing me out, spoke quietly on the doorstep. "Amy tried all her life to do something that old witch would approve. Nothing she did was ever good enough. If a lord offered for Amy, it would have to be a prince for the old woman to be happy. My girl tried all her life to win a word of praise and never one did she get. I'm glad the old woman is gone and that's a fact." He stepped inside and shut the door, while I walked down the path and continued along the road.

Towards the end of it and before I turned off, I glanced back to see a form that looked uncommonly like that of Holmes walking behind me. I halted until he came up with me and I saw that it was indeed my friend.

"Holmes, what are you doing here?"

"Taking advantage of ,your engaging all the attention of the Sandersons, Watson. I wished to have a look inside their garden shed, and in other corners of their property."

"Did you find anything?"

"A few garden tools, an old bee-smoker, and four broken chairs," Holmes noted.

I assumed he had particularly noticed the bee-smoker, being, as he was, fond of bees, and knowledgeable on their lives. I said so but he shrugged as if uninterested in the subject. "It's an old type. However I must leave you here, Watson." And with that, he did so, leaving me to turn my steps to the nearest shop once I was out of his sight and there fell into conversation there, mentioning that I was with the company that had insured the Rosewarne property and was visiting some of the families of those who had died. The elderly proprietor exclaimed and told me much about the Sandersons that I had already heard, as well as providing some additional information.

"A serious lad he were, one that knew his own mind. There's too many as throws their coin about, wasting it on horses and cards. Not young Wintin, no, he saved what he could, his ma died young, her only child he was, his dad went when the boy was twenty-four. It was then he married, his dad leaving him the house and Wintin having a good job."

I asked what he did, to be told that he had started working with the blacksmith, but as the man's work became more involved with automobiles, Wintin had taken over that side of it and finally bought into the business. He concluded: "Aye, he don't make a great play of it, but that house's his, and I reckon he does well enough with the automobiles. Anyways, both his children are still going to school, and no man who's short of money would do that."

I strolled the length of the street, before hailing a cab, and being driven to the Touhy home, while still considering the case of the Sandersons. Violet Stacy had been—to say the least—an unpleasant and bitter old woman. But I saw no reason why any of her family should be involved in her death. She left them nothing, the son-in-law had not seen her in years, the grandchildren were refusing to see her again, and the daughter saw her only out of duty. They could have walked away from the woman at any time, and there was no financial benefit to be gained from her death. I should see if I could discover who *were* her beneficiaries.

I walked far enough to discover an inn that provided luncheon upon request. After finishing a ploughman's lunch of new-made bread, a sharp local cheese, and an excellent ale, brewed by the innkeeper himself, I had a second glass and ordered the blackberry pie with cream, recommended to me by a fellow diner.

Comfortably replete I dallied a while, reading a copy of *The Ampthill and Flitwick Adviser*. As I read I learned such interesting facts as the birth of a two-headed chicken—on a farm to the west of Ampthill, the reporter having seen it for himself and could verify the story—the injuries to a local citizen imprudent enough to step into the road without looking both ways—run over by a trader's van—and a sale—disposal of the estate of the deceased, the well-known, distinguished Mr. Percival Lampton, late of Ampthill parish. Reflecting as a medical man on the chicken, its peculiarities and possible length of life, I hailed a cab and gave the address that I had noted on a piece of paper.

I alighted from the cab at the Touhy's front gate—her daughter had married a second cousin and retained the family name—paused to admire the size and excellent condition of the house, as well as the small but well landscaped grounds about it, walked up the path and tapped on the door. It was opened by a small boy who eyed me in alarm.

"Mum, mum, there's a strange man."

His mother arrived posthaste. She was dressed modestly but her clothing was of good quality, and I began to think that Bess's family were more well-to-do than had been known.

"Yes, sir, was there some way in which I may help?"

I gave her the tale Holmes had provided along with one of the Insurance Company's cards, and was invited in to sit down, offered a cup of tea, a plate of fresh scones, and the lady and the small boy waited to see what I would do or say next. I felt like some rarity being watched by visitors to a zoological garden. I gathered my wits about me, however, and explained the situation further. Her answers gained me no new knowledge and I decided on a bold stroke.

"Your mother—I do hesitate to say this, and have no wish to wound you—but it was known that she did not always pay for the goods she took."

To my amazement the woman who'd introduced herself as Liz - after her mother's oldest friend, as she explained—burst out laughing. "Bless you, sir. I knew that. It was a failing of hers from the time she went blind." She settled into her chair and looked across at her son. "Billy, go and play in your room." Her voice was loving but allowing no refusal, and he went. She turned back to me and nodded decisively.

"My mother always had very poor sight. She didn't marry because of it until she was thirty and found that my father didn't care. Two years after she married my father though, it got worse and they were told that in a few years more she would be completely blind. It was hereditary, the doctor said, just luck that I don't have it too and my sons are fine as well. That was why I'm their only child. Dad wouldn't take another chance. Not that he ever blamed my mother. He loved her and said the two of us were enough for any man. Mum went completely blind nearly seven years later, when I was eight, and it was then she began taking small items. I went shopping with her after the first few times and I'd keep watch; if she picked something up I'd pay for it quietly. All the shopkeepers knew."

"But as they were paid they didn't mind," I said as light dawned. "And you did the same at Flitwick. Did they send you invoices?"

"That's it." She smiled. "It was better for everyone that way. They'd have been embarrassed, you see, calling the police on a blind woman. This way they were paid, and nothing was said. I knew everything she took, as in some ways she didn't hide what she did. Gifts for friends and our family, always small items, nothing really valuable, and it wasn't as if we didn't have the money. Shopkeepers knew that, so they let it be."

She smiled lovingly at a portrait over the mantelpiece. It showed a pleasant-faced woman in her fifties, dressed in a blue gown with a darker blue knitted shawl about her shoulders, and the same loving smile on her face.

Margery Touhy looked at me again. "She was a good mother to me, and kind to her friends. She went to live at the Rosewarne place because she said she was making trouble for me." I looked the question. "It wasn't true." She hesitated. "Although it was, in a way." She pointed in the direction of where the boy had gone. "That's my younger son. The other one is nine and at school. But when he was small, as soon as he started to crawl and move his toys about, mother …" She halted and I saw what she meant.

"A blind person needs everything about them to be in the same place," I said quietly. "Nothing must be moved or they fall over it, but you cannot tell a baby not to crawl about, you can't always be certain that he hasn't left a toy underfoot."

"That's it. Once she fell over him. She hurt her knee and he cried and cried because she'd trodden on his toys and broken two. I think he thought she did it on purpose. We lived with her so I could take care of her, but she saw things straight. She said there was money and I had my own family now, so that we should buy a house that suited us. She'd sell her house and live where her oldest friend lived already. Gail would help her learn the building, and mum would have a lovely suite."

"So she and Mrs. Ashworth were already friends?"

"They'd been at school together. Gail thought the world of mum and mum loved her. Whenever we went to see mum we'd stop in to visit Gail, too." Her face twisted. "I miss my mother so much, and Gail as well. She was like family."

"Were you ever told how they were found?" I asked gently. She shook her head, and I told her how Mrs. Simons had last seen Bess going to make sure her friend was out of the building. How Gail had been found dead on her bed from a heart attack, Bess lying on the floor beside her, and I emphasized that neither died from the flames.

"Your mother could find her way despite the thick smoke that hindered the others," I said. 'She went back into that Hell of smoke and fire to save her friend and was overcome. But I have no doubt that if Gail Ashworth had been alive when your mother found her, she'd have got her out safely."

Bess's daughter wept then, and I talked casually of her mother's suite, the Rosewarne estate, and some of the other inhabitants there until her grief was under control again. She wiped her face with a handkerchief and sat straighter.

"Thank you, Doctor. The coroner didn't tell us that. He just said that mother had been found dead after the fire. We thought she was in her own rooms. It makes it a little better to know she died trying to save Gail. They never said that about the fire either, and we wondered. It was awful to think she might have died ... that way."

I stood. "Thank you for your assistance in answering my questions. You've been most helpful." And as an after-thought I asked, "Did Mrs. Ashworth have any family?"

Margery Touhy smiled through watery eyes. "No, she was married but her husband was a soldier, and he died when they were both young. Gail left her estate to mum, and mum left everything to me. We saw Gail was buried decently in our own family plot."

I took my leave of her after that, musing as I headed for the train, how different people could be. Violet Stacy had been loathed by anyone who knew her well, although morally she was probably upright and honest. Bess was a shoplifter, a condition I thought developed as a sort of compensation for her handicap. She resented her blindness and stole minor items to show that blind or not, she was as clever as any. Yet she, who had ignored the deadly dangers of a burning building, died trying to save her oldest friend. The Bible verse "greater love hath no man than this, that a man lay down his life for his friend," (something I already knew applied to women as well) came to mind, and I was in a sober turn of mind on my return to the inn.

Holmes met me in the lobby with the news that dinner was available should I wish to dine early, and that he was of the opinion that Louise Collins *had* killed her husband. Before I could do more than nod in agreement to the dinner and open my mouth to ask about his comment, he disappeared upstairs, shutting the door to his room once he was within, and leaving me to follow him up the staircase to my own room to seek out a bath, for train travel on these small local lines leaves one excessively grimy.

I enjoyed my bath in good heart. If the lady had murdered her husband, who was to say that if someone discovered that fact she would not have considered the discoverer's death a small price to pay for safety from prosecution, even the gallows? Refreshed by quantities of soap and hot water, I positively bounded downstairs to the dining room, joined there by Holmes. I had chosen the table farthest from the others, in a corner at the back of the room, and outside earshot of anyone else.

Upon my friend sitting I opened my mouth—and found the waiter at my elbow. I dismissed him as soon as dinner had been placed before us, looked at Holmes, opened my mouth eagerly—and found the wine waiter offering us the wine list. Holmes, eyeing me with amusement, gave an order—a pleasant Beaujolais—and we suffered all of the usual nonsense of tasting and approving, before we could be rid of the man.

Once he was vanished into the kitchen fastness I looked about. We were alone. Excellent. I leaned forward. "Now Holmes, tell me all. Were there any suspicions of murder at the time? How is it that her daughters did not learn what she had done? And if they did know, how is it that they are still on such good terms with her? Was the man such a monster that they too approved?"

9

Holmes contemplated my questions and, once he had swallowed, shook his head. "I said that she had killed her husband, not that he was murdered. A fine distinction, but one that I feel applies on this occasion."

I stared in some disappointment. "An accident, then?"

"No, it was deliberate, but I would not describe it as murder, Watson. Tell me, you have seen a man die of stomach cancer?"

I had. It was a terrible death, as all the painkillers we could prescribe could not overcome the agony towards the end. I had seen patients bite lips and tongue until the blood ran, trying to hold in their screams before wife and children. Strong men have begged for death, and when they were cared for at home I had heard quiet reports from colleagues that often the sufferer's death had been ... facilitated—and not always by family.

"I have seen it, Holmes. Is that what Mr. Collins had?"

"It was."

The story he told me was typical in some ways, unusual in others.

Vincent Collins, known as "Vin" to his friends, had fallen, first into friendship with Louise when they were children, and as they matured, friendship had become a deep, abiding love. It was regarded as an unequal match. Her family had money, his were poor farmers. She was intelligent, apparently cold-hearted, and logical, he was a man whose heart was worn on his sleeve, and while intelligent, intuition more than logic drove his actions. It didn't matter. Louise had money of her own, a legacy from her father's mother after whom she'd been named. Vincent inherited his parent's small farm as the only child. They married young, her determination over-riding her parents' initial refusal. The marriage worked, and her money expanded and revitalized the land while his warm and more open nature leavened her darkness.

As he told the story Holmes's voice was neutral, and I was unable to tell if he approved of the events.

"They met at nine when her brother brought him home after school. Everyone I spoke to agreed, the boy took one look at her and that was it. She showed nothing, save to those who knew her well. It was as if she accepted that they were bound together, 'old souls' one woman said to me, two that had loved in another lifetime and found each other again in this life. For all they were so different, they understood each other. They married at eighteen, despite all her parents could do to dissuade her, and went to live on his parents' farm. She spent an inheritance she received five years later to buy up sufficient additional land to make the farm a much better proposition, and modernizing it at the same time. It began to bring in a real profit, and these days it's the showplace of the area."

"Who runs it now?" I questioned.

"Oddly enough, Watson, the elder daughter. The younger went to University, learned science, and works in Edinburgh. The elder daughter wanted the farm. She married another farmer, second son of a tenant farmer, and they have three children, two of them girls. The younger daughter has one child, another girl—the family seems to run more to girls—and to girls who are farmers, since I am told that the farm management will most likely be inherited by the older girl in due course."

I considered that. "How will they divide the farm when Mrs. Collins dies?"

"I'm told that she has money from her parents, an amount that is laid aside from what the farm brings her. That will go to her younger daughter. What they will do in her grandchildren's generation I have no idea.

"But to return to Vincent Collins. He developed stomach cancer when he was seventy-three. They operated and he apparently recovered. The cancer returned three years later, and again they operated. The operation appeared to be a success for a year until the cancer recurred. Upon this third operation being performed they discovered that Collins was riddled with the disease, and there was nothing to be done."

I nodded slowly. I'd had a patient myself with that progression. The initial operation seemed to have removed the bulk of the cancer, but with a deep-seated portion of it having been missed, it had grown back several years later and attacked faster and more vigorously. "So they brought him home?"

"Yes. I'm told that he said if he had to die, he'd do it in his own bed, looking over his own land. Since all they could do for him now was to apply pain relief, the hospital and doctors accepted his demand. He returned home at the start of that autumn and within weeks the pain relief was no longer effective. He was receiving larger and larger doses and sleeping much of the time, waking in agony, receiving the relief, only for it to wear off before another dose was due. The doctor attending had been their family doctor and a friend for many years, and it is generally accepted that he was providing larger and more frequent amounts of the relief than was generally approved."

I knew that it might have not only been for friendship only. It is hard for a compassionate doctor to watch that agony and not feel that it should be relieved. The person is dying; why should they die in such a way when addiction is no worry? I could guess at the rest of the story. Louise Collins was cool-headed and practical. Once she had seen that the drugs ceased to alleviate her husband's pain, she would have acted. I asked Holmes to finish the story.

"Local talk has it that she obtained several doses of greater concentration and called the family, telling them Vincent was dying, and that he was unlikely to last another twenty-four hours. They gathered, said their farewells, and left the couple alone together. Sometime during the night he died. She had earlier called in a second doctor for another opinion—which was that the man was dying and nothing could be done for him. Prior to her husband's death, she had obtained a certificate permitting cremation, and the next morning she had Mr. Collins laid on a pyre on the farm and the body was burned. Her family agreed that it was likely what he would have wanted. The ashes were interred in the farm's private graveyard. By the time the authorities heard what had been done, it was too late. I am told they were annoyed."

I shouted with laughter. "I'm sure they were, Holmes. But that woman is a match for anyone. She had the cremation certificate, she had the opinion of two doctors—I suppose the family friend signed the death certificate—and while it is becoming more rare, burial in a plot on private family land is not yet so uncommon. The amateur cremation was, but we both know how she'd have dealt with official complaints. And with the body destroyed, what could be said or done?" I answered that myself. "Nothing. Did the authorities try to bring charges?"

Holmes's eyes twinkled. "They did. As you surmise, one of illegal cremation. And as you also surmise, the lady looked distressed and asked in what way she had erred. She had the written opinion of two doctors that her husband was dying from cancer, she had a legitimate order for cremation, and she had a listed private cemetery for the internment. If she had not been legally permitted to cremate her husband's remains, why had no one told her of it?"

"Because it never occurred to anyone that she'd do it," I chortled. "It isn't exactly what one would expect."

"Quite so. In the end it was clear to the police and officialdom that while they could charge her, they would find it almost impossible to obtain a conviction. If they did manage to convict, she would most probably escape with a small fine for what would be seen as a technical offence. So they dropped the charge quietly, and let things be. She mourned for half a year, then packed her belongings and moved to a suite on the Rosewarne estate. She arrived when the building became available for such leases and, as her family had known Miss Darna's for some time, Mrs. Collins was informed early and given her choice of suites. We know which one she selected."

He frowned. "I heard other whispers and gossip. They said that now and again she sees things. As you know, Watson, I do not believe in such claims. Those who are supposedly psychic are merely people who subconsciously notice more than most. Mrs. Collins observes events and things about her. She puts two and two together, comes to a conclusion, and calls it intuition. It is only that she is one of those who acts upon it."

I said nothing. On the whole I thought him to be right, but after sharing many of my friend's cases I too had learned not to generalize.

* * * *

I met Miss Darna the morning following Holmes's disclosures. I had breakfasted early, and was taking a stroll in the village. She was shopping, the matron at her side. The lady and I paused to speak, while Matron Dean continued into the shop. Some impulse made me ask a question.

"Did you know Vincent Collins?"

"That was a terrible thing," she said obliquely.

I accepted my cue. "It must have been. As a doctor I have seen such illness, and it only brings terrible grief to the family. A sudden death is hard, but watching one you love dying over many months and in such agony ... Well, there are times it cannot be borne." She inclined her head. "I believe the Collins family were friends of your family?"

"That is so." The matron exited the shop, glanced at us, and dived into a shop three doors along. "My grandfather and Louise's parents knew each other," Darna said. "Louise visited even after my parents' deaths. Knowing something of her circumstances, I offered her a place when we decided to turn the main building into suites."

"And she was interested?"

"Absolutely." Miss Darna smiled. "She received the letter mid-week and drove out that weekend to look over what I was having done. I showed her all of the changes. She walked the whole building, listening to my plans, looking at where the suites would be and stopping now and again to go over one of them carefully. We went upstairs first, and once we descended the staircase she walked right past what became Mrs. Stacy's suite and stopped at the next door. She opened the door, looked in—not that there was anything worth seeing as yet—then walked down that short corridor along the side of the suite to the door that leads outside."

She smiled again, the look of a woman who indulges a friend's fancy. "It was odd. She opened the door, looked outside, shut the door again, came back and looked at the suite door. Then she said, 'This one. If I come here to live, I must have this one.' And that was it. She paid me a five year lease there and then, moved in as soon as the work was completed, and has paid me every two years since."

I made some commonplace comment, said goodbye, and, once out of her sight, increased my pace. I found Holmes in the inn parlor considering the morning newspaper with disfavor.

"Nothing of interest," he said, then looked at me and spoke sharply. "You have something?"

I sat down, dropping my voice so that no one should overhear. "Mrs. Collins may know something of the fire." Holmes raised an eyebrow and I launched into my tale, ending with, "Do you see, Holmes? She chose a suite on the ground floor. One that has, in effect, its own outside exit. She said, and Miss Darna told me the precise words used: 'If she came there to live she must have *that* one.' She paid a five year lease not only before she moved in, but even before the work was done. I find it suspicious, Holmes."

My friend shook his head. "Do you think her to have planned nine years ago to burn down the house? Why? She did not know who the other residents would be, and knew nothing of circumstances that might arise. No, Watson. I think that she chose that suite because it is closest to the kitchen, and food brought to her suite would still be hot. The residents' common rooms are conveniently on the same floor, and as you say, she had, in effect, her own exit, but she is a private lady, who might wish not to have all her comings and goings subject to scrutiny. Then, too, she is a sensible and practical woman, and it may have occurred to her that in an emergency such as fire, what better than an exit so close to her suite? That does not mean that it was she who *caused* the emergency."

I felt like a deflating balloon, and I fear that it showed to my old friend's keen eyes.

"Do not reproach yourself, Watson. The information is interesting, and may yet be useful." I brightened as he continued. "Now, would you care to come with me to discuss some aspects of the fire with Mrs. Collins?"

I agreed at once. The truth of the matter was that I rather liked the lady, and I was interested to hear what Holmes had to say to her.

She was at home, expecting some of her family later, but quite prepared to receive us now. We were offered seats, tea and cake were called for, and she settled back in a way that showed either that she had a clear conscience, or that she anticipated our having nothing with which to accuse her—effectively. The tray arrived, Holmes and I accepted a cup of tea—a very good blend—and a slice of cake, and with the housemaid gone and the suite door shut again, Holmes commenced.

"I would like you, if possible, to go over the events of the fire again. Begin from when something woke you earlier in the night."

She said, as she had done before, that it had been something like a bump.

"Could Mrs. Stacy have been up and dropped something in her suite?" Holmes questioned.

She thought not. "I cannot swear to it, but I had the strong impression that the sound came from outside."

"Some distance away, or close at hand?"

Nearby she believed, yet not directly outside her suite, further along perhaps? Yes, possibly as far as Mrs. Stacy's window. No, she could not recall being woken by such a sound before, but then it had been an exceptionally clear, quiet night. Holmes asked questions, took her back and forth over her recollections, and gained little more. However he appeared satisfied, as if he had gained some valuable information, although I could see nothing of any use in what Louise Collins had said.

* * * *

We walked back together. I was in the middle of writing up an earlier case for *The Strand*, and took the opportunity of asking a few questions that would expand my exposition. When we arrived we sat down to luncheon in perfect amicability, and as we finished the meal Holmes stated that he would be gone again all afternoon. I asked if there was anything he would have me do.

"If you wish, Watson, I would be interested to hear something more of Madame Hartsford's history, if that has been uncovered?"

I reflected grimly that I, too, would find the subject of interest, so I agreed and set out an hour later. I decided to approach the insurance company as the logical place to start, for it had occurred to me that Amelie Hartsford's attempt to defraud them had been quite clever. It was possible that it had not been her first attempt, and any insurance company has a considerable sphere of informants. This one also had a two-man agency in Flitwick, so I went there and was met with something that could almost have passed as enthusiasm. The young man sent to assist me, a Timothy—call me Tim—Thorpe, grinned when I commented on it.

"Yes, Mr. Holmes suggested some time ago to the manager in Ampthill that he—our manager—should see what else could be discovered about the lady, and it turns out that there is quite a lot. The file was sent here so that should Mr. Holmes ask again, we would have that information. A fellow company was most helpful, as were several agents we have in France."

He spread the file out before me and I read, inscribed in meticulous copperplate, with other portions in letters added to the file, a tale of infamy that left me pop-eyed. Upon meeting the lady I had disliked, distrusted, and disbelieved her, but I had not expected *this*.

Amelie Hartsford had been born Amelie Martineau, and certainly not to a wealthy or prominent family as she suggested. Her people had owned a market stall in Paris, and Amelie had early come to see that she would never rise unless she took more direct action. She accordingly ran away with a young man of good family who found himself constrained to wed her when it was revealed that she was under age and her father intended to go to the law. He divorced her quietly four years later, and she was paid off with a large sum on the agreement she leave Paris. She then moved to Dijon, where she posed as a widow. Less than a year later she married an elderly man who died from a heart attack two years after the marriage, leaving her everything, including the loudly voiced objections of his cousins who had expected to inherit.

However the will had been impeccably written, Amelie sold all but her jewels, and, taking the cash, moved back to Paris, renting a pleasant little flat in a moderately respectable area and acquiring a maid. Under her married name and as a genuine widow this time, she attracted the interest of a Mr. Hartsford, currently residing in her arrondissement. At this point I looked up and Timothy placed a second file before me. It was labeled with several names, of which Lane Latimer Hartsford was one. I commenced reading, to find that this third marriage had been a real meeting of true minds, and that the word used in the file for a "police district" had been superbly accurate.

Lane Hartsford had a similar background to that of his new wife. Born in London of poor parents, he had early departed his family to embark on a life of crime. The police knew of a number of events in which they were certain he had been involved, but the man was slippery and the crimes could never be brought home to him. He had been everything in turn from a burglar to a promoter of dubious shares and a suspiciously lucky gambler. He went to France over some trouble involving a man who refused to be silent when he thought himself cheated, and there met Amelie.

I read the next paragraph, turned over Mrs. Hartsford's file and read where events matched, and looked at Timothy. "You now believe that she murdered the man whose accusations were keeping Hartsford out of the country?"

"Yes," he said brusquely. "No proof, and it's been too long to find any, my boss says. But look at the dates. They married in March. In May she comes back to England. Soon after that, Taylor told his friends he'd found this charming woman that understood his every need. He called her by a name that wasn't Amelie or any of her previous surnames, and none of his friends ever met her. In August he was found dead."

"From what?" I demanded.

"Shellfish poisoning."

Well, that wasn't something likely to be mistaken, but it was also something that could be easily caused by carelessness. I told him so and was rebutted.

"She was smarter than that, Doctor. There was an outbreak of toxic shellfish on a nearby beach. The police think that she sneaked down there, gathered a bunch of the shellfish, brought them back and fed them to him. Just think. If they managed to find a believable witness to swear she'd been the man's mistress, and the police did call her on the shellfish, all she had to say was that she hadn't known, that he was so partial to them, and she'd just wanted to give him a treat. He got his treat all right."

"And when?" I asked, "Did the Hartsfords return to England?"

"The next month, in September. Nothing the police could do about it, as the only man that might have sustained a charge against Hartsford was dead. No one had ever seen *her*, and no one back in France was prepared to say she'd been away."

I whistled softly. "An ingenious lady." The rest of the files were more of the same, including two other suspicious deaths—all of which made me conjecture about the elderly husband, as well. Lane Hartsford had died twelve years ago. No question of anything untoward in this case, for he'd had a heart attack in a public bar and been dead when he was picked up. His wife had rented a cottage in Ampthill for eleven of those years before rendering herself deeply unpopular with a woman whose family had considerable influence in the town.

"Started an affair with the wrong husband," Timothy informed me. "It was explained to her she'd do better out of the area and we don't know what was said, but it was effective. She was gone in a couple of weeks. She came here to Flitwick; perhaps someone told her about Rosewarne, and she talked Miss Darna into a year's lease. 'S funny how people see her, Doctor. Either they think she's a sweet woman, helpless and harmless, in want of protection and they rush to help her out, or they see her for what she is and wouldn't touch her with gloves on. A good-looking woman too, doesn't look her age. Not that she's our problem anymore. Mr. Holmes got us out of most of what she expected us to pay, and she's left."

"*What?*"

"Oh, sorry, you didn't know? She packed up some time during this week, called in a carrier, and last night she caught the train. Seems that all the furniture that came with her she sold to her landlady, who's happy with the bargain."

"And you have no idea where she's gone?"

"Not us, and nor do the police. I'm told the Superintendent is saying that she was driven out, and he's quite bitter about it."

I sat up. "Whom is he claiming drove her out?"

The young man looked embarrassed. "Er, he's naming you and Mr. Holmes and Miss Darna. He suggested that you're in Miss Darna's pay, and that you persecuted Mrs. Hartsford to where she was unable to support it any longer and fled. One of his men is a friend of mine. He says the super is furious and telling folks he'll bring that fire home to whoever was responsible no matter what he has to do."

I straightened the contents of the two files, passed them over the desk to him, and rose to my feet. "Thank you for all your assistance." And with that, I turned on my heel and left the office, determined to tell Holmes about this at my earliest opportunity.

He was not impressed, I must say, taking the threat to Miss Darna almost casually, and ignoring too that we had lost one who could rightly be suspected.

"I wished to know more of her background, so she could be found if we wanted any evidence from her. For what motive do you think her responsible for the fire, Watson?"

"She used Miss Reeves in a plan to cheat the insurance company. Wouldn't it have been useful if the lady was dead and all of the contents in both suites destroyed by the time she claimed on her policy?"

Holmes considered that. "Yes, it would, but I have seen no evidence that she could have been guilty. Mrs. Maylon tells me that she sleeps lightly, and she is certain that she would have heard Amelie Hartsford had she risen and left her suite. I examined the windows in Mrs. Hartsford's suite and they are four feet from the floor."

"She could have climbed on something?" I offered.

Holmes comprehensively summed up his opinion on Amelie Hartsford. "I wished to be certain of that myself. The matron says that Mrs.

Hartsford had nothing in the suite that could have been used easily as a ladder. There was no step, no low chest, and while she could perhaps have dragged an armchair over to the window, they are of considerable weight. Besides, no such chair nor the remnants of one were found in that position, nor did anyone see scrapes or bruises on her, as she would have had, had she climbed out that window. And how did she return? The window is higher from the outside, and even more difficult of access."

He shook his head. "I think Mrs. Hartsford fled because she knows that the insurance company are asking further questions about her, and because she doesn't want any trouble. She sold all of her bulkier possessions and took only what could be carried by a porter. I think she has returned to France. In any case, while she is certainly an evil woman who has in the past committed heinous crimes, I believe her, in this case, to be innocent."

I subsided. When Holmes speaks with such certainty on something, he is almost always right. My discoveries had also answered one thing about which I had earlier asked Holmes. Of what type of man would marry such a woman? Now I knew her husband had been the same, and if birds of a feather flock together, well, that tends to apply to jailbirds as well. I only hoped that the wretched woman would come by justice in the future.

10

I was downcast the next morning after Holmes's verdict. We were eating breakfast and I brooded silently on how little we had advanced. We seemed to have investigated almost anyone having to do with the fire. I could still see no way in which it had occurred—either accidentally or deliberately—and ... I sat up, a truly unpleasant thought crossing my mind.

"Holmes?" He turned, brows raised questioningly. I cleared my throat. "Holmes, you don't suppose Blascourt ..."

"It is not impossible," he said quietly, and something in his voice convinced me that the thought had been in his mind, too.

I spoke slowly, considering what I said. "He has had his practice here for seven years and has wished to expand his surgery, attract a second doctor to work with him, and possibly set up a small nursing home with an operating theatre."

"Ah," Holmes said, understanding what I was not saying. "But he has not the money or the land on which to build. However, should a fire clear land that is unproductive according to his own plans, land owned by his fiancée, then his plans might be possible. Upon his marriage he could build, using her money, and with an expanded surgery and the home he would like to own, he could attract another doctor and more medical staff. He could become a man of wealth and influence."

I sighed. "I regard Blascourt as a friend, but I know him. He isn't a bad man, Holmes. However, he likes money, and he has always resented his father's kindness and generosity. His father often did not charge a patient who could not afford to pay. On his father's death, there was little to inherit, save the patients and his right to serve that area. He works very hard and for long hours, and he may believe that an improvement in his circumstances would also benefit those he treats."

Holmes eyed me. "I see no need to tell your friend that we are looking in his direction. I would suggest you merely talk to people that know him. You know the way. And once they are speaking of him, listen."

I nodded slowly. "I have no wish for him to discover what I am about. I'll talk with Mary Whittle first, for I am not entirely sure that she likes or trusts him." And so I set out to meet her as if by accident as soon as I had finished breakfast.

The lady was walking towards the shops when I encountered her, and allowed my company. We strolled along, talking casually about trifles, and I quietly steered the conversation to Blascourt once she appeared comfortable. She hesitated.

"You're his friend." The tone was almost accusing.

"I knew him when we were at medical school. I was learning new techniques, and he was studying. I like him well enough, but I would not say we are close friends. I am aware he has his faults." It was sufficient.

"Aye, he's fond of money, that one. Thinks my Miss Darna doesn't know that's half the reason he's courting her, but I know, and so does she. Other half is that she'd make a good wife for a doctor. Rosewarnes have lived in this area since Sir George Rosewarne moved here from Cornwall near two hundred years ago. The name's known, and people trust it. Miss Darna's good looking, as well, and he could go much further and fare far worse, and he knows it."

"Does he talk of his plans for the future?"

Mary Whittle all but spat. "Talk? He does little else. How he'd do this or that, how he'll be a big man in time, with her money and his doctoring he'll own the county and all will listen when he speaks. Oh, yes." Her grin was a combination of mischievous urchin and a woman who knows something. "Not that I'd count my chickens was I him. Miss Darna's straight as a die; she doesn't hold with lying, and it's what I say when I warn new staff. Tell her the truth and she'll likely forgive you, lie and be caught and you'll be out on the spot—and don't go thinking you won't be caught, because she's uncommonly shrewd, is my lady."

There was a suppressed glee in her voice that alerted me. "And the doctor has a secret, doesn't he?" I said, feeling my way. "He's been up to something he oughtn't, and you have wind of it." I lowered my voice. "Something that would make your lady send him packing did she know?"

"Aye. It would indeed. She doesn't like double-dealing, and she's modest but knows her own worth. She'd not stand for sharing." When I encouraged her to continue, Mary pressed her lips together. "I'll say no more. 'Tis not for me to talk. Let him do that."

And with that remark she walked faster, and I reverted to talking of commonplace events, mentioning the abrupt departure of Mrs. Hartsford, and allowing the suggestion to slip that she had fled ahead of her insurance company's investigation. Mary was amused, but no matter how I introduced the subject I could not return her to Blascourt. At last I gave up, bidding her a good day, before returning to the inn to take stock of what she had said.

I sat in the inn's bar drinking a tolerable cider and thinking. Holmes jokes that I do not always think logically, that I may be swayed by emotion, but I have experienced life, and through my patients have gained some knowledge of how people act and the foolish things they may do. Also, over the years I have known a good number of doctors. If I was not mistaken, Mary hinted that Blascourt had an undesirable connection, one who he might not drop once he was married. I could see how that might not sit well with mistress and servant—*if* it were true. But I must not jump to conclusions.

I finished my cider and set out again. For that day and the next I made myself appear a bigger gossip than any old woman, but it was productive. People talk, and I found something that surprised me: Blascourt was not popular. He was acknowledged to be a good doctor, but he was seen as stand-offish, and even money-hungry. "Not a man like 'is dad," was the general verdict, and since that was so, people were prepared to drop odd tidbits of gossip or comment. I discovered, too, that many disapproved of his attentions to Miss Darna, who was liked and trusted, as he was not. I came down to breakfast triumphant on the third morning.

Holmes eyed me and nodded. "You have found out Blascourt's secrets, have you not?"

"I have, and rather discreditable they are." I frowned. "I know that he, well, I can only say it frankly, that he battens on women. He obtained the money used to set up his house after his father's death two years ago by persuading an old lady to finance him." I poured myself a cup of tea and drank slowly. "I am distressed, Holmes. If those who told me speak the truth, she—a Miss Martin—intended the money as a loan, not a gift. She believed that it would be used to establish a surgery. She was dying, and loaned him the money without recourse to a lawyer or any witness. She obtained it in cash, and when she died four months later and her lawyer asked him to repay the loan, he acted surprised, saying that it had been a gift."

I frowned. "He made it plain to her lawyer that since there were neither witnesses nor a written agreement, the money would not be given up. I talked with the old lady's housekeeper, and she says that her mistress talked often about it in her final weeks, saying the money would build a fine new surgery and that she was happy the local people would benefit. The housekeeper is angry that they did not." I recalled her helpless anger as she spoke. "He be a lying, cheating, toad, that's what he be. She give him all that money so's people would have a doctor. She told me he'd promised he'd never leave here, he'd tend them all his life like his pa. He'm a *toad*!" she snarled. "Him knowing her was dying all along, and a'coaxing of her. Saying his patients would never forget her kindness and generosity. I told her lawyer all of it, and he says as how the doctor don't agree, reckons I must of been mistaken. Lawyer reckons that what I say is hearsay or some such. I got no witness to her telling me, and the doctor, he says as how he'll bring an action ag'in me if I talk." She talked despite that, adding further suggestions and comments such that I could readily suppose Blascourt *would* go to law did he hear her.

"And you have verified some of this?" Holmes asked quietly.

"Not to say verified, exactly. She could be wrong, and have misinterpreted events or conversations," I replied unhappily. "However, she said that her mistress had owned a pair of small Chinese vases. They were valuable and she prized them highly. She had also one of those Chinese horses in jade, and a portfolio of valuable sketches. She noticed they were gone about a month before her mistress died. Miss Martin was either sleeping by then, or mostly incoherent when she was awake. But my informant understood her mistress to say that the doctor had taken the items for safekeeping, having first frightened her with tales of burglars."

"And you saw them in his possession," Holmes said. "In his house I would venture, in his study, and positioned so that they could not be seen through the window. When you commented upon them he said they were gifts from a grateful patient, and asked you not to mention them to others, in case of burglars." I nodded and he continued. "What do you know of the lady's family? Who was named in her will and might resent the loss of their inheritance?"

I sighed. It was a common story for many elderly people who had outlived their own generation and the next. "She left it all to two charities in London. The lawyer said he had discussed it with her. She never married and her parents were long dead. She was the youngest of three daughters and the other two died, one as a child, the other from influenza a week before her wedding. Mrs. Martin inherited everything, and wished to do good with it."

I finished my tea and laid the cup back in the saucer with a small clink. "If what her servant says is the truth, Blascourt got the best of it. The Chinese items and sketches were her only real portable valuables. She had jewelry, but it is mostly silver and semi-precious stones. The money she gave him all but emptied her account. The house is old-fashioned and has not been maintained for years, the furniture is solid—and that was about all that could be said of it. The lawyer told me confidentially that once all the debts were paid, there was a moderate sum to go to the charities, but not what there would have been had Blascourt repaid that—possible—loan."

Holmes understood me. "In other words, Watson, the lawyer believes the servant, and not the doctor." He eyed me keenly. "As do you."

I could only nod. I did, and I found it deeply upsetting. "There's more to come." I stared down at the tablecloth. "He isn't a bad person, Holmes, I'm sure of it. But he sees opportunities and seizes them." His look indicated that I should continue. "He inherited money twice before that," I said. "Not major sums, but useful amounts. Then, too, three of his women patients left him what were described as mementos. I obtained descriptions and they were not the sort of thing I would call mere mementos. In one case what was left to him was a small library—of first editions, Holmes. That is *not* a memento."

He agreed. "Of what sort were his benefactors?"

"Of the same sort as Miss Martin. Elderly people, having only distant relatives, did they have them at all. They lived alone, had few visitors of any kind. They had no large estate and their servants were old, too, and would retire as soon as their employer died."

"No," my friend said quietly. "Nothing to interest anyone. But they had some money, and here and there they had valuable items. The sort of thing that is often put away, and of which few know the value. They have it as a family inheritance and do not think what it may be worth. You saw the library?"

"Yes. It too was in his study. I observed the beauty of the bindings, and recognized several of the works, commenting on them. He said his father had inherited the library. It was a lie, Holmes. His father has been dead two years and the woman who owned the books only died last year. I ..." I faltered.

"You fear that there may be more to his inheritances than is obvious. That he may have seen to it that once a will was made, the maker would not go back on his bequest."

"That is my fear," I acknowledged miserably.

"Then you may leave go of it," my friend said firmly. "I have met Blascourt a number of times and I see him as an opportunist, not a killer. Consider the situation. He takes up practice in a country area where there live a significant number of elderly women and men. They all trust him, for his father is known as a good man, and how could the son not be so as well? They are not rich, but they have large, moldering houses on two or three acres of good land; they have some money, and scattered about their houses they have family treasures. And they are lonely, Watson. That is the key. They used to shine in society once, and now all they have are old servants. No family, few friends, and fewer visitors. Into their lives comes a good-looking young man, a doctor, educated, friendly, and apparently interested in talking to them—and listening. Never underestimate the influence of a good listener, Watson."

I was cheered. "Then you think that all he did was persuade them into leaving him money or certain items?"

"I do. It is unethical but it is not criminal, save for the case of Miss Martin, and there is no proof. I think wrongdoing may not have been initially intended. She loaned him the money, then she died and he suddenly saw a way he could keep it. There were no witnesses to any conditions, nor was there any written contract. Her lawyer knew nothing of the money until he came to settle the estate and queried the amount paid out only a few weeks before her death. Blascourt knew he could not be made to repay the money, and with Miss Martin gone, no one knew on what conditions he had received it. So he built the house of his dreams, and in that spacious study he places other trophies of his ability to charm."

"Miss Darna would not like any of that if she knew," I commented.

Holmes pursed his lips. "I would not be so sure she does not. If she is ignorant, someone else may not be. Remember Miss Whittle's comments. She said 'better to tell her the truth and be forgiven, than be caught out by her in a lie.'"

"Ah. And she said that Miss Darna was shrewd." I recalled the woman's words. "I thought at the time the way she said that suggested that they *both* knew something of Blascourt. Or it may be that Mary knows, and Miss Darna only suspects."

"Quite so, and being a woman she will find out. I do not think that once she has done so she will forgive, or that she will be inclined to wed a man who enriches himself in that way."

"No," I said with satisfaction.

Holmes turned the subject and we parted when we left the inn: I to speak with others on the Rosewarne estate, and Holmes to catch the train to Ampthill.

* * * *

I found Flora Maylon at home and chatted with her once I was settled in her suite, a tea-tray on the small table between us. Holmes's final suggestion had been that I should endeavor to find out if Blascourt had tried his wiles on any of the Rosewarne estate's well-to-do women. I had chosen Mrs. Maylon as the one most likely to know, to tell me honestly, and then keep silent. I had judged the lady to be the type who did not appreciate obfuscation so, I spoke openly.

"I am going to tell you something that must not be passed on. I ask your promise that whatever is discussed here, you will not speak of it elsewhere."

Her look was steady, and after a few seconds she nodded. "I shall say nothing—unless it is to save a life. I cannot swear to keep silent if someone is in grave danger."

I agreed to that and disclosed to her some of what I had discovered about Blascourt. "He does not harm them," I assured her. "But he comes in the guise of a friend, of someone who enjoys their company and finds them interesting. He would hint at his appreciation for some small possession, suggesting that it would be valued as a memento of a friendship he cherished."

"I see. And many women of that type would not honestly know if the item is valuable or not," she agreed. "Older members of the family die and they inherit. They do not know the painting is by an artist who now sells for large sums. They think of it as 'that painting Great-Aunt Alma's husband bought her on their honeymoon in Italy and that was left to my mother who liked the scene, and thence to me.'"

She smiled. "I admit to having some possessions of my own of that sort. Considering what you tell me, I think I shall have them valued again and list them separately in my will, rather than as part of the furnishing." She focused on me with abrupt intensity. "I can tell you something useful to your inquiry. Three years ago, Doctor Blascourt began to visit me more often. I thought nothing of it at the time. I had been unwell and I was grateful for the company. He listens, as you say. He stopped coming so often once my family heard of my illness and began to visit, staying overnight regularly at the inn where you and your friend are staying."

Her smiled hardened. "Before that, however, he had mentioned several of my small but valuable pieces of furniture. He did not ask for one, nothing so vulgar, but he did mention another patient who had left him her father's library. They were only books, he told me. But they looked well in his study and he valued them, since he had liked the patient and remembered her each time he saw them or read one." I drew in a breath. "Yes," she said. "If those are the first editions of which you speak, then they are far from being of little value. So you may therefore count me as one he tried to persuade into leaving him a 'memento.'"

She fell into thought briefly before glancing up again. "I do not recommend you speak to Louise. She is likely to tax him with it, if he approached her in that way. Not that I think he would. He would not be able to persuade her, and he would know it. But Miss Reeves would not talk if she gave her word. She can be gullible, as she was with that Hartsford woman, and could have been a suitable subject for the doctor's wiles." I accepted the suggestion and making my farewell, I went at once to tap on Miss Reeves's door.

Miss Reeves was willing to promise silence, but could recall little of talk of mementos. Yes, the doctor had admired her row of ornamental figures. They had been inherited from a German great-grandmother and she would never sell them. Leave them to someone in her will? Certainly. They had been left to her oldest friend, to go in turn to her daughter, who had often admired them as a child. Yes, she had stated it in the document.

And also—no, it was true they had spoken of wills, and she had assured him that she had one, updated each year after consultation with her lawyer. Her lawyer? Oh, a man of rectitude, whose family had been lawyers for three generations and been lawyers to her family as long. Yes, the doctor had commented on her attractive jewelry. She had told him the truth, that it was mostly paste, and that where it was not, it was listed in her will.

Why, yes, she supposed that for some months the doctor had been quite attentive, then his visits had fallen away. It *might* have been after those conversations, she couldn't recall. No, she had assumed that he had merely become busier. It was a pity he worked so hard. But that was the man he was, unsparing of himself. She rambled on until I could extricate myself, leaving with the thought that the woman would never know how lucky she was to have a good lawyer who kept an eye on her.

It quite put me out of countenance to meet Blascourt on the way out. He was coming in, smiling at Miss Whittle and making some joke to which she responded with a blank stare. He turned to me.

"Good to see you, Watson. Any news on the cause of that fire?"

I said there was not.

"Oh, well, I'm sure you are on the trail of some criminal."

Indignation welled up and possessed my tongue. "That is so. I have heard from a number of people that there is a man who persuades lonely, elderly women into giving him money and items of value. A shocking thing," I said acerbically. "They are asked for as mementos. However, some relatives plan to make official complaints. Mind you," I added, as if in belated caution. "I merely heard some gossip from a police friend. I have no idea whom it may be, other than a professional man." I managed a jocular grin. "Not you I suppose, Blascourt?"

"Certainly not!" he snapped, almost thrusting past me. A sheen of sweat appeared on his brow and I departed, well-satisfied with my day thus far. His guilty conscience might make him less ready to encourage and accept bequests for a while. He would be too busy listening for a knock at the door—and each time someone *did* knock, he would fear who might stand there.

11

I returned to the inn, and made only a moderate luncheon, being still distressed about Blascourt. How could I have been so wrong about the man? I'd liked him. If asked, I would have said that I trusted him. Yet all the time he had been quietly—was stealing the right word? Not quite. His patients were grateful for his time and care, what they gave they gave voluntarily, but how much of that had been his insidious coaxing, his prompting, and their fear that if they did not he might not come as often? Still, his visits had delighted and occupied them, and without that promise of reward he would not have visited beyond normal duty and they would have been lonelier. My thoughts went around and around until I felt sick.

That afternoon I went out and walked mile after mile. I am a doctor. To my mind that is one of the highest callings a man may have. I relieve pain, heal the sick, or, if I cannot, I can alleviate their distress. I have held the hands of the dying and known that my presence made them more able to accept their departure. I have consoled those left behind, and they have understood that they had done all they could, that those they loved were now in the hands of the Almighty.

And at last, after I had walked myself into near exhaustion, I came to a conclusion. What Blascourt had done was unethical. Criminal it might not be, however, it was morally wrong. Not in the receiving of his 'mementos'—many doctors were left small bequests by grateful patients—but in what amounted to his demand for them. To him it was an exchange. Leave me something of value and I will spend time with you, I will listen to your stories, flatter you with my presence, and allow you the illusion that you have a friend. Refuse and you will receive nothing but the presence of a doctor who wastes no time with you bar the minimum his profession demands.

I returned to the inn, weary in body but more settled in mind, to discover Holmes had returned. He looked up at me as I entered the parlor between our bedrooms and I saw a concerned expression flicker across his countenance.

"Watson, what is it?"

I told him everything.

My friend poured me a cup of tea as I talked, listening in silence until I was done. Then he sighed. "Yes, I had come to that conclusion from things I heard elsewhere. I did not wish to mention it to you since you are right. He has done nothing illegal, and some would say that he is not unethical. Do not clerks, typists, laborers, and the police sell their time? If it is moral for them to do so, how is it wrong for a doctor to exchange his spare time for items of which the giver will soon have no more need? Yet, you are also right on another thing you said. He preyed upon the lonely, and he took advantage of being a doctor—a man who was freely welcomed into their homes—to do as he did."

"There is nothing that can be done about it," I stated, half hoping he would tell me that I was wrong.

Holmes's lip curled. "Not under criminal law. But since it distresses you, Watson, I may have a word here and there. Nothing may come of it, however, so expect nothing."

I ate dinner in better heart and went to my bed that night and slept peacefully. I had no idea what my friend might have in mind, but Holmes is not a man to arouse false expectations.

* * * *

I rose and joined him over breakfast the next morning, and as soon as I had enjoyed my bacon and eggs, I asked for the day's program. He sobered.

"Upon my return yesterday evening, I was given a note. It is unsigned, but we can both guess the writer."

Here he produced the single sheet of paper and passed it to me. It was written in a hand that had essential education, the letters being well enough formed, but the language that of a man speaking simply.

Dear Sir,

there's trouble with that Frenchwoman. Someone came that says he speaks for her, and he complains Miss Darna attacked her and caused her to lose property. It isn't lawful for that it isn't her complaint with her not here, but the super wants to listen and he won't wait much longer. If you can find something soon he'll have to leave it be.

It was unsigned.

I looked up from it. "Joe the policeman?"

"So I would think. It matters not who wrote it. The question is, is the information true? I believe it is. Here, as I said some time ago, Watson, is the 'friend' whom she has induced to make mischief on her behalf."

"What do you plan to do?"

"Our writer says we have no time. On the contrary, I will make time. The Superintendent is unaware of the true character of Mrs. Hartsford. I will make it my business to enlighten him."

"He may not take that well," I warned.

"Maybe not, but he will stay his hand while he investigates the information I shall give him, and while he does so we shall have time to see out the final act."

I felt a leap of exultation. "You know!"

"I do. I have known for some time in broader terms who it must have been, although I saw from the beginning how it was accomplished. Yesterday I made other inquiries and I now know the person responsible. As yet I have insufficient proof. I have an agent collecting that, and in another day I believe I shall be in a position to unmask the killer. Yes, Watson," he said at my raised eyebrows. "It was murder."

"But who was the intended target? Five died."

"Ah, Watson, you know my methods, and I prefer not to reveal the solution prematurely. But the other deaths … Yes, that was the unintended camouflage for the death of the important one. It succeeded so far as the police were concerned. They did not accept that the fire was a crime—despite the superintendent's claim that Miss Darna was responsible for her servants' actions—and even had they accepted it was not an accident, they would not have understood the motive or recognized the method used. The killer was clever, and I understand why they did as they did. However, they cannot be permitted to escape." (I noticed that he was being careful to use no pronoun that might identify the one of whom he spoke.) "When a murderer is successful and remains undiscovered, it often leads them to murder again and again as a solution to their difficulties, until it may become the only solution they consider. I will not permit that. But for now let us go and bespeak the Superintendent."

* * * *

Superintendent Bartholomew Goodbody was in his office and graciously agreed us a moment of his time.

"And have you come to confess yourself baffled, Mr. Holmes? Now I am not, for I am finalizing charges upon a recent complaint, and I hope to have others to lay against the same person shortly."

Holmes appeared downcast. "In that case, you must be busy, and it is doubly good of you to see us. I will be brief, Superintendent. The insurance company for which I was asked to make inquiries subsequently uncovered certain information on the background of one who was involved in the Rosewarne fire. I thought that you should be apprised of it. I am sorry to say that it reveals the immoral character of one who does not appear so, but I serve the truth and that must always be admitted."

The Superintendent's chest swelled. Here, he was undoubtedly thinking, was the verification that Miss Darna should be prosecuted, that she was not the innocent miss she appeared to those about her. He seized the file and began to read avidly. The first document—the confession of attempted fraud that Amelie Hartsford had signed—produced a rising tide of red, which slowly suffused his face. He said nothing but moved on to the details of the woman's birth, marriages, and career. By the time he was done reading, the file's contents straightened, and the folder placed neatly on his desk, he had command of himself again. As he faced us, I saw that there was more to him than prejudice and arrogance.

"I am indebted to you, sir."

Holmes shook his head. "On the contrary. A policeman detests the deaths of the innocent. It is his duty to see if a death was not accidental. In my experience, when a major event occurs into which the police must inquire, all sorts of minor acts come to light. Some are criminal, some are unethical, while others may merely be the stumbling of one taken in a snare by those that are more clever or cunning. Such is Miss Darna. Yet she had begun to see through her tenant, and had refused to renew her lease."

"Do you think the Hartsford woman to be responsible then?"

"I do not. I think she is exactly what that file shows her to be. A thief, a trickster, maybe a murderer, but when she acts, she does so more directly and for immediate profit. There was no profit in burning the house. She was soundly asleep when it occurred, and would she risk that if she had set the place afire? No, I believe that her plans were indeed to cause a fire at some later time, but not one that would imperil herself." The superintendent looked interested at this and Holmes expounded.

"I said that her lease was not renewed. I believe she knew it would not be and accepted that action, for all her protests and refusal to move. I am told that before the fire she had already, very quietly, made arrangements to rent and paid the first month for the cottage to which she removed herself after the fire ..."

Superintendent Goodbody broke in with the air of a man upon whom has come revelation. "Yes, yes, of course. She would establish that there was considerable animosity between her and Miss Darna, and that she was the injured party. She would make it appear that she was being driven out of her home, suggesting perhaps that it was a matter of money. She would reluctantly move to the cottage, and one evening when she was away from home at some well-witnessed event, a fire would break out. All of her possessions, so many of great value such as were listed in her insurance policy, would be lost to her. The cottage was not hers, so she would owe nothing there ..."

"She could, on the contrary, say that the fire had been caused by some laxness in her landlady's responsibilities," Holmes noted.

"And she could take an action against *her*, while claiming large sums for property said to have been lost," the Superintendent finished up triumphantly. He brooded briefly on that. "She might have even persuaded someone into taking up a collection for a poor lady who had lost everything through the malice of one woman, and the carelessness of another." His fist slammed down on his desk. The superintendent let loose a ripe oath. "And I was foolish enough to swallow that act."

"You and many others in the past," Holmes said dryly. "I would not blame yourself. They were a clever couple, and his death does not seem to have rendered her less eager in her pursuit of profit. You may note that here in Flitwick she did not succeed, where she did so in many other areas, including France, where their laws are less scrupulous on guilt or innocence. Let you congratulate yourself on that."

The Superintendent eyed him. "Thank you, Mr. Holmes, you are generous. Now, if you will excuse me, I wish to have some few words with the man who came here on her behalf. He may be another dupe who was eager to aid a much put-upon lady, or he may be a confederate in her confidence. Before he is allowed to depart I shall uncover which he is, and if the latter, I shall take steps against him."

Holmes nodded, stood, gathered the file from the desk, and indicated that I should follow him. We departed the office, noticing as we walked away that on a seat in the corridor sat a small, meek-looking man who glanced at us as we passed. I observed that for all his timid appearance he had a pair of very sharp eyes, which widened slightly at the sight of my friend. I walked towards the door and exited behind Holmes. My footsteps had gained an echo. On turning, I saw the mild little man on my heels. He muttered something, slid around the corner of the building, and vanished from view. From the open window I heard the Superintendent roar.

"Gone? What do you mean, he's gone?"

"Holmes, do you suppose that man was the complainant?" I asked. "He seemed to recognize you as we passed."

"He should," was Holmes's reply. "That was 'Humble Humphrey.' He makes a good living at certain applications of the badger game, and he is excellent in falling in front of a building, and complaining that the owner was negligent. He can dislocate several joints at will, and his piteous moans will melt the hardest heart." He chuckled. "He would not have been pleased to see me there. He guessed the game was up and got out before he could be taken by the police."

I remembered the roar of rage and frustration. "The Superintendent wasn't pleased."

"No," Holmes agreed. "He has lost all around. The lady whom he believed has been shown to be untrustworthy, the lady he wished to find a charge against now looks to be innocent, and his final quarry has disappeared from his very station. However, I have something that may console him. While I was in Ampthill yesterday I spoke to the Chief Constable. He listened courteously to my request and agreed to it."

"Surely that is unusual?" I protested.

"Not in this case. Five years ago I was able to assist him in capturing a man who had attacked his young daughter. A very dangerous man, who went on from that to attack other women, ending with the deliberate murder of the last one. He came of an old family, but even so the scandal could not have been silenced had not the man, once I had him at bay, broken down completely when he saw no way of escape. He was removed to an asylum without the need for a trial.

"The Chief Constable is grateful that his daughter's attacker was apprehended and his criminal career stopped, and also that he had no heroic decision to make as to prosecution. In turn, upon my explaining my reasoning as to the events at Rosewarne, and my assurance that there was, and was likely to remain, insufficient proof to obtain a conviction, so that a confession before witnesses was all that could be hoped for, he agreed that I might do things my way. In the morning I shall send a note to all those who are deeply involved, including the Superintendent, requesting that they gather at Miss Darna's home where I wish to provide them with further information about the fire."

I walked beside him, considering the reason the Chief Constable had agreed to this. The case Holmes mentioned was not one I knew, and I was trying to think how I could reopen the subject and hear more about it when Doctor Blascourt strode towards us. His face bore a terrifying glare and his fists were clenched as he halted before me

"How could you betray me in such a way?" he snarled, thrusting his face towards mine. "We are colleagues!"

At his shoulder Holmes spoke quietly. "You mistake the matter, Doctor Blascourt. It was not your colleague who informed some of your victims' relatives; it was I."

Blascourt spun to face him. "You, sir? Why, and for what motive? I did nothing illegal, as many doctors receive small bequests from patients. By what right do you object to a common practice and blacken my name?"

"By the right of any man to warn sheep that a wolf is amongst them," Holmes said coldly. "If the relatives of those you fleeced"—here I choked slightly—"choose to protest your inheriting family heirlooms then that is your and the law's concern. Charities too have their rights, and I may say that some were not pleased to discover a sadly diminished inheritance. They may not be able, all of them, to obtain justice, Doctor. But their voices will be heard."

Blascourt stood there a moment longer, breathing heavily in his rage. Then he turned on his heel and strode off.

Holmes looked after him. "Well, Watson?"

"Very well," I assured him. My friend had spoken no more than the truth. Blascourt's actions had been legal, but that would not matter a jot once word of what he had been doing was known about the towns. People expect a doctor to adhere to a higher standard, and in this Blascourt had signally failed. Others, some of whom had assented, and others, such as Mrs. Maylon, who had not, would remember his hints and suggestions as to their will and that too would become common knowledge.

"And once Miss Darna hears all of this, her marriage may not take place either," I said with satisfaction. Holmes nodded and we walked along the street, each understanding the other. The law demands proof, but public opinion has its own methods. I deplore such conclusions as it may sometimes produce, but in this case, I believed it would enact justice and I was content.

12

The morning was dull, overcast and gray, yet there was a muggy, smothering feeling in the air, and I thought that soon the day would become very warm. A fitting morning on which to announce Holmes's conclusions. The brief notes summoning people to a meeting mid-morning had gone out before breakfast, and I doubted that any would refuse. He had carefully tailored each letter to the person or persons receiving his request. Then there had been the one written by the Chief Constable, that would bring the Superintendent and likely one or two of his men with him—probably all of them arriving early, and wishing to quiz us.

Ten minutes before time we walked into the large parlor belonging to Miss Darna, and I saw that I was correct. The Superintendent was there, seated solidly on a large, sturdy armchair, Joe in the corner, notebook in hand. Holmes walked to the small outside door and opened it.

The Superintendent roused. "*Now* what are you about?"

"The room will become stuffy," Holmes said calmly.

"Why? How many others have you asked?"

Before Holmes could answer or be interrogated, we heard a bell ring and footsteps in the passage. One by one those summoned filed in and sat on the chairs Miss Darna had commandeered from several rooms. Her parlor, fortunately, could be expanded by the simple device of moving a long bamboo screen. And with that taken away, I could see that originally the room had been intended as a large dining room. That table, if it still existed, had been removed, and now the room was encircled with two staggered lines of chairs to which Holmes was waving the arrivals.

Miss Darna had arrived first with Mary Whittle, but hard on her heels were Flora Maylon pushed in her wheelchair by Louise Collins, with Esme Simons behind them. Matron Dean arrived shortly after that. Holmes had summoned only those who might have a part to play. However, it seemed that he wanted representatives of some of the deceased as well, since Bess Touhy's daughter Liz entered, then the Sanderson clan, Violet Stacy's family, complete with son and daughter, arriving last along with Bill Lewes.

They sat, and Holmes moved to face them from by the doorway. "The police have never accepted the conclusion of the coroner," he said quietly. "Which was that the fire which destroyed the main house on the Rosewarne estate was caused accidentally? On the contrary, they believed that it occurred either by negligence or malice, and it was those possibilities I also set out to investigate. The general belief was that the fire had begun when a live coal rolled from the fire in the small downstairs office."

He turned to Louise Collins. "You, however, in the course of the two days prior to the fire had passed and re-passed the open office doorway. You told us that at no time during those two days did you ever see the fire alight. Am I correct?"

"That is true. I would swear that I did not, and I believe that I would have noticed it. On some occasions Mrs. Maylon was with me and she too did not see a fire in the office," was her composed reply. Flora Maylon nodded agreement.

Holmes's gaze swept the two lines of listeners. "The office fire was not lit at any time during the two days prior to the fire," he agreed. "That evidence was also given by Matron Dean," she nodded, "and by Miss

Darna, who had entered the office briefly on both days. Furthermore, there was something that went unnoticed." He slightly emphasized his next words. "The triangular mark on the outside of the building directly opposite the office fire."

The matron spoke first. "Then it *was* the office fire that caused it somehow."

"No, for if a coal had been flung from the office fire and set the floor alight, the fire would have burned *into* the building. It would not have left such a mark on the outside planking. This mark means the fire started from the outside. Do you see? Something caught fire immediately beneath that outside wall. Flames ran along under the floor, catching the driest timber. It ran deeper into the house to where, between the kitchen and the back of the inner staircase, it surfaced."

I saw Superintendent Goodbody's face. He knew the layout of the house well by now. He'd walked it several times, and however reluctantly, he understood the likelihood of my friend's assertions.

Holmes nodded at him. "The question is, what was there to catch fire, and how could that have occurred? Someone carelessly tossing away a cigarette end? No, for Miss Darna, in order to prevent weeds, had seen to it that fine gravel was laid in a bed that reached well under the house edge, to some three foot outside that. A butt casually tossed on that would have burned itself out without harm. No, I did what other investigators did not bother to do. I observed the mark, and by dint of digging out some of the gravel I was able to lie flat beneath the outer edge of the building ..."

From the look in the Superintendent's eyes, some investigator was going to pay for his oversights. During all this the room was growing warmer. I was glad Holmes had opened the door to outside, as it was all that was keeping the atmosphere tolerable.

"And once there," Holmes said, his gaze flicking from person to person, "I was able to observe a circular burned area, such as would come from a source of sustained heat being placed against the tinder-dry floor-boards. Upon forcing myself deeper underneath and directing the light farther in, I could see that the marks of burning widened, leading to the area between the kitchen and the back of the inner staircase. I went to that area and pulled up a number of the floorboards. From there the fire had flowed back on an angle to Mrs. Stacy's suite, and also upwards, to fire the upper floor. It was not until sometime later that it broke through into the corridor there, but the fire was eating through the lower part of the inside staircase and it brought that down early on."

He looked at his audience. "Fire was applied directly to the underside of the floorboards outside the office windows. This was no accident.

Murder of more than one person may not have been intended, but the actions of the arsonist caused the deaths of five people, and great destruction of property. The law is unlikely to say that because the death of only one person was meant, let us forget the other four."

Louise Collins spoke, as if considering a mathematical problem. "How did Violet die?"

Mr. Sanderson glared. "It was said at the inquest. She died from breathing smoke."

"Yes. How did the person who set the fire know that would happen?"

Holmes nodded, "A good question—if Violet Stacy was the intended victim and her killer cared *how* she died rather than that she merely did so. I doubt they had any idea how the fire would travel, or what it would do. I do think it may not have occurred to this person that the whole building would catch alight. They may have thought the fire would move slowly, so that most would easily escape it."

"Foolish, then!" The Superintendent was scornful. He fell silent as I could see an idea dawning on him, born of Holmes's comments. His lips thinned in anger.

"Naive," Holmes corrected.

He turned to Louise Collins. "You woke earlier in the night." It was an invitation to repeat what she had told us and she did so, glancing about the circle of interested faces.

"I woke early that morning. I do not know why, although I have a vague memory of a bumping sound. Only once, but sufficient to wake me. I listened but heard nothing more. I drifted off to sleep again, but I did light a candle to look at the time. It was just after one o'clock."

"Yes," Holmes agreed. "It is my opinion that was when the fire was lit. But note this. At one o'clock Miss Darna was still in company. The matron was asleep upstairs and her assistant, having been given leave of absence, was some distance away and awake, caring for her sister who was ill, as can be also attested. The other household staff were in their beds. How do we know that? Because the four women who slept in a cottage for the staff are all adamant none of them was out at that time. It is possible all four could be lying, but the police have made extensive inquiries and are inclined to believe them. This leaves Mr. Lewes, gardener and general handyman, who can tell us something since he was taking a walk at that time."

Every gaze in the room swiveled to Bill Lewes who, nothing loath, spoke up. "I were out walking. Sometimes I don't sleep so well, and when that's so, I go for a stroll, like. I heard someone walking too, coming down the drive they were, just as I were close to the estate boundary. T'would have been about one o'clock I reckon, or a mite before. They moved light-footed, and careful. I guessed whoever it was to be familiar in a general sort of way with the lay of the land. Like one that's come to the place a few times, mebbe a number of visits, but only in daylight, never at night. Whoever it were walked easy for the direction, not easy for the footing with it being so dark. I didn't see them, nor I didn't know who they was. But there were someone there all right, I don't make no mistake about that."

Holmes nodded. "So, we have a person who set the building alight on purpose. They were familiar to some extent with the estate, and while they may not have intended to kill so many, they did not care if they did, and they came in from the outside. What resident or member of the staff would have walked beyond the estate, only to return?" Most present inclined their heads in agreement.

"So, it was an outsider, but someone with a motive that drove them to kill, to kill a particular resident, someone they feared and hated, and someone who was doing them a great injury and would not cease. In the end, they acted to prevent further abuse." Holmes wheeled. "You, Mrs. Sanderson! You feared and hated your mother, Violet Stacy. All your life she dominated you, and only once did you defy her, to marry the man you loved. And even then she would not let you be. She insulted him to his face at every turn, and she spread false rumors about him. You persuaded her to remove to the Rosewarne estate where your husband never visited and you and your children came no more often to visit than you must."

He ignored the growing fury in Sanderson's face as he addressed the shrinking woman. "You and he could live with her abuse of you both, but then she began on your children. Your daughter she named openly as a whore, and she said to others that your son was mentally deficient, an idiot. Neither accusation was true. Your daughter is a decent girl, but you knew that such lies may be believed by the foolish or small-minded. Your son, far from being slow, is an intelligent boy who does well at school. Nor is your husband the fervent adulterer that she claimed. In fact she lied, constantly, continually, and damagingly to those you loved. And after so many years you determined that it should not continue."

He pointed a finger at her. "You crept out of your house, you travelled here, you knew the estate and even in the dark you were able to reach the house. There you crawled partway under the building with the bee-smoker your father-in-law had left in your shed. You placed the nozzle of that against the timber and, using dry material that produced fire rather than smoke, you set the boards alight. You chose the place where the office wall runs alongside that of your mother's suite, and to make certain of her death you whittled a gap between the nearest two floorboards of her suite before you started your fire. That would draw up the smoke."

I noticed out of the corner of my eye that Joe had moved to stand behind the Sandersons. He placed a large hand on the husband's shoulder and held him down, as the man would have sprung at my friend. "Easy now, sir. We don't want any trouble."

I thought that he was wrong there. From the look on Sanderson's face that exactly what he wanted, but Joe had the strength, the weight, and the leverage, and Sanderson, strong man though he was, perforce remained seated.

Holmes looked at Mrs. Sanderson. "For the murder of five people there is no doubt that you will hang ..."

My attention was drawn to young Michael Sanderson, for the blood was draining from his face and in a moment, I thought, he would faint.

Holmes frowned. "How came you to think that no one else would be injured by your actions? Or did you not care? Are you so callous, so vicious? Never mind, a judge will have the final say, and he'll have no mercy. It all comes together: the bee-smoker, your familiarity with the estate. I suppose that you drugged your husband that night?"

She opened her mouth but emitted only a small, pitiful moan of denial.

Her son leapt to his feet, facing Holmes like a young lion. "It wasn't her, it was me! Nobody else knew about it. I burned the old cow. I'm sorry about the others; I didn't think the fire would spread like that. It was *her* I wanted dead—and she is. You don't know what it was like. Every time mum went there she'd come home and cry and cry. We kept hearing rumors about Vee, and others would say that dad put it about. No, the adults weren't talking, but the kids were. I got into fights and got blamed for starting them. That last day ...." He choked in his rage.

"That last day," Holmes repeated. "She said something so terrible that you couldn't stand it any longer. What did she say?" He voice was low, his tones understanding, and Michael Sanderson replied as if bent to my friend's will.

"She laughed and called Vee a slut. I said she wasn't, she was a decent girl, she was my sister—and—and I love her. She looked at me and sort of leered, it made me feel sick. Then she said, of course I did. Any boy thinks he loves the girl when he's on top." I saw his chest heave in an involuntary retching. "My sister, she said me and Vee ... I said I'd kill her for that, and she said I was like my dad, no guts, all talk and nothing doing."

He straightened. "I showed *her*. I said I'd kill her and I did. I hope in the end she knew she was dying and that I did it. I'm sorry about the others; I never meant to harm them. I'm so sorry."

And with that he was gone. His father had tried to wrench free as Michael leapt for the door, but Joe was too occupied to realize that the boy was escaping. When he made a grab for the flying figure, it was already too late.

Michael had been closest to the open door, and dashed through it. Before Joe could disentangle himself from the lad's father, Michael had reached the line of bushes and vanished. Joe charged after him, returning subsequently to confess he'd lost sight of the boy, could hear no footsteps, and had no way of knowing where he had gone. The superintendent grunted.

"No matter. He's thirteen with no money and no friends as soon as they hear why he's wanted. We'll pick him up in a few hours."

The gathering broke up in chatter and confusion. Joe and his superior went to start the hunt, while others, including the deeply distressed Sandersons, departed. Holmes and I stayed with Miss Darna and Mary, who turned to us.

"They won't take him alive, will they?"

Holmes shook his head. "No. I saw him thinking it through as I spoke. He'd decided what he would do before ever he rose to confess."

Mary nodded. "You knew it was him. All along, you knew."

"I did."

"He's nobbut a lad."

"He was old enough to kill five women," Holmes said quietly. "And murder is addictive. Had he not been found out, what would he do the next time someone outraged him? Murder becomes easy once the first killing is safely accomplished. He intended it never to be known as murder, but even when it was suspected, he never imagined that he would be found out. Yet he was still decent enough not to let another take the blame. His mother might have done so, for I saw her realizing who it must have been once I talked of the bee-smoker,. Had he not spoken first, I suspect she would have accepted the responsibility."

"Poor boy," Mary Whittle said. "I don't know that were I him I wouldn't have killed that woman myself."

"Murder is rarely the answer," I said, from my knowledge of Holmes's many cases. "I suppose they'll find him and he'll hang."

"They'll find him, at least," Holmes said.

* * * *

They found Michael Sanderson as Holmes said. He had made his way to a local wood, climbed the tallest tree he could find, and jumped. His neck was broken.

I looked at Holmes when we heard the news.

"You opened the door, and you seated the family by it."

He nodded. I said nothing more. I too would not have wished to see the boy hang, but he'd killed five women. It was true that four of the deaths were in ignorance, not malice, and as for his grandmother, I could understand how a sensitive boy had been so sickened and disgusted by her accusation that he determined she should die. Boys of that age tend to be unstable, especially if they are so wrought up they cease to think of consequences.

As for my friend, he'd begun to know who might have committed the crime almost at the start. He'd even mentioned that inverted triangle burned into the outer wall of the building. I had not understood what it meant, nor had the police or anyone else of the scores who had seen it.

I was musing on this case and the one before it later that evening. I spoke of my distress that both times it had been a family member who had been the killer, and Holmes glanced at me.

"It is those we know best that best know how to drive us to commit crimes we might otherwise not have committed."

I nodded. "Yes, such are *familyar* crimes."

I emphasized the way I pronounced the penultimate word so that he took my meaning, and his rare smile flashed out.

"Indeed, Watson. Such crimes are *relatively* frequent."

I groaned and departed to my bedroom.

* * * *

Three days after Michael Sanderson was found, Holmes received a generous sum for solving the mystery and we left the inn, returning to Baker Street. Now and again I heard of or saw mentioned in the news-papers some of the people we had come to know, however, and I was pleased and often amused by the information.

Miss Darna did not marry Blascourt. As I'd thought, gossip and ru-mor spread, and while he was charged with no crimes in the end, what he had done was known and heartily disapproved by all in Ampthill and Flitwick. I do not know where he went, only that he sold his house, most of his less portable possessions, and left the area. Miss Darna married three years later, a slightly younger man from a collateral branch of the family, a man who came to visit a distant relative and found a closer relationship. I believe they are happy.

Miss Reeves died two years after the fire, for her heart, I heard, had always been a little weak. Mrs. Maylon and Louise Collins remained living in the guest cottage—until Mrs. Collins's death at the good age of ninety-six—and Mrs. Simons moved back to join them. Nothing more was ever heard of Amelie Hartsford by that name, but a woman of similar description was executed in France five years later. She had married an elderly man, claiming to be a Madame Elisse de Tandor. The husband died soon after under suspicious circumstances, and the police determined it to be murder. Her claim, that it was a *crime passionale*, was laughed out of court.

Mary Whittle continues to care for her Miss Darna, although this year she reverted to her original position as children's nurse since there was a new addition to the family. The Matron retired, and Miss Halpern was promoted to that position. Bill Lewes returned to employment as the estate prospered, and the housemaid, Janet Blane, married her young man from Ampthill.

The Sandersons had been distressed almost beyond bearing by the revelation that their son—and brother—had killed five people. They quietly received his body and moved away. Holmes was told privately that they had gone to Sussex, where distant relatives of Mr. Sanderson lived, and that they had taken a smallholding. Holmes thinks the boy to have been buried there, sanctioned or not.

That was the end of the case. The ruined building was razed as planned and has become a rose garden, and few remember much about the events any longer. They had a small ten year service at the rose garden last year, however, only a handful of immediate family and friends attended. As for Holmes and I, we were currently too busy to attend. I had seen publication of my account and that would do. (I quietly burned the papers left me once that was done.) In any case I rarely hark back to such events once they are done, unless I am writing another occurrence that reminds me because of items in common. This reminds me, there was such a one recently that I must begin writing up momentarily. That all started when ....

CPSIA information can be obtained
at www.ICGtesting.com
Printed in the USA
BVOW04s1317050517
483334BV00001B/13/P